ESSENTIALS OF MURDER

BOOK 1 IN THE AROMATHERAPY APOTHECARY
MYSTERY SERIES

KIM DAVIS

ISBN: 978-1-963705-90-4

Published in the United States of America by Harbor Lane Books, LLC.

www.harborlanebooks.com

For my husband, Dan, my number one fan and cheerleader. I couldn't have written this book without your encouragement and support.

In memoriam of Dawn Dowdle, literary agent extraordinaire. She was a true champion of authors and gave us the faith to believe in ourselves. She is greatly missed.

CHAPTER ONE

"Mom, you have to do something. Go to City Hall and complain." The voice next door dropped for a moment, then rose again, loud enough for me to hear the end of his rant. "...put you out of business."

"Stop harping." Victoria Lewellyn's gravelly cough interrupted her tirade. "I don't see Carissa's shop as competition. We can work together with enough business to go around. I've already discussed collaborating with her on a few items."

"If you don't believe she'll steal your customers, you're blind." A door slammed. "If you won't do something about it, I will."

Over the past two weeks, I'd heard the same cringey argument nearly every day. I had a hard time concentrating as I tried to tame my shop into some semblance of organization before my grand opening. I turned up the music to drown out their ongoing bickering. My aromatherapy shop wouldn't steal customers from Victoria's candle shop. Our products complemented each other, but Russ Lewellyn refused to listen to reason.

Bright sunlight made the pastel-hued glass jars glow on the shelves in front of me. I arranged them by color in the front window of Aromatherapy Apothecary. The display was meant to entice customers at the shop's grand opening in two days. In the meantime, there were more than enough last-minute details to keep me working late into the night.

The bells on Mystic Valley Candles' door jangled like they were angry at the world. Russ stopped in front of my window, saw me standing there, and punched his fist toward me. A dark scowl cut through his bushy black brows, and his beefy face and neck turned a mottled red.

I jumped and knocked a jar off the shelf.

The sound of glass shattering on the polished concrete floor echoed through the store. When I looked up from the mess, he was staring at me. My heart stopped. I couldn't shake the feeling that nothing but hatred filled the man's soul.

He sneered, then turned and stomped down the street toward City Hall.

I'd done nothing he could complain about that would jeopardize my business. Still, I worried he might fabricate something that could postpone my opening.

The scent of lavender spread throughout my shop as I carefully wiped up fragments of glass that scattered across the floor. Sweet almond oil, infused with lavender, had splashed on the wall, the legs of the tables, and in a growing circle on the floor. I didn't have time to make sure all the grease was cleaned from the floor, but the last thing I could afford—or want—was for someone to slip and fall. Insurance was much more expensive than I'd expected, especially without placing a claim the very day I opened. I'd planned to fit in time distilling a new batch of lavender essential oils. I wanted to tinker with my Celebration blend for the grand opening, but the cleanup was taking up a lot of the time I'd allotted for those tasks.

When the last shard of glass had been wiped up and my floor felt squeaky clean, a soft knock sounded on the locked adjoining door that separated my shop from Mystic Valley Candles. I stood and brushed a tendril of curly raven-black hair that had escaped the elastic band holding my thick ponytail away from my face. Droplets of perspiration dotted my moon-shaped face, despite the air-conditioning that hummed. It was much too hot for early April, and I worried about what summer held for the small town of Oak Creek Valley in Southern California.

I hurried to unlock my side of the connecting door and pulled it open.

Victoria eased into my shop and handed me a plate of chocolate chip cookies. She'd already found out my favorite.

"I'm so sorry about my son's behavior. I don't know what's gotten into him." Her washed-out gray eyes were red-rimmed. A generous amount of crow's-feet framed her eyes and lines marred the skin surrounding her thin, chapped lips. "Ever since his father left, he seems to fly off the handle for no reason."

"It's not your fault." I held up the plate. "Thanks for the cookies. Can I fix you a cup of tea?"

"That would be nice. Thank you." Her hands trembled as she reached up to pat her gray bob.

"Please, sit." I motioned to a padded black leather barstool at the narrow island that ran down the center of the shop. It didn't take long for me to fill the delicate floral-patterned tea cups with cinnamon tea I'd brought in a thermos carafe with me that morning. I placed a cup and saucer in front of her.

She sipped her tea, and I bit into a gooey chocolate

chip cookie. It was the perfect ratio of chocolate to cookie, and I liked how she'd added a mixture of regular-sized chocolate chips and mini-sized chocolate chips. I reached for another cookie and watched as her gaze swept around my shop, taking in the disorganized stacks of diffusers, aromatherapy kits, and jewelry. My neighbor appeared much older than her fifty-four years. Her skin was more sallow than usual, and worry lines mixed with her normal wrinkles.

"I've talked to Russ until I'm blue in the face. Why can't he understand business will be better for both of us if we collaborate?"

My face warmed. I didn't want to tell her about her son's behavior. She had enough worries over him already.

She lifted her pointy nose in the air and sniffed. "I have customers who would pay more for organic and natural scented candles, like the lavender you're scenting the room with. Do you have a diffuser running?"

"No, I, uh, accidentally knocked over one of my sample jars."

"You should think about using diffusers or something to scent your store with seasonal fragrances. The lavender is lovely, but it might be a bit too calming. Citrus will be popular during the summer and cinnamon in the fall." Victoria's eyes regained a bit of their spark. "On days when it's not too hot, prop your door open and use a fan to blow the fragrance out onto the sidewalk area. That'll bring in customers."

"Is that what you do?"

"Never underestimate the power of the schnoz." She pointed to my freckled nose. "Let me know when you do that and we can coordinate our scents."

"Uh, sure." Great, one more thing I needed to add to my

to-do list. Maybe my dad had an extra fan tucked away in his garage.

"Rumor around town has it you've set up a distillery in here." She mimed tossing back a drink. "Are you doing anything illegal that I should know about?"

"No! Absolutely nothing illegal is going on here." Heat flooded my face again. Before I moved back to Oak Creek Valley, I had enough accusations thrown at me to last me a lifetime. "I'm distilling some of the essential oils I sell, which should help the bottom line. Lavender is one of the key ingredients along with citrus from our local Pixie tangerines."

My mentor, Mariska Kemp, had talked me into purchasing a copper distiller. While distilling my own essential oils was more work than I bargained for, Mari made a good point. With organic fields of lavender, flowers, and herbs, plus orchards of tangerines, lemons, oranges, avocados, and olives readily available within fifty miles of my shop, I could get quality ingredients at reduced prices and pass those savings on to my customers.

"Using local ingredients will be a good selling point. Once you open, I'll buy some of your tangerine essential oils and try it in a batch of candles." She gulped the tea remaining in her cup. "Maybe we can do some cross-promotion that way and get Russ off my back."

"I'll give you some right now so you can start experimenting." I walked over to a stack of boxes, rummaged through them, and handed her a vial. "Let me know what you think."

She uncapped the vial and took a sniff. Her eyes widened. "I can't wait to try this in a candle. It'll be a huge seller, especially in the summer months."

"If you like that, you'll have to try my Celebration

Blend once it's perfected." I had experimented with numerous essential oils and had narrowed down the mixture to include jasmine, geranium, coriander, and rosemary essential oils along with our local Pixie tangerines. I was close to figuring out the exact ratios for the uplifting fragrance, but the blend still wasn't quite what I'd envisioned. "In fact, I'll commission you to make Celebration Blend candles to sell in my shop, if that's agreeable to you."

"That works for me." She nudged her teacup and saucer away from the edge of the counter. "I've taken up enough of your time. You probably have a lot you need to get done before your grand opening."

"There aren't enough hours in the day, but I'm opening, one way or another."

"Stay optimistic and let me know if there's anything I can do to help."

"The cookies were the perfect pick-me-up." We walked to the adjoining doors. "I appreciate it."

"My pleasure." She tilted her head. "You'd better make sure you keep this door locked from your side. I'd hate for my son to sabotage your new business before you even open."

CHAPTER TWO

Victoria closed her side of the connecting door and turned the deadbolt.

My mouth gaped open.

She was worried about her son destroying my shop? What in the heck had I done to deserve his malice?

I shut my connecting door harder than I intended. The bang reverberated around the walls and echoed off the polished concrete floors. I jumped, then turned the deadbolt to lock the door on my side. I hoped she didn't think I'd done that in anger, but deep down I knew I had. Russ wasn't the only one experiencing anger management issues. Ever since I'd been arrested nine months ago, it didn't take a whole lot to tick me off—or make me jump.

I closed my eyes and took several deep, calming breaths, then unlocked the cabinet in the island and pulled out two small bottles of oils—patchouli and lemon. I extracted two drops from each and placed them in a tiny glass bowl, then eyeballed three-quarters of a teaspoon of sweet almond oil and a quarter teaspoon of local organic olive oil into the mix. The smell of patchouli wasn't entirely pleasant, but the lemon oil made it bearable. I massaged half the mixture onto my arms, applying with long, gentle strokes.

As my skin absorbed the oils, I plopped down on the floor and kicked my shoes and socks off. I worked the remaining mixture into my soles, applying extra pressure along the line horizontal to the balls of my feet. I sighed as some tension slipped from my body. With the hectic schedule of opening the shop, I'd neglected practicing reflexology, and my body had paid the price.

A key turned in the lock of my front door and the chimes hanging on the handle jangled as it pushed open. I jumped and the now-empty glass bowl skittered across the floor.

"Carissa? Are you here?" Mari entered the shop and locked the door behind her.

"I'm putting on my socks and shoes."

Mari peered over the countertop. "Is everything all right?"

"Eh." I rocked my hand as I looked up at the nut-brown, deeply wrinkled face of my friend. Her jet-black hair was cut short, the ends spiked up with gel. "The stress is getting to me. A quick massage with some patchouli and lemon helped."

"Do you have time for a longer reflexology session?" She walked around the counter and pulled me to my feet. Despite her tiny size and advanced age, she was remarkably strong and energetic.

"I'll be fine. Can I take you up on that offer after opening day is over?"

"Absolutely. Don't forget to take care of yourself in the meantime." Mari studied my face with her golden-brown eyes. "But the stress isn't from all that needs to be accomplished. What happened?"

"How do you do that? You can always tell when something's wrong."

"You're an open book, darlin'." She patted my round cheek. "Now, tell me all about it, and let's see if there's something I can do to help."

My friend, my mentor. Mari had rescued me many times over the last four years. I would have still been floundering in life—or worse, in prison—if she hadn't taken me under her wing. Her gaze never left my face as I told her about my run-in with Russ and his mother's warning. She glanced over at the adjoining door. "He's a troubled young man. Keep that locked."

I snorted. "I do. He's in his thirties. He's beyond being a young man and should have grown out of that."

Mari frowned and shook her head. "Some people would have said the same of you, my dear. Look past the actions and see what's beneath the surface that creates those actions."

I shouldn't be so quick to judge, but I felt threatened by him. "You're right. His mother said Russ started the angry behavior after his father left."

"How long ago was that?"

"I didn't think I should pry, so I didn't ask."

She rolled her eyes. "You mean to say you didn't *think* to ask."

Ack. She knows me too well.

I hung my head. "I'm trying to be sensitive. But when I get stressed, it all flies out the window."

"It doesn't matter. He'll see reason within a few weeks when he finds your shop is bringing them new business and profits." Mari tugged me toward the distilling room, where my copper still occupied a long butcher-block table. "Show me your new concoction. I'll help figure out

what needs to be done to make it worthy of the celebration."

We worked together for an hour, Mari's sharp nose and intuitive nature pinpointing the adjustments that needed to be made. I crossed my fingers as we left the still to do its magic through steam distillation. The system held enough water to run for several hours, so I didn't have to babysit it. I'd turn it off after two hours and allow the resulting concoction to rest overnight before separating the oil from the hydrosol and bottling it in tinted vials. I'd use the hydrosol, which was basically the scented water extracted from the plant material, to perfume the warm towels used during reflexology appointments.

Mari departed to have lunch with a friend at one of the historic downtown arcade cafes, known state-wide for its innovative vegan food. Omnivores and herbivores alike lined up for the delicious meals. Despite having a few cookies earlier, my stomach rumbled, reminding me I hadn't eaten lunch. I eyed my PB&J sandwich, but it wasn't very appealing. Instead, I was tempted to stroll down the block to Jean-Luc Patisserie for a cup of coffee and a croissant sandwich.

Purse in hand, I locked the door and turned right onto the wide sidewalk toward the patisserie. I waved at Victoria as I passed the candle shop, then dodged around several tourists who stood clumped together, their heads bent as they consulted a map.

Oak Creek Valley—located about two hours north of Los Angeles in normal traffic—was home to artists, New Age enclaves, and spas, as well as award-winning wineries. With plenty of warm sunshine year-round, tourists flocked to our valley. Downtown Oak Creek wasn't very big—just a few blocks of shops and restaurants, and a large park that held an outdoor amphitheater.

I pushed the glass door open and stepped into the cheerful interior of the patisserie.

Lunchtime was over, but several people waited in line.

I glanced at the enticing desserts in the glass case and reminded myself that I was here for lunch. I didn't want to admit to myself that I was really here for the delicious baker, Jasper Whitby. My heart beat faster when he stepped through the kitchen door. He focused his attention on the patron placing an order, and I returned my gaze to the tempting pastry case with the mouthwatering mounds of delectable desserts.

I knew better than to think he'd noticed me as anything other than a chubby customer who enjoyed gobbling up his delightful goodies, or at least a cup of coffee, just about every afternoon. I couldn't resist admiring his green eyes flecked with gold or his slow smile that ended with a dimple appearing in his left cheek whenever he took my order. His deft hand at making utterly sinful Triple Chocolate Rolls ratcheted my admiration to the stratosphere. I reminded myself, again, that I needed a sandwich and not a pastry.

By the time it was my turn to order, the butterflies in my stomach were performing cartwheels and went into over-drive when Jasper flashed his bright smile at me.

"What can I get for you today, Carissa?" His slow drawl made the words sound low and husky.

I wanted to fan myself. "Do you have any croissant sandwiches? And a cup of coffee too." I fumbled in my purse for my credit card, keeping my gaze on Jasper.

"Will turkey and smoked provolone work for you?" He accepted my card and our fingers brushed.

I hope he didn't notice my trembling hand. "That would

be great. Thanks." I took the card back and dropped it into my purse. "Can I get it to go?"

"It'll be ready in a few minutes." Jasper turned and spoke to the pimply teenage boy working at the espresso machine. The kid went back into the kitchen for a moment, then returned.

He ignored the line, looking at me instead. "Are you all set for your grand opening?"

"I'm getting there. It's not quite as organized as I'd have liked, but it'll work well enough."

"I'll be happy to drop by this evening and give you a hand. Just say the word."

Before I could say thanks, the elderly woman behind me interrupted. "Excuse me, but I don't have all day to wait to place an order."

"Pardon me. I didn't mean to hold up the line." I moved to the side to wait for my sandwich.

Jasper's interactions with the other customers made me smile. As an apology for making them wait, he included a free cookie with each order. He gave each of them a wide grin and made them feel like he was honored they'd stopped by his patisserie.

I'm delusional if I think he's interested in me any other way.

It didn't take long for the kid to hand me a white bakery sack and a to-go cup.

Jasper met my gaze again, and he winked.

Heat flooded my face, but before I could react, his attention was back on the ordering customer.

I juggled the bakery bag and coffee on the way back to my shop. At the door, I fumbled with my keys. The lock clicked open and just as I'd reached for the door handle, I saw Russ sauntering down the sidewalk. He had a smug smile and his steps were jaunty.

What changed his mood?

I wasn't sure if he'd noticed me, so I flung myself into the shop, secured the deadbolt, and hid behind the wall that separated the front door from my window display case. I waited a few minutes, then peeked out the window.

He stood there, staring in, like he'd waited for me to look.

Startled, I yelped and the bakery sack and full cup of coffee tumbled from my hands.

He raised his hand and formed his thumb and finger into the shape of a gun. "Bang. You're dead."

CHAPTER THREE

By the time I'd found my cell phone in my purse, Russ was gone. I didn't think I was in any real danger, but his actions rattled me, so I made a call that brought my twenty-seven-year-old self tremendous embarrassment.

"Chief Carmichael, here."

"Dad?" I wrapped my free arm around my stomach. "I, uh, I think someone just threatened me, but it's probably not serious. Just thought I should run it by you, you know, in case."

"Where're ya at, Carissa? Are you safe?" His radio squawked in the background.

"I'm safe in my shop. He ran away already."

"Stay where you are. I'll be there in ten."

Dead air filled my ear.

My dad, Police Chief Robert Carmichael, had served the small town of Oak Creek Valley for over fifteen years. Everyone knew him. Some loved him, some feared him, and a few wanted him out of the way. My scandal almost brought about his downfall. The only thing that saved him was that it happened in San Francisco, several hundred miles to the north, and I was eventually cleared of the charges. Barely. And my straight-laced dad had spent a lot of his retirement savings to get the best lawyers for me. To say our relationship hadn't fully recovered would be an understatement.

While I waited for him to show up, I mopped up the spilled coffee and tried to get the milky brown stains out of my leggings. My sneakers were soaked but there wasn't much I could do about that, except dab at the moisture. They'd need to take a spin through the washer. I made a mental note to bring a spare change of clothes and shoes to keep in the shop should further mishaps occur. With an appetite that had vanished when Russ startled me, I tossed the coffee-soaked sandwich into the wastebasket. If I got hungry later, I could eat my PB&J. Missing a meal wouldn't hurt me, though.

Dad used his key to let himself into my shop. He paused a moment, perhaps to look at his only child, who had increased in girth since her disgraced return home several months ago. Or perhaps to figure out what to say to said daughter. In the end, he resorted to interacting with me in an official capacity.

"Are you okay?"

I nodded twice.

"Was there any property damage?"

I shook my head.

"Tell me about the threat. Is it the first time, or has it happened before?"

I hated to admit it, but now that my dad was here, my nerves calmed down and the shaking subsided. I gave him all the details I could remember, from overhearing their loud voices to my conversation to Victoria to the pretend gunshot.

"Why don't you lock up for the day and head home? I'll chat with Mrs. Lewellyn and see if I can track Russ down."

"Daaaaaddd. My opening is in a day and a half. I can't leave. There's too much work to do." My inner whiny four-teen-year-old self was back in full force. "Are you gonna tell me to move back in with you so you can keep me safe?"

"How many times do I have to explain it's not safe living out there in that orchard all by yourself? There are too many deadbeats looking for an easy steal or an isolated place to crash." He grimaced. "I don't know why your grandmother decided to give you the house and property instead of selling out and leaving the money."

"I'm sorry. I shouldn't have said that. I know you worry about me." I'd hit a sore spot, and I wasn't proud of it. I also knew my dad had arrested some squatters who had moved onto the property after my grandma died and before I'd moved back to Oak Creek. His concerns were justified. "But Gram loved her farmhouse and orchard and knew I loved it almost as much. It's brought me a lot of comfort being there."

He scrunched up his nose and let out a deep breath. Words—and especially emotions—didn't come easy for my dad. "Cari-girl. It's hard to see you as a grown woman making it on your own." He scratched his ear, but his use of my childhood nickname encouraged me. "I lost your mama almost five years ago, then my mama just over a year ago. I couldn't bear for anything to happen to you, so I'm trying to keep you safe."

He'd brought in the big guns.

My mama.

Who I still sorely missed every single day.

Her demise at a much too early age, cheated from a long life by the dreaded C word, had left a hole in my heart that would never be whole again. My dad still mourned her, even if he had an occasional date. And then to lose his mother not that long ago. How could I add to his stress and worry?

"How about I keep my door locked at all times? I promise I won't go anywhere. Then, if you believe it's necessary, we can meet here so you can follow me home. I'll spend the night at your house if that will make you feel better."

So that's what I did. The afternoon proved uneventful, and I was happy Mari had helped me figure out the ratios for the Celebration Blend essential oil. My dad didn't find Russ, but he didn't allow that to put a damper on his mood during our evening together. I even slept without night-mares since my dad was in the house, there to protect me if necessary. I woke refreshed, ready to finish putting my shop together and decorating for tomorrow's grand opening party.

Nothing will stop me now.

CHAPTER FOUR

When my dad turned on the water for a shower, I snuck out of the house and drove a few short blocks to my shop. He had insisted I wait for him to escort me to work, but in the bright early morning sun, I was sure I'd overreacted the day before. I checked up and down the sidewalks, making sure Russ was nowhere in sight, then opened the door to Aromatherapy Apothecary.

The overpowering smell of lavender greeted my nostrils.

Did the still malfunction? I know I turned it off before I left. I hope there isn't a huge mess to clean up. I've got too many other pressing things on today's list.

I locked the door behind me and turned to look around the store.

The connecting doors between my shop and Mystic Valley Candles were wide open.

"Hello? Victoria? Are you here?"

Silence hung in the aromatic air.

"Hello?"

No one answered, so I headed toward the room that

contained the still. In the doorway, a polished copper vessel glinted in the bright overhead track lighting.

Dang it. Russ must have forced the lock and let himself in to sabotage my business.

I reached for my cell to call dispatch but froze.

Just beyond the copper condenser was a shoe that appeared to be on a foot. I inched closer and saw a leg attached to the foot. The leg wore pants that looked eerily similar to the ratty blue jeans Russ had worn the day before.

I took another small step and poked my head into the room.

Sure enough, Russ Lewellyn lay sprawled on the floor, dark eyes staring straight at the ceiling. Not moving.

A large, dented copper pot lay next to his body.

I backed away from the room and swallowed the bile that roiled in my stomach. With trembling fingers, I called 9-1-1 on my cell phone and rushed to the front door.

"What's your emergency?" The crisp, efficient voice of Peg Godwin matched her no-nonsense self. She'd worked with my dad for at least fifteen years and knew me well.

"Peg, it's Carissa. There's a man in my shop. I think he's dead. He might have been murdered." I shuddered.

"Carissa Carmichael?" Peg's voice faltered. "Honey, are you safe?"

"Yes. I locked my shop, and I'm heading to the patisserie down the street. There'll be people there."

"Okay. I'm sending out the full cavalry." Voices squawked in the background. "Do you want me to stay on the line with you?"

"No. I've got to call the chief before he hears about this from anyone else."

"Good luck with that, kiddo."

This wasn't the hardest phone call I'd ever had to make. That honor went to calling my dad when I'd been arrested. This call, however, took a close second. He'd specifically told me he wanted to open the shop with me this morning and make sure nothing was wrong. Instead, I'd snuck out of the house like a willful teen.

"Get yourself down to the bakery and stay put." Chief Carmichael was in full command mode the second he answered his cell.

"How did you—" I closed my eyes. *Of course, he already knows.* "Sorry, Dad."

"I'll be there in a few minutes." His voice was gruff as his siren switched on.

The phone clicked off, and I hustled outside.

Before I stepped into the patisserie, two squad cars, an ambulance, and the fire department's paramedic unit roared to a stop in front of my shop. They all had their sirens screaming and lights flashing.

A crowd of people rushed out of the patisserie and pulled me back toward Aromatherapy Apothecary. This wasn't the kind of attention I'd wanted my shop to receive. Word would get out that a man had died there. No one would visit my store.

I hung back with the crowd and watched as my dad opened the door with the key I'd given him. He withdrew his gun from the holster belted around his waist before stepping through the doorway. The people gathering on the sidewalk craned their necks to get a better look. I was grateful the body was in the back room so no one could see the gruesome sight.

Chief Carmichael motioned for the paramedics and his other responding officers to enter. Russ was dead, so there wasn't anything they could do for him. Or had I been so freaked out I thought he was dead but instead he was only injured? I pushed through the group of onlookers and walked into my shop.

Two paramedics stood with their arms crossed against their chests by the door that led to my distilling room. When they noticed me standing next to the long counter-top, the older one stepped toward me.

"Ma'am, you must leave. This is a crime scene."

"I'm the owner. I have a right to be here." Now that my dad was here to protect me, I had to know what had happened.

"Carissa, he's right." Dad put his hand on my shoulder. "Go on back to my house. Mr. Lewellyn was murdered. You won't be opening anytime soon."

"But—" I stopped when I saw my father's disapproving glare. "Have you told Victoria yet?"

"No. What time does she usually arrive?"

"Around nine." *Poor Victoria. She'll be heartbroken. I hope she has family close by to help her through this tragic time.*

"We'll keep an eye out for her. Now get on home." My dad's shoulders slumped. I think it hit him that it could have been me lying on the floor.

I edged out the front door and back onto the sidewalk.

"Carissa, what happened? Why are all the emergency people in your shop?"

I closed my eyes for a second, then slowly turned to face Victoria. "You're here bright and early."

"Russ didn't come home last night." She brushed a limp lock of hair from her face. There were blue smudges beneath her eyes and her face was almost gray. She wasn't wearing even a trace of her usual rose-colored lipstick. "I worried he'd gotten up to no good. He didn't do something to your shop, did he? Is that why they're all here?"

I swallowed hard and glanced back at the closed door. *I don't want to be the one to break the news to her. Where's my dad?*

She tugged on my T-shirt sleeve. "Well, what happened?"

I gulped. "There was an accident. I found, um, well, somehow Russ got in my shop, and—"

"What are you trying to tell me? He isn't hurt, is he?" Victoria rushed to my door, flung it open, and ran toward the back room, where the paramedics stood.

"Victoria!" I followed close on her heels.

"Russ! Are you okay?" She tried to push past the paramedics, who blocked the doorway. "Russ. Answer me, son. Are you hurt?"

My dad appeared behind the paramedics, his cell phone pressed against his ear. Between Victoria's cries for her son, I caught a few of his words. It sounded like he was speaking to the medical examiner. He held his index finger up to me.

I rested my hand on her arm and tried to pull her away from the doorway. She didn't need to see her son like that. "I'm so sorry to tell you, he's dead."

She whirled around on me and pulled her arm from my grasp. "You killed my son. You couldn't bear for anything to happen to your precious oils, so you killed him."

"No! I didn't do anything." My face flamed hot. *This can't be happening.* "He was here when I opened this morning."

Victoria shuffled out the front door and into the crowd.

I ran to catch up with her, but stopped in my tracks. Several members of my community glared at me. It wasn't hard to read their minds.

They thought I was guilty of murder.

CHAPTER FIVE

Officer Bryon Zabor, my father's right-hand man, followed me to my dad's place.

I was grateful I hadn't been placed in the back of his patrol car behind the wire mesh. The memory of handcuffs, flashing cameras, and a wire cage from several months earlier still haunted me. Oak Creek's gossip hotline would be burning up the airwaves about the chief's daughter being escorted home, even without the visual of me being driven away like a perp.

Bryon had been a fixture in my dad's life for over fifteen years when he joined the department after serving four years as an Army military police officer. Even though he was ten years older than me, his smooth skin and rosy cheeks gave him a baby-faced freshness. He kept his light blond hair in a short military-style cut. I'd never seen him in anything other than crisply pressed clothing, whether it was his uniform or jeans.

He made me sit in my dust-encrusted blue Subaru with the doors locked while he walked into the two-story house. I looked around the yard and realized it had aged along with me.

My parents bought their home when I was an infant. The wooden siding had recently been sanded down and repainted a soft yellow. Dad said the color would show less dust than the white it had been. The dark gray shutters framing the windows added the only accents to the house. When my mother was alive, colorful flowers bloomed year-round in the yard and in the planter boxes that hung below the lower front window. Nothing had survived but the grass and an ancient oak tree in the middle of the yard. I had spent many years swinging from a tire Dad had roped around a thick branch in the stately tree, but that too was long gone.

When Bryon exited the front door, he was holstering his gun.

I shuddered to think there might have been a reason he needed to use it.

He motioned for me to unlock the car and then opened my door. "It's all clear."

"The alarm was still set?"

He nodded. "I turned it off, but you'd better reset it once you go in. Make sure you keep all the doors and windows shut tight. Can't be too careful with a killer on the loose."

This was going overboard, but I didn't argue. He was only passing on my dad's instructions—or what he thought my dad would tell me.

"Thanks for checking out the house."

Bryon waited until I'd entered the front door, then climbed into the black-and-white sedan. I watched him drive away until the taillights were no longer in sight, then I made sure I engaged the deadbolt.

I fumed. Would I have to shutter my shop before it even opened? Given the glares the onlookers had thrown my way, it was a safe bet no one would want to buy anything from me.

I hauled myself up to my old room and curled up on the faded baby-blue chenille bedspread that had covered my childhood bed for most of my life. I started a to-do list of things that needed to be done to cancel my festivities. First on my list was notifying Mari. She wasn't supposed to meet me at the shop until later, but I wanted to hear her soothing voice and gather strength from the comfort she always offered.

"Oh, darlin'. I'm so sorry you had to be the one to find him." She clicked her tongue. "It's a wicked world to take such a young life."

"He had to have broken into my shop to sabotage my opening. But why would someone follow him in and kill him there with my still?" Everyone in town was aware of my earlier scandal and most probably now believed I was guilty of murdering Russ. "Do you think the killer tried to make it look like I killed him?"

"It's worth considering. What does your father have to say?"

"I haven't had the chance to talk to him since he sent me to his house with Bryon as my escort." I sighed. "He'll probably be unavailable for hours—if not days—with the investigation. I suppose he'll need to interview me at some point since I found the body."

As a daughter of a chief of police in a small town, I knew my dad had several long days ahead of him. It happened every time there was a crime, major car accident, or natural disaster, such as floods or fire. His first priority was serving the community and keeping the residents safe.

His family came second.

"Let me reschedule a couple of things and I'll be over in about an hour. You shouldn't be by yourself."

"You don't have to do that. I've got calls to make to cancel tomorrow's festivities, then I'll take this downtime to review the applications sent in for the sales clerk position." It would be impossible to work ten hours a day, seven days a week without some help. Nor would I be able to schedule reflexology appointments, which would leave the shop unattended. Several applications had sat in my email inbox, unopened, for the last two weeks. I'd been too busy and, to be honest, too overwhelmed by everything that needed to be done for the opening. Being stuck at home was the perfect opportunity to weed through the applicants.

"Are you sure you don't need me to come over?"

"I'll be fine. Knowing you're there for me brings me comfort enough."

Second on my list was calling the patisserie. I hoped Jasper would answer the phone. I didn't want to talk to one of his part-time helpers.

"Jasper speakin'." His soft Texas twang floated through the phone. Jasper wasn't French. But when he'd purchased the patisserie from his retiring Francophile employers, both who had trained at an exclusive pastry school in Paris, he'd kept the name.

"Hi. It's Carissa." I cleared my throat when my voice turned squeaky. "I need to talk to you about the order of cookies for tomorrow."

"Hey, y'all okay down there? I heard about the commotion going on down at your place."

"Uh, yeah. I'm okay. Listen, I have to cancel my grand opening tomorrow." I gulped, unsure what I'd do with two hundred cookies if he wouldn't hold my order. I crossed my fingers for good luck. I needed all the help I could get. "Is there any chance I can postpone my order?"

There was a long pause. "It's that bad, huh? Sure, no problem. Just tell me when you're ready to reschedule."

"Thank you. I'm so sorry this is at the last minute, but, well, it was an unforeseen thing."

"Don't worry about it. I planned to bake them this afternoon." Jasper lowered his voice. "Can you tell me what happened? Gossip's already flying around here, something fierce, and I don't know what to believe."

My dad hadn't told me not to tell anyone. Several people witnessed Victoria accusing me of killing her son too. It was bound to be all over town before lunchtime. "I found Russ Lewellyn inside my shop. Dead. Murdered. But I swear I didn't do it."

A low whistle filled my ears. "No kidding? The only thing that surprises me about Russ is it's taken this long for someone to kill him."

"What? What do you know about him? Who wanted to kill him?"

"I've gotta run. Customers are lining up." He chuckled. "My business will pick up with your new scandal to keep folk gossiping."

He disconnected, but not soon enough. I overheard his customer asking if he'd heard anything about the murder that happened in Carissa's place.

I cradled my head in my hands.

Can today get any worse?

Apparently, it could. My dad called and told me to expect Detective Harvey Miller within the hour to interview me. The tone he used when he said the detective's name made me think they were anything but friends.

"Why can't you interview me?" I didn't know anything

about Russ nor why someone would have wanted to kill him.

"Conflict of interest. You're my daughter. So they've sent Harvey up from Thousand Oaks to take over the investigation."

"They're kicking you off an investigation happening in your town?"

"They're just taking me off the lead." His chuckle was humorless. "I'll have the honor of fetching reports and coffee for the illustrious detective."

"That doesn't seem fair."

"Life's not fair, and that's a fact." Dad cleared his throat. "Listen, Cari-girl, if you ever feel like Harvey crosses the line and makes you uncomfortable, you tell him you want an attorney present before you answer any more questions. I'd tell you to get an attorney right off the bat but with my position, it wouldn't look good."

"What do you mean by uncomfortable?"

"Let's just say he's predisposed to either thinking you're guilty or wants you to be guilty."

"How is it possible he was assigned to investigate? Can't you complain and request someone else? There have got to be dozens of other investigators in the county who could step in."

"I wish it were that easy." His sigh filled the airwaves. "Someone with a lot of clout requested him and made it clear to my superiors that my relationship with you has clouded my judgment."

"What in the heck am I supposed to tell him?" I panicked, afraid I'd be hauled off in handcuffs again. *This can't be happening.* "Can't you be here when he comes?"

"You'll be fine. Just stick to the facts."

Yeah, facts that Detective Miller wouldn't believe

because, apparently, he had it in for my dad. "What about my alibi? Only you can confirm I wasn't anywhere around my shop when the murder took place."

He took a sharp breath in. "How do you know about the time of death?"

I shook my head. "It had to have happened after you and I left the shop together yesterday and before I showed up at seven-thirty this morning."

"Harvey will doubt your alibi, but tell him the truth about everything that happened—including Russ's threat against you yesterday," Dad grunted. "I'll most likely end up a suspect, given that threat. I gotta run, but I'll send you a text with my attorney's contact information first. Call Alfred if he hassles you too much."

CHAPTER SIX

After wading through several job applicants, none of which sounded promising, I made a pot of tea and helped myself to a few of my dad's fig cookies. I didn't care for them that much, but it was all he had. My sweet tooth was craving a treat, like Jasper's chocolate rolls, and I couldn't ignore its demands.

The doorbell rang, and I wiped crumbs from my mouth, then rinsed my hands. I didn't care if the detective had to wait. If my dad had issues with him, then so did I. And I'd do everything to make him sorry for inserting himself into the investigation.

I opened the door and froze. When my father mentioned his name, I envisioned a gruff, grumpy man wearing a trench coat and nearing retirement. This tall, golden Nordic god was much too young and too, um, hot to be named Harvey. I might have swooned a little before I found my voice. "May I help you?"

"Ms. Carmichael?" He stuck out his hand. "I'm Detective Miller."

I shook his hand, his grasp firm but not too strong.

"Would you like to come in, or did you need me to come down to the station for the interview?"

"Here is fine." His light-blue eyes sparkled. "I'd hate to inconvenience you."

I led the way to the living room and tried to make sure I didn't have any lingering crumbs on my face. Why hadn't I bothered to put lipstick on? My hand flew to my springy curls, and I tried to tame them with my fingers. No such luck. They bounced right back up.

"Can I offer you some tea or coffee?"

"No, thank you." He motioned to one of the faded over-stuffed armchairs. "Please have a seat, unless you'd like to get something to drink first."

"I'm fine." I tried to sit straight up in the chair, but my bottom sank into the soft cushion. My legs wanted to fold up beneath me. This was my favorite chair to read in, all curled up and snuggly beneath one of my grandmother's crocheted afghans.

He sat back against the couch cushion and crossed his ankles. He held an iPad Mini in his left hand and his right index finger hovered above the screen. "How long have you been business neighbors with the Lewellyns?"

"Technically, it's Victoria's shop. Russ doesn't—*didn't*— have ownership. He didn't even help out when she needed assistance." I twisted a strand of hair around my finger. "I signed the lease about six weeks ago and met Victoria a few days after that."

"And you got along with her?" His gaze fixated on the iPad screen and he tapped it a couple of times.

"Yes. She's been very friendly with me."

"What about Russ Lewellyn? When did you meet him?"

The day I met Russ was vividly etched in my memory.

He'd gone out of his way to make me feel unwelcomed, but I'd keep that information to myself if I could. "He showed up at his mother's shop two weeks ago."

"And?" He looked up and circled his index finger in the air. "How was your relationship with Mr. Lewellyn?"

"We didn't have a relationship, but I can tell you he was unhappy about Aromatherapy Apothecary opening next door to his mom's shop. He was afraid I'd take business away from her. Which, by the way, won't happen since our businesses complement each other."

"Tell me about any altercations you had with Russ." His voice was calm and his demeanor polite.

"We didn't have any altercations." Truth be told, I tried to stay out of his path as much as possible. There may have been a time or two I'd stuck my nose in and told him to lay off harassing his mother, but I wouldn't call that an altercation. "It was difficult to not overhear his displeasure with my shop when he complained to Victoria."

"Did you at any time feel threatened?"

"Up until yesterday, the only thing Russ did was make sure I overheard his complaints. Yesterday was the first day he threatened me." I explained what had happened.

He spent a minute tapping on the iPad, then lifted his gaze to meet mine. "Tell me how you came to find the victim."

I shuddered. I didn't want to relive that awful discovery and I feared it would haunt my dreams for a long time to come. "When I unlocked the front door, the scent of lavender was overpowering. I walked in and saw the doors between my shop and Mystic Valley Candles wide open. I went to check on the still, and that's when I found Russ on the floor. My copper still was lying next to him."

Detective Miller asked a few more questions, pulling

details from me about what I'd seen. Not once did I worry he had "crossed the line" or given any indication he considered me guilty. Instead, he was respectful.

When he stood up, I followed suit. He shook my hand. "Once the report is typed up, I'll call you when it's ready for your signature."

"Thank you. I hope you can find who did this."

I wasn't sure if he'd held my hand a second or two longer than necessary or if it was a wishful fantasy.

I closed the door behind him and ran to the window. With the curtains shielding me from view, I watched him walk to his unmarked sedan parked at the curb. His lean body filled out his slacks just right, and his broad shoulders strained just enough against the fabric of his light-blue dress shirt to tell the observer he worked out.

I shook my head and looked at the T-shirt that hid my expanding muffin top. There was no way he held my hand longer than necessary. Someone like him would never look twice at a woman like me. I promised myself that as soon as my shop was up and running, I'd start taking better care of myself.

Instead of working late into the night, my dad came home just after five.

I had waded through half the applications and needed a break, so I poured a glass of locally grown Sauvignon Blanc for myself and opened a bottle of Dos Equis for my dad.

He took a long swig and settled onto the chair at the kitchen table. "Are beans and franks good for dinner? I didn't know you'd be staying with me, so I hadn't planned anything else."

I inwardly groaned.

My dad ate the same thing every Friday night for longer than I can remember. They definitely weren't my favorite...

but I would never tell my dad that. To him, it was a tradition passed down by his dad. To my grandmother, it was something she'd tolerated because she loved her husband and her son.

I did the same because I loved my dad. "That sounds great, Dad. I haven't had beans and franks in, like, forever."

His eyes brightened, and he didn't look as tired as when he'd come in. "Maybe we oughta make it a tradition for the two of us every Friday night? My treat."

"Uh, yeah. Sure." I agreed because I didn't want to hurt his feelings. And once my shop opened, Friday night dinners at home wouldn't exist for me anymore.

"How'd it go with Harvey today?"

"He didn't tell you?" I had assumed the two men would talk about the investigation after I'd given my interview.

"Nope. He had me running all over the place." Dad took another swig of beer, then stretched out his legs. "He didn't hassle you too much, did he?"

"Not at all. In fact, he was super nice about the interview." I took a sip of my wine. "I'm sure we don't have anything to worry about."

My dad groaned and slapped the palm of his hand against his forehead. "Don't tell me charmin' Harv conned you."

"What? No, not at all. He was very professional."

"That man's smile has been known to get a confession out of a nun." Dad shook his head. "You didn't confess to anything, did you?"

"No! I'm innocent, with nothing to confess." I pressed my lips together. *What is he talking about?*

Detective Miller had been the epitome of professionalism with the utmost politeness. It hadn't hurt that he looked like a Nordic god, either.

"Are there two Detective Millers? Because this guy didn't seem at all like you described."

He groaned again. "I can't believe you fell for his spiel. I thought you were smarter than that."

"Excuse me?" I narrowed my eyes. "I didn't fall for anyone or anything."

"Did you stick to the facts like I told you to do?" He took a longer swig of beer. "That's why he's sent to interview the women. They fall for his handsome face and polite words."

"If that's the case, you should have warned me." I glared at my father. "I was expecting a man twice his age with gray hair and horns sprouting from his head."

Dad relaxed and chucked my chin. "Well, let's hope he didn't pry any of your deep, dark secrets from you."

"Secrets? I don't have any secrets. Mari says I'm an open book." I went to the refrigerator and grabbed another beer for my dad. "You can relax in the family room and watch whatever it is you like these days. I'll fix the beans and franks plus a salad."

He got up and kissed my cheek. "Thanks, sweetheart. We'll hope for the best when it comes to Harvey."

"When can I go back to my shop?"

"You can plan on Monday. I already called a cleaning crew to come in on Sunday." He paused at the kitchen entryway. "You'd better order another still. Yours is being kept for evidence. It was the murder weapon."

"I figured as much. I'll contact my insurance company and see what's covered."

CHAPTER SEVEN

After my dad left for work the next morning, I finished reviewing the job applications and set up a couple of interviews for Sunday. The young woman said she could only meet at eleven for thirty minutes. The other, a man, told me he was free whenever it was convenient for me, so I scheduled him for an eleven-thirty interview. I told the two applicants to meet me at Starbucks. I didn't want them to see the cleaning crew at the shop and freak them out about the murder.

I was just about to switch my laptop off and head out to my farmhouse to pack up some clean clothes and other essentials when a new application came in. The name rang a bell, and I wondered if it was the same Ashley Price who had been my friend from grade school through high school.

Heat flooded my face as I remembered how I'd cut myself off from my friends when I left for San Francisco to attend college. Why had I discounted my old friends and embraced new ones who turned out to be false? I knew why, even though I'd told no one else...I had sworn I'd never move back to Oak Creek Valley. I wanted to leave everyone, aside from family, behind. The town and the residents had seemed so small, so stifling, as I grew up. Big city life suited me better—until big city life chewed me up and spit me out.

The applicant, Ashley, seemed to have an appropriate amount of retail service experience. And she was local. It astounded me that several of the applicants lived over an hour away. The commute through the valley pass from the beach town of Ventura moved at a snail's pace on the single-lane highway, especially on the weekends. The pay I offered didn't seem like it would be worth the time and gas it would take. Were jobs that scarce? Or had they wanted to relocate to our quaint town?

Expecting to connect to voicemail, I stuttered a greeting when she answered the phone call. "H-hi, Ashley, it's Carissa from Aromatherapy Apothecary. Thanks for taking my call."

"Carissa!" she squealed. "Oh-em-gee. It's been, like, forever. I couldn't believe it when I heard you'd moved back into town and now you're opening a shop. You should have contacted me when you first got back. We need to get together for drinks and catch up."

She was the same vibrant, bubbly person I'd known ten years ago. "I'd love to get together. But the reason I'm calling is I just received your application."

Ashley turned uncharacteristically quiet.

When she said nothing, I jumped in to fill the silence. "I'd love to hire you."

Wait, what? Why did I say that?

I crossed my fingers that she would be a good fit. If she wasn't, how would I be able to fire a friend?

"You have no idea how much this means to me. Thank you, thank you." Her voice wavered. "When do you want me to start? What hours? I can work any time except late afternoons on Sundays. Otherwise, whenever and however long you want, is fine. My mom says she'll watch Hunter as much as I need her to."

Hunter? Did she have a son? I felt like I'd cut off my nose to spite my face by turning my back on my friends when I moved away. "That's terrific. Can you meet for coffee tomorrow afternoon, say around two? We can go over the job description and schedule. And if you're available, you can start Monday morning and help me prep the shop for the grand opening."

Ashley cleared her throat. "Wasn't your grand opening today? I meant to get down there to congratulate you and buy a couple of things, but Hunter was being a pill, and I never got out of the house."

"I guess you should know before you accept the job, a man was killed in the store yesterday. But professional cleaners will be there tomorrow, and it'll be as good as new. You'll never be able to guess something like that happened."

"Oh-em-gee! Get out! Who was it?"

"Russ Lewellyn."

"Oh. I guess it was bound to happen one of these days." Ashley covered the phone with her hand and said something to someone in the background. "I hate to cut this short, but I really need to tend to my son. I can't wait to catch up with you tomorrow!"

Driving to my farmhouse, I couldn't stop thinking about Ashley. When I pulled up to a stop sign, I glanced at myself in the rearview mirror. "What do you think? Do I need to tell Ashley about my scandal before she starts working at the shop, in case she doesn't want to be associated with a jailbird?"

I did a mental face slap. *Who am I trying to kid? Everyone knows that story backward and forward, including Ashley. Could fate be trying to tell me it's time to put down roots here in Oak Creek Valley instead of looking for something bigger and better?*

The dusty oblong green leaves of the avocado trees greeted me as I drove down the quarter-mile gravel road through the orchards to the farmhouse. I remembered the excitement my grandmother had displayed when she bought the house and orchard right after my grandpa died. I turned the last corner and drove into the large clearing that held the house.

A black-and-white patrol car sat parked at an angle across my driveway, the door gaping wide open. The vehicle was empty and the red and blue light bar flashed on and off, on and off.

CHAPTER EIGHT

My heart pounded hard, and my hands turned clammy as I gripped the steering wheel.

It was my dad's car.

Was he in danger?

Or was I, for that matter?

I wasn't sure if I should lock myself in my car or see if my dad was okay, so I called Peg.

"What's your emergency?"

"Hi, Peg, it's Carissa again."

"Good lord, don't tell me you've found another body."

"No! Nothing like that." Did she know my dad was at my house in his patrol car? I didn't want anyone to accuse him of doing something he shouldn't be doing. "Sorry to call nine-one-one, but I needed to see if you know where my dad is."

"You tried his cell?"

"Um, no." I guess it would come out anyway. "His car is at my house with lights flashing and the door wide open. I can't see him from where I'm parked and didn't want to go wandering into a gunfight or something."

"Oh, honey, gunfights don't happen in Oak Creek Valley. Course murder in an aromatherapy shop doesn't happen either." She muttered something. "Let me try to get him on his radio. Hang on."

She put me on hold and I listened to Muzak for what seemed like forever. "Sorry about that. There's a small brushfire that broke out around Camp Comfort. Some kids were playing with firecrackers."

"Oh no. How bad is it?" A chill slithered up my spine. Wildfires were a huge worry for a town surrounded by a dry brush and oak-tree-filled wilderness. Oak Creek Valley had miraculously been spared when it had been surrounded by an out-of-control wildfire a few years back. There had been mass evacuations and several properties on the outskirts had been consumed by the flames. No one wanted a repeat of that experience.

"There's no wind, and it sounds like some parkgoers dumped a cooler full of water and ice on the flames as soon as they noticed it. It appears to be out, but the fire department is on their way to make sure it stays out. Dang kids." She sighed. "Let me get ahold of your dad. I'll be back with you as soon as I can."

Hold music played in my ear again, and my mind went back to that horrific disaster. I lived in San Francisco at the time and had remained glued to my computer, hunting for updates and news reports. Dad worked round the clock for days on end until the danger had been contained. My grandmother was one of those who had to evacuate. Some trees had been scorched on the edge of her property, but thankfully, fire crews had been able to contain it. While my dad handled the massive destruction surrounding his town, my mama and grandmother had to fend for themselves. Not only had their strength seen them through the inferno, but I learned they had helped organize shelter and food for those who had lost their homes.

As soon as firefighters had contained the massive wildfire, I drove down the coast to visit my parents. It was as if I'd entered a war zone. Charred stumps and limbs marred the landscape, where stately oak trees had reigned. Some of the oaks had been centuries old. Solitary brick chimneys jutted from soot-covered rubble. Burned-out shells of cars and trucks stood beside piles of debris that had once been someone's cherished home. It was a sight that would haunt me till the end of days.

"Your dad saw some taggers defacing your house, and they took off in the orchard. He tried to chase them down, but they outran him. He said to give him five minutes. He'll meet you in the house."

"Thanks, Peg."

Why had they picked on my house? I hadn't been gone long enough for anyone to know it was empty.

"No problem. Take care now."

I disconnected and grabbed my house keys. My purse often stayed in the car but, given my recent company, I decided I'd better take it with me. I let myself into the ranch-style farmhouse, tossed my purse on the entry hall table, and then went back outside to inspect the damage. My mouth gaped open, and my heart fell into the pit of my stomach. When Peg said taggers, I assumed kids had spray-painted gang-style graffiti or obscene words.

I was wrong.

Someone had taped a sign to the side of my house.

**KILLERS BELONG IN JAIL
NOT OAK CREEK**

Red paint, the color of blood, had been splashed around the sign. The paint dripped down the wall, all the way to the flower beds. My future in Oak Creek Valley didn't look quite so promising.

How could anyone who knew me think I was capable of murder? Was the killer trying to heap more suspicion on me?

My dad walked around the corner of the house and headed toward me. His face was beet-red, and sweat soaked the collar of his uniform. "It's too hot to be chasing punks." He bent at the waist and took a few shallow breaths. "I suspect I need to add more cardio to my exercise program."

"You've been exercising?" I'd never known my dad to exercise when I'd lived at home.

"I've got a strength training routine, but I avoid the cardio. That's why I didn't catch the perps." He straightened and pointed at the sign. "I'm sorry you had to see that. I planned on having it checked for fingerprints and getting the paint cleaned up before you got here."

"Come on in and let me get you a glass of ice water." I led the way into my house.

It was cool and stayed that way even in the summer. My grandmother said the original owner, from the early nineteen hundreds, had used thick adobe blocks for the walls.

"I guess I'd rather hear what people are saying about me than be oblivious."

"No one's saying you killed Russ." He gulped down the glass of cold water, and then poured a refill.

"Well, someone's saying it. You can't misinterpret that sign."

"I wish I could have caught one of 'em." Dad's shoulders sagged. "At least I stopped them from doing any more damage. Lucky for you, I decided I'd better check on your house since most folks know you're staying with me."

Yeah, lucky me. "How many were there?"

"Three."

I was glad my dad hadn't caught up with them. They could have been the killers and harmed my father. I shuddered. I hated to admit my dad was right. Maybe I did need to sell my house and move into town, where I wasn't so isolated. Except I loved my grandmother's house and the four-acre avocado orchard that surrounded me.

Will a dog give me extra security? I made a mental note to visit the animal shelter sometime in the coming week and see if they had a dog that would work. It seemed like I was settling back in Oak Creek for the long haul and getting a dog would solidify my decision.

My dad had been in law enforcement for a long time and knew how to do his job. Still, it was becoming harder for me to stand by and allow people to accuse me of murder while I did nothing. It was time to ask questions and try to find answers to what had happened.

"Were the taggers kids?"

"They coulda been older teens or perhaps early twenties. Hard to tell with the hoodies they wore. Long sleeves and hoods pulled over their heads."

"In this heat?"

"Crazy, huh?" He collapsed into a kitchen chair. "Guess they didn't want to be recognized."

"Would you guess they were all guys? Or could there have been a woman?"

Dad dipped his head and stared at me. "What is this? An interrogation?"

"No. Nothing like that." I bit the corner of my lip. "I

thought if you described them, I might recognize who they were. Just trying to be a helpful citizen."

"Uh-huh. Don't you go getting involved in this investigation. Leave it to the professionals."

"You mean like the professional who seems to have a vendetta against you?"

My dad brushed his hand in the air to wave away my concern. "It's not as bad as that."

"You sure made it sound like it yesterday. What's the deal between you and Detective Miller?" I still couldn't get past his name. "And what in the heck is up with his old-fashioned name?"

"It's actually Harvey Edward Miller, the fourth, or it might be the fifth. Anyway, he's just as pretentious as his name."

"Still, what happened between you two to make you so antagonistic?" There had to be a story that went beyond a personality clash. "You've obviously worked with him before this."

"It's nothing I need to talk about. We have bigger problems to figure out, like who killed Russ."

"Daaaddddd." I stuck my lower lip out. "I need to know what happened between you two. I'm dying of curiosity, especially since you won't tell me."

"Oh, for Pete's sake, Cari-girl." He took a gulp of water.

Once again, I bit my tongue and waited.

"He wants my job." Dad blew out a long-held breath. "There. Are you satisfied?"

"Nope. I need the details."

"Has anyone ever told you that you're incorrigible?"

"Yep. You tell me that whenever you think I'm being too nosy." I shook my finger at my dad. "C'mon. Spill it."

He stared at the ceiling for a long while and blew out

another breath. "You can't let this color your interaction with him during this investigation. Promise?"

"I promise to be completely professional about it."

"I should wait until all of this blows over."

"Dad. No way."

"Harvey was the force behind trying to push me out of my job when you had your little, ah, escapade up in S.F." He pulled at his ear, then scratched his nose. "For whatever reason, he wants to be chief of police here in Oak Creek. I'm afraid he'll try to use this murder, and your involvement, to end my career."

CHAPTER NINE

I was stunned. My poor judgment in boyfriends shouldn't have impacted my father's career. His long years of exemplary service should have been more than enough to secure his job. Tears stung my eyes when I realized the harm I'd brought to him. "I wish I could go back in time and make better choices. I never meant to hurt you or jeopardize your career."

"You're not to blame, Cari-girl. I hope you know I've never blamed you." He handed me a tissue from the box perched on my counter. "You're sweet and surprisingly gullible, especially since you were raised under my roof and around your grandmother. It's refreshing since I've dealt with so much skepticism and strife day in and day out. But I regret I didn't prepare you for the world better, before I let you spread your wings."

I dabbed at my eyes with the tissue. That was the most personal talk I had with my dad since the "escapade," as he called it. Deep shame had made me want to avoid the issue. I was sure it had mortified my father when I'd been arrested. It reflected poorly on his parenting skills and perhaps even his law enforcement ethics.

"It's not your fault. You prepared me just fine." I took a deep breath in then exhaled slowly. "I could hear you talking in my head, telling me to ask questions, be more observant, and be wary of something that appeared too good to be true. I just didn't want to listen to what you had taught me. I wanted to be sucked in by the glamor and the money."

And my ex-boyfriend, Vincent, had reeled me in. Hook, line, and sinker. Now my family was paying the price.

He reached over and squeezed my hand—the one that wasn't clasping a soggy, shredded tissue. "We'll get through this. You and me. We're the survivors."

I gave him a small smile, tears filling my eyes. "Thanks. You know I love you, right?"

"Yeah, baby girl. I love you too."

That brought on more waterworks, so my dad set the box of tissues in front of me and busied himself filling our glasses again. I pretended not to notice when he grabbed a tissue before he turned his back to me.

Dad sat the glasses on the table and plopped back down into his seat. He looked around my cheery kitchen, buttercup-yellow with a chain of white daisies painted above the chair rail. My grandmother had painted it all. By hand. I always wished I'd inherited her artistic skill.

"I've been thinking..." He looked around the kitchen again, then drank a gulp of water.

I stiffened, preparing myself for the speech about me selling and buying a house close to him—or even moving in with him.

"I realize how much this house means to you. And honestly, it means a lot to me. I'd never seen my mama happier than when she bought this place and moved here."

Personally, I thought her happiness might have come about because of the little green plants my grandmother grew in the middle of her orchard. But I'd never mention that to my law-abiding father.

"You and your grandmother probably assumed I wasn't aware of her little garden." He closed his eyes and took a deep breath. He exhaled and his shoulders drooped, then he turned to gaze out the window. "I chose to turn a blind eye as long as I knew she wasn't corrupting a minor or selling. I was never more relieved when California voters saw the light. If you thought your escapade in San Francisco got tongues wagging, it would've been nothing compared to someone discovering the plants. That would definitely have been the end of my career, but unfortunately, it might come back to haunt me."

"What do you mean? That was a long time ago. Those plants are long gone."

He sighed and rubbed his face. "It seems like Harvey caught wind of what I chose to ignore way back when. Plus, there's the issue of those squatters trying to sell the plants that sprouted from seeds. He's insinuating I was part of the distribution. I should've used weed killer on the ground, but I didn't want to damage the avocado trees."

"I don't see what he can do. There's no proof."

A frown flickered across my dad's face. "Harvey's threatening to report me if I don't give him free rein on this murder investigation. A couple of your grandmother's friends are still around. It would only take one of them being tricked into giving him enough details to make my life miserable. I could fight it, but there are other things I'd rather not be brought to light."

"What do you mean?" I gave my full attention to my dad. I'd never heard him speak like this.

"I'm not going to get into it." He shook his head. "Harvey doesn't have any proof about anything, but I'd rather lie low and let him run with the investigation as long as he doesn't throw you in jail."

I had hated keeping secrets from my father, but it appeared he'd been doing the same. I wouldn't pry now but, one way or another, I'd find out what else he was hiding. "I'm sorry he's making your life miserable, but I'm glad you allowed Gram to enjoy the end of her years."

"She never told you, but she suffered from excruciating pain the doctors never diagnosed. Her garden harvest helped control it. When you were in middle school, she was on a heavy dose of opiates those idiot doctors prescribed. She was a complete mess. Couldn't eat, couldn't function. She was done-in and ready to call it quits. It took months to wean herself off those pills, and she swore she'd never take another one. I had to ignore the law to keep my mama alive."

"But couldn't she get a prescription for one of the medical marijuana dispensaries instead of growing it herself? It was legal back then." As a young teen, I'd been aware of the law but hadn't questioned why my grandmother grew her own, even after she'd sworn me to secrecy.

"Our county wouldn't allow any dispensaries to open and none of her doctors would write a prescription for her to take to L.A. to get filled." He rubbed his face with the palms of his hands. His five o'clock shadow made scratching noises in my quiet kitchen. "Besides, it was painful for her to sit in traffic for that long of a drive, and I suspect she was also sharing with her friends in need. It was one of those situations that if you don't think you'll like the answer, don't ask the question."

It made me wonder again what other laws my father had ignored and if someone would find out about it.

CHAPTER TEN

Dad tapped the tabletop with his fingers, the sound echoing in the quiet room. "If you're determined to stay out here by yourself, how about we find a dog for you to adopt?"

"I was just considering that idea earlier." I wondered what types of dogs were at the shelter. "Will you go with me to choose one?"

"Yeah, I'll go with you, but I doubt you'll need my input." He rolled his eyes. "No Chihuahua though. I'll freely give my opinion if you choose a yapper dog."

"Should I get a large dog? You know, for security?"

Vincent had owned a Doberman Pinscher until he was convicted. Even though the dog had never been aggressive toward me, I'd been thoroughly intimidated.

"A medium-sized dog can make plenty of noise and warn you if there's a problem." He patted my hand. "Let me take you to the range next week and get some shooting practice in. You're probably rusty on loading and getting the shots off in a short amount of time."

Dad was right. I hadn't handled a firearm since high

school. "Um, I'm not sure how comfortable I am with a gun."

"Nonsense. You grew up with them. Take appropriate precautions and practice safety, and it's not a bad thing to have in case of an emergency."

I considered the acres of avocados surrounding my house. I really was isolated if someone with bad intentions caught me out here. "All right. Can we do it after work sometime next week?"

"You bet. I'll get your gun out of the safe and oil it up." He rubbed his hands together. "Remember the target competitions we used to have? I'll bet you ten bucks you'll hit the bullseye within five minutes of practice."

"How about you give me twenty if I hit the bullseye, and if I don't, I'll cook a steak dinner for you?"

"Make it a ribeye with all the fixings." He reached out his hand to shake on the deal.

I left my dad in the kitchen to rustle up some PB&J sandwiches for us while I piled clothes and shoes in a suitcase. He'd insisted I stay with him until the killer was apprehended. I didn't argue. The sign the taggers had left freaked me out. Not only was I a potential target or scapegoat for the killer, but some townspeople appeared to be against me.

As we ate our sandwiches, I talked about hiring Ashley. My dad frowned at my hasty offer, but as soon as I told him she had a son and seemed to really need a job, he became supportive. I hadn't canceled the two other interviews scheduled for Sunday afternoon. Even though I wouldn't hire them, I'd buy them a cup of coffee and a pastry, and at least I'd have a comparison, should I need to replace her in the future. I hoped it wouldn't ever come to that.

Dad stacked the dirty plates in the sink. "I'll wash lunch dishes and you can finish packing."

"My suitcase is ready to go. It's in my bedroom." I nudged him away from the sink with my elbow. "I'll wash up and you can load the suitcase into my car. I hope it's not too heavy for you."

He flexed his arm. "I should be able to handle it unless you packed bricks."

"Nope. No bricks this time. I even left out my hardcover book."

I watched my dad load the suitcase into the car he had deemed most safe when I'd passed my driver's license test in high school. My Subaru was a little dented in places and desperately needed a wash, but it still ran great even after all these years.

After making me promise to be careful, Dad went back to work to pick up the fingerprint kit and stuff to clean up the mess the taggers had left behind.

I stayed a while longer to wash the lunch dishes. Since my grandmother had never installed an automatic dishwasher and I'd never gotten around to it, I hand-washed and dried the dishes. Once they were tucked away in the cupboards, I called Mari.

"Hi darlin', I was just thinking about you." She didn't give me a chance to identify myself or even say hello. "Is everything okay?"

"If you're home, I'd love to come by and chat for a while." I picked at a hangnail, a habit I only did when I felt stressed.

"Come on over. I'll have a glass of chai waiting for you." Without waiting for me to acknowledge, she disconnected the call.

Fifteen minutes later, I parked in front of the charming stone cottage. Mari had found the place on Airbnb and signed a lease for six months. Touted as an artist's retreat of sorts, it was small, but offered all the amenities an elderly retired woman would need. Plus, it took mere minutes to walk to downtown Oak Creek Valley.

Mari flung the door open and waved me in.

After settling in with iced chai and chilled mango slices, she turned her golden-brown eyes to me. "So, you've finally come to solicit my help in solving the murder."

I choked on my drink. "Are you a mystic?"

Her laugh tinkled in the thick, warm air. Even though her cottage had air-conditioning, she refused to run it. "No. The town gossip mill is running rampant. Half the folks believe you killed Russ while the other half is waiting to pass judgment. Which means they're not convinced you're innocent."

A whimper might have escaped my mouth. It was even worse than I'd imagined. My grand opening would have to be postponed until I could prove my innocence.

"Don't worry, darlin'. We'll figure it out." She refilled my glass from the carafe sitting on the low coffee table in front of us. "Rumor has it Russ wasn't well-liked. In fact, many folks might have had reasons to do him in."

"I've heard the same thing from two other people." I took a sip of my tea. "But so far, no one's telling me who or why."

"I'm running into the same problem. It's because we're outsiders."

"But I grew up here. I'm not an outsider."

"Yes. You are." She patted my knee. "You left for almost ten years. It's why they're not so sure of your innocence in this matter. And, well, your other problem in the Bay area doesn't help."

"No one will ever let me forget it happened." I bit at my hangnail.

"Give it some time. A few years down the road and you'll be a part of this community again. They'll forget it was ever connected to you." She opened a small wooden chest sitting beside the teapot and extracted a small vial, and uncapped it. "Let me have your hand."

I gave her my hand that wasn't nibbled on.

"No, your other hand."

I wrinkled my nose. "Let me go wash up."

"Don't be silly. Just give me your hand."

She took it in her warm palm and sprinkled a few drops of oil from the vial onto my chewed thumb. With gentle pressure, she massaged it into my cuticles and over the rest of my hand and wrist. A floral fragrance with undertones of citrus wafted around me. I closed my eyes and inhaled deeply, held for a few seconds, then slowly exhaled.

"Relax your jaw, darlin'." Her voice was gentle.

No wonder I was tense. I settled back into the cushion of the couch, and the stress left my body. "Thanks. I needed that. What oil blend did you use?"

"Ylang Ylang, bergamot, and a small amount of avocado oil."

"Hmmm, it's perfect."

"You need to take better care of yourself." Mari rose and went to the kitchen and washed her hands. "Eat better, start exercising, and practice stress relief with your oils. Have you considered getting a dog?"

"Actually, my dad is going with me to the shelter on Tuesday to look for one. Did he tell you to talk me into following through?"

"No. It just seems like a logical thing to do. You'll be giving a worthy companion a loving home and the dog will inspire you to walk and play. Plus, research has shown dogs are great stress relievers."

"Why don't you have a dog, then?"

She gestured around her quaint cottage. "My life is in flux right now. I'm not sure where I want to settle, and I might want to do some traveling before I make that decision. It wouldn't be fair to make a pet part of the family and then abandon it when it's time to move on."

"I hope you find Oak Creek Valley becomes home. I love having you here." I grasped her small hand.

I should have been moving back to a place that contained my vibrant mother and grandmother. Mari made that move so much easier now that they were no longer here. I'd emotionally adopted her as my surrogate grandma, and I didn't want her to leave.

"It'll always be like home as long as you're here, but there might be other places to go and things to do before I'm ready to call it quits." She straightened up. "Now, let's figure out a game plan to clear your name."

"Jasper—you remember, the owner of the patisserie?—and my friend, Ashley, both said they weren't surprised that someone killed Russ."

She raised her eyebrows.

"I'll quiz Ashley when I meet her for the interview and see if she has any information about who might have wanted Russ dead."

"You're interviewing Ashley for a job at Aromatherapy Apothecary?" She took a drink of her chai.

I nodded. "I guess interview isn't the right term. I kind of offered her a job over the phone and we're meeting up to go over duties and hours and get reacquainted."

"And Jasper?" She wiggled her eyebrows. "Are you going to interview him as well?"

My face heated. "No! I'll stop by in the morning for coffee and a chocolate roll and..."

Mari narrowed her eyes.

"Fine, I'll order coffee and something with fruit in it." I'd rather she remind me to eat healthier than have her guess why I frequented the patisserie. But given her facial expressions, anytime I brought up his name, I wasn't fooling her in the least. "I'll try to go when there isn't a long line. Maybe he'll know who might have had a motive for killing Russ."

"I'm going to the farmers' market tomorrow morning with some of my friends. I'll see if I can get them gossiping about Russ. You know how we old ladies love to wag our tongues."

I left with plans to meet up with her Monday morning at my shop. She would bring scones for breakfast, and I would provide the tea. I drove down the main thoroughfare and slowed as I passed my shop. Yellow crime scene tape was still strung across the front door. The weekend tourists gawked as they walked by. Would anyone ever want to buy anything from me?

It was after four, so I knew Jasper wouldn't be at work. He'd once mentioned he was up by three every morning to start the baking and candy making. He served nothing but fresh pastries, cookies, and bread, along with a chocolate confection of the day, which was why his bakery proved to be a huge success.

Dad sent a text and said he wouldn't be home until late, but wanted to make sure I locked all the doors and windows. I wondered if his late evening was work-related or if he had a date. He didn't talk much about his social life, but I'd heard snippets of rumors he'd been seen dining with an auburn-haired woman a few times. It wasn't any of my business, but I hoped he was enjoying life and not grieving.

Aside from my dad and Mari, who both lived full lives,

my life was empty. Since moving back, I'd first allowed myself to wallow in self-pity for a couple of months before immersing myself in planning, locating a retail space, and now setting up the shop. I had assumed it would keep me busy day in and day out, so I hadn't reconnected with old friends. But I didn't have my shop, and I still didn't have any friends. A pity party was headed my way, so I went home, poured a glass of wine, and found a good mystery to read—after I made sure all the doors and windows were secure like my dad ordered.

CHAPTER ELEVEN

Sunday morning dawned bright and clear, with birds chirping and squirrels chattering in the oak tree. Another hot day was in the forecast. I rummaged through my suitcase and found a slightly wrinkled sundress and hung it in the bathroom. The steam from my shower would make the dress a little more presentable. I hated to iron.

With some light makeup and comfortable sandals for walking, I tiptoed out of my childhood room. My dad's bedroom door was closed, so I assumed he'd had a late night and was still asleep.

I quietly let myself out of the house and walked to the patisserie. My plan was to get there early, before the church crowds swarmed for their fix of caffeine and sugar before Sunday services. I felt a twinge of guilt. It'd been several years since I set foot in church, not since my mother passed away. Instead of feeling closer to her during worship at her home church, it made me realize how much I missed her. Perhaps I hadn't dealt with my grief after all.

Shaking off the melancholy that threatened my mood, I picked up my pace.

Jasper would be a welcomed sight to brighten my day.

The door chimed when I pushed the ornately painted glass door open.

A broad smile appeared on the baker's face. "Carissa, how're you holding up?" He handed his only customer a pink bakery box. "I missed seeing you yesterday."

My cheeks heated. I wasn't sure if he meant he missed my daily purchase of his pastries or if he missed me as a person. "I'm doing okay."

"When can you get back into your shop? I noticed the crime scene tape is still there." He poured coffee into a large stoneware cup and added a liberal amount of milk to it.

"A cleaning crew is scheduled to come this afternoon so I can access it tomorrow. I have no idea when I'll be able to open for business, though. I guess it'll depend on how the investigation goes."

"Here. It's on the house." He handed me the cup. "Should I plate up your usual?"

"Thanks, I appreciate it." My usual...a sinful Triple Chocolate Roll, probably a thousand calories in a delectable, melt-in-your-mouth, pastry. My mouth watered and I couldn't resist. Despite Mari's nudging, I'd treat myself today and promised to eat healthier the next day.

I sat down at a small, round bistro table.

Jasper filled another mug with coffee and brought the plate and mug over to the table. After setting the plate in front of me, he sat down and took a sip of his coffee. "You're out and about early this morning if you can't get into your shop."

He wanted gossip, which was just the opening I needed. Except what I really needed first was a bite of the roll sitting in front of me, with its melty chocolate oozing down the sides. A moan might have escaped my lips when I bit into the sinfully delicious treat, and I closed my eyes to fully appreciate the bittersweet chocolate that mingled with the sticky, sweet topping.

When I opened my eyes, his gaze was locked on me, and his huge smile showed perfectly straight, white teeth. "Thanks, Carissa. You just made my day. I've never seen anyone enjoy my roll quite as much as you."

Heat flooded my body from the top of my head to the soles of my feet. I hadn't meant to show my enjoyment in such a public manner. "Err, well, your rolls and all your pastries are the best I've ever tasted."

"Like I said, you've made my day." He took another sip of coffee, his gaze never straying from my face. "Where are you headed off to so early this morning?"

What was the best way to word it so he wouldn't think I was hitting on him? Especially after my PDA with the pastry. "Um, I actually came to see you. There's something I want to ask you."

Jasper leaned forward. "Okay?"

"You mentioned the other day about not being surprised someone killed Russ. Can you tell me what you meant?" I was getting more flustered by the moment.

He didn't move away from me, and we ended up in a staring contest. I finally blinked and looked out the window. When I turned back, he had relaxed into the chair and held his coffee mug.

"My customers like to talk, so I hear all sorts of things." He gestured around his empty patisserie. "Such as you had a lot of reasons to kill Russ."

"No! I mean, I didn't. I wouldn't. That's not what happened." *Shut up already, Carissa.*

He laughed a deep, sexy laugh that made my stomach drop. "I'm positive you're not a killer."

It wasn't smart to ask, but I couldn't help it. "How do you know that?"

He sat his coffee mug down and closed the narrow space that separated us. "Anyone who can enjoy my chocolate rolls the way you do can't possibly have it in them to do something like that."

Is he flirting with me? That sounded a lot like flirting to me. My stomach plummeted even more, and I wished my face didn't have to flame like it did. Even with my olive-toned skin, I was aware pink colored my cheeks, which caused my freckles to become more noticeable. "I'm glad you believe in my innocence, but if I didn't do it, who else had a motive?"

He jumped up when a customer came through the door. "Be right back."

While he poured coffee and boxed up more pastries, I took a few more bites of the roll. When the customer departed, Jasper refreshed my mug with hot coffee and fresh milk, then sat back down. He brushed his thumb against the corner of my lip.

Can this morning get any better?

"There was some chocolate there." His smile was lopsided, and a short curl of strawberry-blond hair seemed to spring up from the top of his head.

I resisted the urge to smooth it back down. *Oh-em-gee. He really is flirting!* I smiled back then closed my lips, worried I had chocolate stuck in my teeth. I took a sip of coffee. "Have you heard any other rumors?"

He gazed at the ceiling for a moment, and then looked back at me. "Are you investigating?"

"Um, no. Just asking some questions. There seem to be quite a few people, present company excluded, who think I might be guilty."

"Isn't that your dad's job?"

I shook my head and my black curls bobbed against my bare shoulders. "Conflict of interest. The detective now in charge has reasons of his own to make sure I'm found guilty."

"How is that possible? And why?"

I shrugged. "Nothing I can explain at the moment, but that is what's happening. Anything else a customer might have told you?"

He studied me for a moment. "Well, there wasn't any love lost between Russ and his mother. Someone overheard Victoria threatening him."

"Really? From all their incessant arguing I've had the misfortune of hearing, it sounded like he was doing the threatening."

"Why do you suppose they argued so much?" He ran a hand through his strawberry-blond curls.

I looked at him over the bridge of my nose and shook my head. "Russ was Russ. Need I say more?"

He guffawed. "Yeah, he was a piece of work. Not to speak ill of the dead, but what exactly did you overhear?"

"He didn't want to work and expected his mother to support him. He was always harping on her to hand over money." I drank my coffee. He had fixed it exactly the way I liked it. "And Victoria frequently nagged him about being slovenly, but I don't see her bashing her own son's head in with my still."

Another customer entered the patisserie and Jasper went behind the counter to serve the elderly man. I took the opportunity to down the remaining crumbs of the chocolate roll while I admired the baker and his smile.

CHAPTER TWELVE

Once we had the patisserie to ourselves again, Jasper sat down and leaned in toward me. "Rumor has it that Mystic Valley Candles is in financial trouble and Russ went through all her money, which backs up their arguments over her supporting him. I'm only passing on what I've been told since I didn't actually hear her threaten him."

"Have you heard about anyone else having issues with him?" I eyed the smear of chocolate left on the plate but resisted the urge to scrape it off with the fork and eat it.

He rested his chin on his balled fist. "Let's see...accusations went around about a year ago that he stole quite a lot of expensive equipment from North Valley Trading Company. Almost put the owner, Seth North, out of business."

"How is that possible?" North Valley Trading Company was a sporting goods and outdoor recreational equipment store. One man wouldn't be able to shoplift enough merchandise to jeopardize the company.

"If Russ did it, he didn't do it all on his own, and I don't think he was smart enough to mastermind it. But, shortly after he quit working there, a large tractor-trailer cleaned out Seth's warehouse. Whoever stole the stuff knew how to disable the alarm and must have known when the security company made its nightly rounds."

"It was never proven?"

"Nope. The police questioned Russ but never charged him. Not long after that, he moved away for a couple of months. Seth barely scraped by. He only avoided bankruptcy by selling off several acres of his family's lemon orchard." Jasper's face darkened. "A developer snatched it up, and rumors are going around that there are plans in the works for some large housing developments and a retail complex. People around here aren't happy about that."

That didn't surprise me. Residents liked the small-town atmosphere and resented outsiders taking that away. Oak Creek Valley's mayor and council members had a reputation for being anti-development, but perhaps times had changed since I last lived here.

However, this scenario opened up the suspect list since anyone might have blamed Russ for paving the way for the development company to get hold of the acreage. It was a long shot, but it gave me something to look into. "Thanks for the information. At least there are a couple of other people around here that might have killed him, aside from me."

"Oh, I have one more rumor for you. You'll love this one."

He dragged the suspense out. I wouldn't give him the satisfaction of knowing I was on pins and needles.

Except, the longer he sat there and smiled, the more it piqued my curiosity. "Well? Are you going to tell me before another customer comes in?"

The words were barely out of my mouth when the door chimed as a family spilled into the shop. Two little boys ran to the pastry case and pressed their hands and faces against the glass to get a better look. I was sure they would leave sticky smudges behind.

I silently groaned as the little boys changed their minds a half-dozen times about what they wanted. My curiosity was killing me about who the third suspect might be. Yet, all the while, Jasper smiled and chatted amiably with the parents and gave the boys a few samples to try. The patisserie was nearing its busy time, and I needed to get out of the way. I'd been lucky to have as much uninterrupted time as it was. Arriving at six paid off, and I congratulated myself.

When silence returned to the bakery, Jasper sat down, and a wistful expression passed over his face. "Cute kids. They come to town to visit their grandmother at least once a month."

"That's really sweet." I wasn't sure what else to say, and my mind was screaming to get on with finding out the third suspect. "Now, about that third person."

"I love it when you're so impatient. But, okay, I'll play nice." He flashed me a grin. "You have to keep in mind this is only gossip. I guess Russ started spreading it around that Beatriz Torres, the mayor of our fair city, had an affair with him, then paid him to keep quiet about it."

"If she paid him, why would he spread the rumors?"

"He wanted more money, but she couldn't afford it because her husband dumped her."

"What? That's terrible. I can't see anyone having an affair with him. He wasn't, um, all that attractive." I pursed my lips together. "Even if she didn't, he still ruined her marriage."

"And her reputation. She's up for re-election this fall, and some residents are mighty unhappy about her fallen-woman status."

"That's not fair. Even if she had an affair, and I'd bet money she didn't, it's none of their business."

"Welcome to small-town politics."

"Do you think Mayor Torres is someone who could, you know...."

He wiggled his hand back and forth. "She's got a short temper and is feisty as all get out. But murder? I don't think so."

"How about her husband? Would he have wanted revenge?"

"Hard to tell. Last I heard, he already had some arm candy. Doesn't seem like he's all broken up about the alleged affair."

The door chimed again, interrupting our gossip session.

Jasper rose and leaned forward to whisper, "Write down your cell number and leave it at the register. I'll text you if I learn anything new."

And with that, the stream of Sunday morning customers began.

I swallowed the last bit of coffee, then wrote my number on a napkin and wedged it next to the cash register. I waved and pointed at the napkin before I walked out the door. I stepped onto the sidewalk and I decided I'd cook a proper Sunday morning breakfast of waffles and eggs for my dad. It was time to express my appreciation for everything he'd been doing for me.

While I walked, I opened my phone and Googled the mayor. The city website loaded, and her photo popped up in living color.

Mayor Torres had deep auburn hair and a striking

smile. Even in her mid-forties, she was still an attractive, fit woman.

Hadn't I heard somewhere that my dad was dating a woman with auburn hair?

No, it couldn't be.

CHAPTER THIRTEEN

I rounded the corner that led to my dad's block and there, across the street from his house, the mayor was climbing into a black BMW SUV. My dad, the chief of police, stood on the front steps of his home, barefoot, hair wet from a shower, wearing a white undershirt that pulled across a muscular chest, waving as she drove off. I stopped in my tracks, turned around, and power-walked out of sight. Neither of them needed to know I had seen them together.

I also saw my dad in a new light. He was handsome with slight graying at the temples of his copper- hair. He had a strong, square jawline and clear, blue eyes. And he'd be a catch for any woman. I'd never noticed that before.

My mind turned over all the possibilities of why Beatriz would have been at our house this early. Had her SUV been there when I left? I couldn't remember. My focus had been on the questions I wanted to ask Jasper and not on what was going on around me. If my dad knew I'd wandered around town without being aware of my surroundings, he'd lecture me for the rest of the day.

His voice echoed through my head with past instructions. "Scan your environment. Notice who's around you. Be prepared with keys gripped in your hand to protect yourself in case of attack. Never park in a dark corner. Always park under the security lights." The list went on and on.

I understood his concern, and it was all sound advice, but when my mind was puzzled by a problem, I tended to not focus on where I was.

What should I do? Take a walk around the neighborhood? Walk home and act like I didn't see anything? Ask him about it? I ended up walking home and pretended I hadn't seen a darn thing. He'd tell me about Beatriz when he was ready.

Waffles and eggs were soon on the table, and Dad read the Sunday paper while I reviewed my interview applicants and noted questions to ask. It surprised me he hadn't asked me where I'd been that morning, but I wasn't about to bring it up.

I checked the time, collected a notebook and pen, and kissed Dad's cheek. "I'm heading to Starbucks for a couple of interviews. Need anything while I'm out?"

He looked up from his paper, his eyebrows pulled together. "Didn't you hire Ashley, or did that fall through?"

"Ashley's still hired, but since I'd already scheduled the others, I decided I'd better keep them. I might be able to hire them down the road when the shop gets busy." *Which will never happen if I don't open.*

"Hm, okay. Be safe out there and watch your surroundings."

He couldn't turn down an opportunity to give me the safety talk.

"Are you working today?"

"I need to do some paperwork at the station a little later

on. Not sure how long I'll stay, though." He waved me away and put his nose back in the paper.

It didn't take long for me to reach Starbucks—or to pick out the young woman who waited for me. She was in her early twenties and had long, straight blonde hair. For the interview, she had dressed in a short, tight black miniskirt and a hot-pink cropped tank that showcased her flat abs and a sparkly navel piercing. When she reached forward to shake my offered hand, she tottered on her four-inch wedge sandals.

"Samantha? I'm Carissa." I pulled my hand away from her sweaty palm. Or maybe she had just applied scented lotion because the scent of synthetic cherries assaulted my nose. I covertly tried to wipe my hand on the backside of my dress. "Thanks for meeting with me today."

"Sure."

"Can I buy you a cup of coffee or a pastry?"

"No thanks. I don't drink or eat that stuff." Samantha seemed to look me up and down as if she judged me for consuming it myself.

"Okay, then. Let's grab a table out here and we can chat."

She followed me to a table that had an umbrella to shield us from the sun. I asked her a few questions about her past employment and she indicated she'd lost her job when the store went out of business.

She asked me a few questions about my product and nodded like a bobblehead toy while I explained what my shop sold.

"Can you tell me why you're looking for a job in Oak Creek when there are plenty of retail jobs in Ventura? I worry the commute might prove too long."

"It's not that bad of a drive. Like, you know, it only took

me thirty minutes." She looked at a chip that had appeared in her hot-pink nail polish. "My roommate commutes to LAX, and it takes over an hour and a half some days."

I shuddered, not wanting to imagine sitting in bumper-to-bumper traffic that long, five days a week, just to earn a paycheck. "Why do you want to work at Aromatherapy Apothecary?"

Samantha—or Sam, as she preferred to be called—twirled the ends of her blonde hair around her index finger. "Oh, well...I've heard you can meet a bunch of celebrities in Oak Creek Valley and, like, you know, I want to get discovered—or at least meet a rich guy."

Okaayyy...this application is going in the trash. I glanced at my watch. I still had twenty minutes before the next applicant was supposed to show up. "Sure, we see some celebrities in the restaurants now and then, but they don't come to the valley to shop."

"They don't?" Sam pouted her hot-pink glossy lips. "Where do they shop?"

"Rodeo Drive, I suppose." I wasn't exactly telling the truth, but I didn't want to encourage her.

Oak Creek Valley was home to many celebrities and, with our close proximity to Los Angeles, we were known for weekend getaways. Not only that, they often used our town for location shoots for television programs and movies. It wasn't unusual to have a street or two closed down and see film crews with their massive trucks and equipment blocking the road. As a result, the crews, including the actors, often descended upon the town's restaurants and shops during their downtime.

"Oh." She bent her head and checked her cell phone, then straightened up and looked over my shoulder. "I'm meeting a friend for brunch, so I'd better go now or I'll be late."

I stood and offered her my hand, which she shook. "I appreciate you taking the time to meet me for an interview. I'll be deciding on hiring personnel within the next two weeks."

"Thanks, but I really don't think this is like, you know, the right fit for me." Sam turned on her wedge sandals and walked down the street.

I shook my head and walked inside to wash my hands. Sam had definitely overdone the cherry-scented lotion. My hand reeked.

CHAPTER FOURTEEN

My next applicant, Dillon Andrews, showed up three minutes early, accepted my offer of coffee and a muffin, and sat ramrod straight. He was younger than I'd imagined him to be.

"Tell me about your experience working at the sporting goods store, Dillon." I glanced down at his application. "I see you've been working there since last August."

"That's right. I decided I needed to work a year and save up some money before starting college." He grinned. "Not only did I get all the hours I needed, but they gave their employees a good discount on merchandise. It came in handy over the ski season."

"But you're looking for a new job now?"

"My mom's work transferred her to Oak Creek Valley, so we moved here a couple of months ago." He ran long fingers through his light brown hair that had been trimmed short. "Commuting to Ventura for the job isn't all that bad, but once my college classes start in late August, the sporting goods store wouldn't agree to accommodate my request for a part-time schedule. I saw your ad and thought now would be the right time to look into other employment oppor-tunities."

I hadn't considered a part-time employee. "Once you start school, you're looking for a flexible schedule? Part-time only?"

"Yes." His hazel-colored eyes made direct contact with me. "Of course, weekend work is preferable, but I should be available for any evening hours as well. I don't have a class schedule yet to know how early or how late my classes might be."

I nodded. "What kind of duties do you perform at the sporting store?"

"I help customers find the merchandise they're shop-ping for, and I have to explain the features of whatever it is as well. I can run the cash register along with ordering and stocking merchandise." He paused a moment and his cheeks reddened. "I'm fully capable of doing janitorial duties, such as unclogging restroom toilets and cleaning up, the, ah, problem."

"In other words, no task is too menial for you?"

"That's correct, ma'am." He flashed a smile. "I'm grateful to have a paycheck at the end of the week, no matter what it takes to earn it."

I liked this kid, but he'd have to learn to not call me ma'am. I wasn't *that* old...yet.

I gave him the details about my shop.

He nodded enthusiastically. "My aunt in Santa Cruz is into essential oils, so I've learned quite a bit about it. Not how to make it, though."

"I'll be doing the distilling and blending. I'm looking for someone to help stock shelves and sell the products to clients."

"I used to get colds several times a year when I was a

kid. My aunt gave me a concoction I spray on my feet every night. I've only had a couple of colds in seven years since I started using it." He looked sheepish. "I'd wear it during the day, but it makes me smell kind of like Christmas. It got a little embarrassing."

This kid already knew about essential oils and believed in them. Still, I had the teeny-tiny little problem of not having a functioning retail store. "How soon do you want to start a part-time job?"

"My mom says it's customary to give a two-week notice when I quit." He looked worried. "But if it meant losing out on an opportunity, then I'd figure something else out with my old company."

"No, that works. What I meant to say is I'm very interested in hiring you, but my shop ran into a little snafu, and I'm not even open yet."

"You're the one who had a man murdered in your store, aren't you?"

Oh boy. Word sure got around. "Uh, yes. That'd be my store."

"Cool." His dark brown brows furrowed together. "Except, well, my mom will probably want to talk to you about safety and all that."

It sounded more and more by the minute I'd hired this kid and he'd accepted. How the heck had that happened? "I understand. You said your mom relocated here for a job?"

"Yes. She's the new sheriff's deputy assigned to Oak Creek Valley." He hung his head and looked at me over the bridge of his nose. "So you can see why she'd be wanting to talk to you about safety."

"I completely understand. My dad's the chief of police."

"Really? You're Robert Carmichael's daughter?"

"Do you know him?"

"Of course. He and my mom, well, they go out." He scrunched his nose up. "I guess I missed hearing your last name. He hasn't said anything about my mom? Sandy Andrews?"

"I recently moved back to town and we've been, ah, kind of too busy to talk about anything personal."

Actually, it was because we'd both avoided talking about anything personal. I didn't want to talk about my arrest or Vincent, and he obviously didn't want to talk about his love life.

"That's right. You were in San Francisco." Dillon snapped his fingers as if remembering something. "My mom said if I ever pulled a stunt like that, she'd skin me alive."

Why, oh why, couldn't my past go away and leave me alone?

"Oh. I'm sorry." The tips of his ears were bright red. "I shouldn't have brought that up. I have a little problem with a mouth filter sometimes. Especially when I'm nervous."

We both had that in common. "Don't worry about it. I'm sure my dad wanted to do the same thing."

He took a sip of his iced coffee.

I did the same, then exhaled the breath I'd been holding in. "Dillon, here's the thing. I'm really interested in hiring you, but until my shop opens, I'm not sure how much help I'll need or how many hours I can offer you."

He looked dejected. He probably assumed I was mad about him bringing up my past and he'd just blown the interview. "No problem. Thanks for your time."

"No. Please wait." I gestured for him to sit back down. "It's not anything you said. It's just that I didn't expect for my shop to remain closed for so long and then, well, I'm sure you've heard...people think I killed Russ. I'm not sure how successful Aromatherapy Apothecary will be if I'm not proven innocent."

Dillon bit his lower lip. "Yeah, I kinda heard the rumors going around town. My mom wasn't sure I should even interview. Although, I'm positive she didn't know the owner is Robert's daughter. That'll put her mind at ease."

"Or forbid you to ever speak to me again." This time, I laughed to let him know I was joking. "Seriously, if you can find another part-time job you like, take it. Otherwise, I'll call you as soon as I straighten this mess out."

And if I got my wish, it'd be sooner than later because if I didn't start making money, I'd have to sell off the avocado orchard to keep from declaring bankruptcy.

"Thanks. I guess the good thing is I still have a full-time job and don't need to quit until August."

"That might work even better, as long as you don't mind continuing on at the sports store. It'll give you a chance to put some money in the bank before you start college." I tapped my forefinger against my lips. "If I find I need some extra help, perhaps you can work a few hours for me here and there and when school starts, you can work here. I'll be happy to figure out a flexible schedule for you."

Where is my filter? I needed to work details out with Ashley first, open my store, and *then* worry about part-time help. Yet, here I sat with two employees and zero sales. But something inside told me, in very strong terms, that I needed to hire this kid.

I thought back to when Mari hired me. After my mom passed, I dropped out of college. Not knowing what to do with my life and refusing to move back home, I started work as a temp, doing menial tasks. Working at a bridal trade show for a vendor, I stumbled upon Mari's essential oils booth when the fragrance drew me in. She took one look at my dark chocolate-brown eyes and said she'd hire me full-time if I was willing to work hard. I started the very next day. It was the same feeling I had with both Ashley and Dillon so, somehow, it would all work out.

"Thank you, Ms. Carmichael." He held out his hand to me. "I appreciate the opportunity."

"Please, call me Carissa." I shook his hand. "Welcome to the team. I'll be in touch when the store is open and we can discuss details then."

"Cool. I can't wait to tell my mom."

And I couldn't wait to grill my dad about one Sandy Andrews.

Once Dillon and I parted ways, I meandered past the patisserie–it was still crowded–then down through the historic arcade. I admired its graceful arches and Spanish-tiled sidewalks that reflected the town's heritage. Across the street, the farmers' market was in full swing, with tourists stocking up on produce and local arts and crafts to take home. With a population of less than eight thousand residents, Oak Creek Valley relied heavily on tourism. Visitors, including famous notables, flocked to our town to experience the serene beauty nature had to offer, indulge in world-class pampering, or enjoy one of the many festivals revolving around music, art, and food. We had a little of everything.

For lunch, I grabbed a street taco from one of the food trucks at the farmers' market. Fresh homemade maize tortillas were wrapped around juicy *carnitas*. I topped the melt-in-your-mouth pork with garden-fresh *pico de gallo* and cubed avocado. Mari's advice about eating healthier whispered in my head, so I added fresh shreds of cabbage and a squeeze of lime instead of cheese and sour cream. By the time I had downed my taco and slurped my iced tea, it was time to head back and meet up with Ashley.

CHAPTER FIFTEEN

Ashley flung her arms around my neck, rocking me back and forth in a bone-crushing hug.

Tears stung the corners of my eyes. I wasn't worthy of her affection, yet it melted some of the melancholy I had experienced the night before.

She held me at arm's length and looked me up and down. "Look at you, girlfriend!"

My face heated. *Uh, yeah. Look at how much weight I've gained. Thanks for pointing it out.* I looked her up and down. Still the same gorgeous blonde I'd known in school. "You haven't changed a bit. How is it you haven't aged a day?"

Her tinkling laugh made the men in our vicinity stop and stare. She was hard not to notice with her wavy curls that fell halfway down her back. Her low-rise skinny jeans and the tight T-shirt she had tucked into the waist emphasized a generous bosom and tiny midsection. No one would ever guess she'd had a kid with her perfectly proportioned body. If she wasn't such a nice person, I might've been jealous.

She gazed at me with her baby-blue eyes. "What? No way. But you...you look fantastic." She grabbed my hand and twirled me around in a circle.

My sundress billowed out, and I pulled a shoulder strap back up when it slipped down my arm. I was speechless. *Did she really just say I look fantastic? Me?*

She must've noticed the surprise—or more likely shock —that crossed my face. "You've filled out. You have curves now instead of bony angles. Not that there was anything wrong with being skinny in high school."

I still didn't know what to say. I was chubby but my friend said I looked fantastic?

"Carissa, you've blossomed into a woman."

"Um, thanks?" It was impossible to wrap my head around her version of who I'd become. "Should we grab a table and order some coffee? My treat."

"I have a table for us." She pointed to a black satchel on top of a table shaded by a dark green umbrella. "I'll take a plain black iced tea, if you don't mind."

"Would you like a pastry or cookie to go with that?"

"I'd love a cake pop. The one with the pink frosting." She flashed a smile at me. "Just a little treat without over-doing the sugar. I'm trying to teach my son that concept, so I'm having to learn it myself."

I gave her a thumbs up and stood in line at the counter as the siren scent of cinnamon coffee cake called me. Her advice was something I should incorporate for myself. Despite what she saw as womanly curves, I didn't want to get any larger, so I needed to make some lifestyle adjust-ments. Living in town had its advantages. I'd walked almost everywhere since staying with my dad. Perhaps I *should* consider moving.

It was finally my turn to order. In no time at all, I

carried two unsweetened ice teas and two pink birthday cake pops back to her table.

"That cake pop looks amazing. Thank you."

I waved her off. "It's my way of saying thank you for meeting with me to talk about the job offer, especially on a weekend. It's the least I can do."

"Thank you from the bottom of my heart. You have no idea how excited and, to be honest, relieved I am that you hired me." Her lower lip quivered and her eyes turned shiny. "I'm not here to make you feel sorry for me, but this couldn't have come at a better time."

"If you need to talk about it, I have a good listening ear."

"Not now. I'll be fine." She gave me a half-smile. "Tell me about your shop. When will you be able to have your grand opening?"

That was when grim reality set in. Until I was making a profit, I couldn't afford to pay Ashley a full-time wage. I still had a decent nest egg left over from my grandmother's inheritance, but I had to remind myself I couldn't spend it just because I felt sorry for or connected with an employee. Like Ashley and Dillon.

"Well...obviously, there's been a bit of a setback with the death."

Ashley's face fell from hopeful to distraught.

I plunged forward, ignoring the grownup voice that whispered to take it slow. "However, I will still open and need all the help I can get to organize for the grand opening."

"That sounds good." She took a nibble of her cake pop, so I did too. "Do you have an opening date in mind? Or you might consider a soft opening, like on a Thursday or Friday, to give yourself a day or two to work out any bugs before tourists descend over a weekend."

And that was exactly why she was hired, with no looking back. She had a natural talent for retail that I lacked. It made so much sense to me, that I mentally kicked myself for not planning a soft opening myself.

"Unless the investigating detective says otherwise, should we shoot for a soft opening on Friday and the celebration on Saturday?" I hesitated since we hadn't talked about the hours or days she wanted to work. "Let's talk about your schedule and what hours you can work before we decide. I'm a bit gun-shy about opening, even a soft opening, since it appears there are quite a few people who are sure I'm guilty."

"We can do the soft opening a couple of different ways: by invitation only, or open the doors to anyone who happens to walk by."

I pursed my lips together while I thought about the two scenarios. Invitations would add extra time I didn't have to my workload. And, to be honest, I worried the townspeople would ignore it and leave me with an embarrassingly empty store. "Let's open the doors for anyone to walk in. Fridays aren't too busy, since tourists generally don't start their serious shopping until Saturday."

"Leave it to me. I'll start the word of mouth, and there'll be plenty of people in there. Do you think Saturday will be your grand opening?"

"Can you give me a couple of days to think about it? I'm worried about the investigation..." If I was in jail, I couldn't very well open the doors to my shop. I finally remembered my manners. "I don't know what to say except thank you for your advice."

"You're welcome. It's the least I can do." She brushed a crumb from the tabletop with the tip of her finger. "How did you get into the aromatherapy and reflexology business?"

"I got lucky and met Mari Kemp in San Francisco. She ran a shop there and hired me, and now she's consulting on my shop here. You'll love her!" What I didn't want to share with her quite yet is that after my mother died, I'd floated around with no purpose. I'd relied on temp jobs and my grandmother's financial gifts to keep me going. I'd broken Gram's heart by refusing to move back to Oak Creek, but I couldn't bear to be in this town without my mom back then.

"C'mon, spill the details. You don't go from working in Mari's shop to having your photo splashed across national newspapers without there being a story." Ashley narrowed her eyes and leaned her face close to mine. "And why in the heck didn't you cover your head, or at least your face, for that perp walk? Girlfriend, that was one dreadful photo of you!"

I covered my face with my hands, embarrassed to be reminded of something I'd tried so hard to forget. Between my Medusa hair and the smears of mascara beneath my eyes, I looked like a demented raccoon as I was hauled off in handcuffs. "They never gave me a chance to do anything, and once the cuffs were on, I was helpless. Then the police were screaming at me and pushing me toward the cruiser. They didn't let me say one word."

She placed a cool palm on my shoulder and rubbed it in small circles—something my mom used to do to soothe me when I was a child.

I lowered my hands from my face and tried to smile. It probably looked like a contorted grimace.

"Mari had nothing to do with my arrest. It was all my ex-boyfriend's fault." Property developer Vincent Huber, with his jet-black hair and striking blue eyes, had sucked me right in. I'd been so stupid to be taken in by his flowery flattery, posh restaurants, and trips to the wine country on a private jet. And when he bankrolled the expansion of my reflexology business, effectively cutting off my association with Mari, I hadn't given it much thought. Vince had, unbeknownst to me, used me to carry bribes and city bid information between my clients. After the lawyers got the charges against me dropped, I left San Francisco and slunk home to Oak Creek Valley with my tail tucked between my legs.

"Yeah, I read all the news accounts. But he's still in prison, right?"

I shivered. "He'll be in for several years, but I worry about his threats of getting even with me. He blames me for busting up his scam."

Ashley waved away my concerns. "He's in the hoosegow. Forget about him."

"Hoosegow? Where'd ya get that?" I giggled.

She smiled. "Mom and I love watching those old black-and-white movies from the forties. I guess some of the language stuck to me."

Anxious to change the subject, I took the opportunity to ask her about her life. "So, you have a son. Hunter?"

"Yes. He's two-and-a-half and keeps Mom and me jumping." She twisted a napkin between her fingers. "I might as well tell you...Hunter's dad was killed while serving in Afghanistan...so I'm a single mom. I never even had the chance to tell him I was pregnant."

"Oh, Ashley. I'm so sorry." That explained why she desperately needed a job.

She nodded and blinked several times.

"Where did you meet your husband?" I rested my hand on her arm.

"Bruce was stationed in San Diego, and I met him at a friend's party." Her voice quivered and her eyes turned glassy.

"Did you live there the entire time, or did you have to transfer elsewhere?" I knew all too often military families rarely stayed in one place for long.

"We lived in several places, all over the country." Tears threatened to roll down her cheeks. She shook her head and blew out a ragged exhalation. "I'm sorry. It's still too hard to talk about."

"That's alright. I'm sorry for being so nosy."

She flashed a quick smile. "You're not nosy. Your questions are normal, considering we haven't seen each other in a long time."

I gave her arm a squeeze, then grabbed my iced tea. "Tell me what your ideal schedule would be, and let's try to make it work."

"For the most part, weekdays are best, although I could work Saturdays if you need me. My mom works late Sunday afternoons and evenings and I don't have anyone else to watch Hunter if we're both working." Ashley jiggled the ice in her now empty cup. "While I can work some evenings, I'd prefer to be home by dinner so I can be with Hunter for the evening. Bath time and story time are important to us both."

"That shouldn't be a problem for any of it. I'm not planning on keeping the shop open later than six and I should be able to handle it on my own for an hour."

"I know my mom will be relieved to hear that. It's a long day caring for Hunter all on her own." Ashley twisted her lips. "If you have special events or need me to stay longer, I'm happy to work. I'll do anything you need me to, just as long as I can keep the job."

"I'll keep that in mind. For now, we should be able to get you home in plenty of time to spend dinner and the evening with Hunter."

I didn't feel quite so bad about offering Dillon a part-time job since he could work the weekends to accommodate his college schedule. When the business was firmly established, I was sure I'd need their help and then some, if other shops in the area were any indication. Well, except for Mystic Valley Candles.

CHAPTER SIXTEEN

"I'm curious about your comment yesterday when you mentioned you weren't surprised someone had killed Russ. What did you mean?"

Ashley's face flushed pink. "Oh, that's just the gossip floating around. I really don't know anything."

"At this point, I'm happy to hear all the chatter I can get about Russ. According to Dad, Detective Miller seems to believe I did it." I gave an exaggerated shudder, hoping she'd get the hint I needed some information. I didn't care if it was based on fact or speculation.

"Well, his own mother was about ready to toss him off a cliff. He was a real piece of trash, if you know what I mean."

I nodded. "Someone mentioned that. But can you see Victoria conking him in the head until he was dead?"

"Oohhhh. Is that how he was killed?" Ashley's blue eyes opened wide. "Did you find the murder weapon?"

I gave myself a mental forehead slap. They hadn't released the cause of death. Although come to think of it, Jasper hadn't acted surprised when I'd mentioned the still.

I'd have to remind him to not spread gossip about the cause of death. "Promise me you didn't hear that. Pleeeasseee?"

"My lips are sealed." She held up her pinky. "I pinky promise. Plus, I really, really need this job, and I'd never do anything to make you fire me."

I grasped her pinky with my own and then released it.

"Well, did you hear that our delicious baker had it in for him? At least five people told me Jasper threatened to kill him."

I grabbed onto the table and licked my dry lips. My voice came out in a whisper. "Jasper? What did Russ do to Jasper?"

"According to these eyewitnesses," Ashley rolled her eyes, "Russ stomped into the patisserie and wanted his pastries and coffee comped because they were retail neighbors."

I snorted. "Yeah, like he ever worked a single day at Mystic."

Ashley laughed. "Exactly. So Jasper threw him out when he refused to pay. He stuffed half the pastry in his mouth and told Jasper he'd stuff the other half up his you-know-what."

I grimaced. "So what happened next? Is that when Jasper threatened him?"

"No. Jasper was cool as a cucumber and ignored him." She had a glint in her eyes. "The next day, the health inspector shows up and says someone called in an anony-mous complaint that the bakery was infested with roaches."

"That's not possible."

"Unless someone sabotaged it and planted the roaches before calling."

"Oohhh…Heebie-jeebies!" I shivered. "Seriously, that's what happened?"

"Yep. And the health department shut him down for a week until they could schedule a new inspection. Obviously, Jasper had no proof who did it, but it doesn't take a rocket scientist to figure out it was Russ the Rat." Ashley turned serious. "That's when Jasper threw off his apron and stomped down to Mystic. He grabbed Russ by the throat and said if he ever stepped foot inside the patisserie again, he'd kill him. Again, that's according to five eyewitnesses."

"Yikes."

Jasper hadn't mentioned this altercation. Instead, he'd tried to lob Victoria off as a viable suspect.

How on earth had I been so gullible? Again...Apparently, I hadn't learned my lesson in matters of the heart.

She touched my hand. "Are you okay?"

I shrugged. "Jasper and I had coffee this morning and talked about the murder. He didn't say a word about his problem with Russ."

This time it was Ashley who snorted. "What? You expect a man who's smitten with you to tell you he should be a suspect in a murder investigation?"

"Where'd you hear he's smitten with me?"

"Oh, Carissa, you've been away from Oak Creek for way too long." She giggled. "You can't go to the patisserie every single day for a Triple Chocolate Roll and a cup of coffee with milk and Jasper giving you your 'usual' without people gossiping. Out of the eight thousand souls who live here, you're the only one he asks if you want the usual."

She knows what my usual is? Which meant everyone in town knew what my usual was. That was it. I had to find something new to order. I wasn't strong enough to stop frequenting the patisserie cold turkey. "Maybe I'm the only one who's so boring and orders the same thing day in and day out. Most people don't go there every single day like, um, me."

"Trust me. You go there because you're infatuated..."

"I'm not—"

She held up her hand. "And you go there because oh-em-gee those pastries are to die for. On the flip side, Jasper looks forward to seeing you every day. Have you not noticed the googly eyes he gives you when you're in line?"

"How do you know that?"

She rolled her eyes. "Don't tell me you're looking at the pastry case instead of at him or the other customers?"

My face turned hot. "Um, yeah. That's exactly what I'm looking at since he's always busy when I walk in. Besides, I want to see if I should try something new."

"Ah-ha. So you admit it."

"That's not what I said." I huffed. "Okay, so I might be. But that doesn't mean he's smitten with me. I'm sure that's far from the truth."

Her laugh reminded me of Tinker Bell. "Honey, when you walk through the door, it's like whatever customer he's waiting on doesn't even exist."

"That can't possibly be true."

He gave each of his customers individual attention, which was one of the reasons his shop was so popular.

"Take my word for it. It's one hundred percent true."

Had I been an ostrich these last few months, wallowing in my self-pity over the scandal I had been caught up in? I had no idea which way was up or if he was trying to hood-wink me and set me on the trail of suspects to take the spot-light off himself. Out of all the scenarios of who might have killed Russ, his was the most plausible.

I cradled my face in my hands.

"Hey. Are you all right?" She touched my arm. "I didn't mean to upset you."

"It's fine. I'm glad you told me." I lowered my hands into my lap. "It's just been a...difficult year."

"And then some, from what the gossipers say."

I lifted my gaze.

Ashley winked at me. "Ya know what we need, girlfriend?"

I shook my head.

"A pitcher of sangria." She jerked her thumb toward the parking lot. "C'mon. Grab your nightie and pillow and come out to my place. I'll mix up a batch or three. We both deserve it."

"What about your mom and Hunter?"

"Hunter goes to bed, like clockwork," she looked at her watch, "in three point five hours. And my mom will be more than happy to drink her share and fix some barbecued ribs for us."

My mouth watered. Memories of Ashley's mom, Mrs. Price, flitted into my mind. She had made the best melt-in-your-mouth, stick-to-your-ribs barbecue ever. Then it hit me. Ashley used her maiden name. Plenty of women did that for professional reasons, but, as far as I could tell from the job application, she'd held minor retail clerk positions, which never lasted more than eight or nine months. I wondered why that was. I hoped she'd confide in me once we spent some time together. "Okay. I'll meet you at your house. What can I bring?"

"Just yourself. Give me your phone?" Ashley entered her address into my cell phone's GPS app.

"It'll probably be an hour before I can get to your place. Does that work alright for you?"

"It's perfect. I'll have the first batch of sangria chilled and waiting for you."

I walked home at a brisk pace and gathered the overnight essentials I'd need. Rummaging through my dad's junk drawer, I finally found a pen that kind of worked and scribbled a note telling him where I'd be.

Going to Ashley's for dinner
Don't wait up!
Love you!
P.S. Don't worry. I'll be careful.

CHAPTER SEVENTEEN

I turned down a gravel road bordered on each side by lush, green-leafed tangerine trees laden with bright orange Pixie tangerines, just like the GPS directions told me to do. I rolled down my window to breathe in the fragrant fruit. Ashley had warned me I needed to follow the gravel road for about a half mile, even if it felt like I was lost in the middle of nowhere.

When I exited the orchard and drove into the clearing, I almost slammed on my brakes. Their home still showed the cruel ravages of the fire that had swept through this area a few years ago. The charred corpse of a pickup truck, its twisted metal angling toward the sky, still sat to the side of what used to be the garage. A grim reminder of all they had lost.

Ashley met me at the front door and swept her arm around. "Awful, isn't it?"

I nodded, wondering why they hadn't hauled the charred truck away or had the garage rebuilt. "Were you living here at the time?"

"No. I was back east. My mom barely managed to evacuate before the fire hit." She shuddered. "The winds were horrific, and the blazes jumped the fire lines before anyone had any warning. Our garage was completely engulfed in flames by the time Mom was even halfway down the gravel road."

"At least the fire crew saved most of your house." I glanced around the homey interior.

A tow-headed little boy sat on the couch watching a cartoon. He turned his head and gave his mama a huge smile. His blue eyes widened when he spotted me, and his smile disappeared before he turned his attention back to the television.

"True. It's given us a place to live." Her mouth pressed into a hard, thin line and her eyes darkened. "At least for the time being."

"What do you mean?"

Ashley walked over to her little boy, kissed the top of his head, and smoothed his hair down with her fingertips. She turned toward me and forced a small smile. "It's nothing. Let's go to the kitchen and drink sangria. Mom's out back grilling."

"I didn't mean for her to do extra work on my behalf. I should have brought takeout or pizza."

"It's no problem. She planned to grill anyway." She opened a modern refrigerator that looked out of place with the nineteen-fifties-era stove and speckled gray Formica countertops. She sat the pitcher of ruby-red sangria on the scarred wooden farm-style table, along with three acrylic wine glasses. Chunks of oranges, strawberries, and green apples floated in the wine.

"You can pour." She opened a cupboard and pulled out a package of water crackers, arranging them on a plate next to slices of cheddar cheese, pepper jack cheese, and thick slices of salami. She plopped down on the chair beside me and lifted her glass.

"Here's to friends." We clinked glasses and took long swigs of the fruity concoction. "So, Cari, what are we going to do about the investigation?"

"I can't let you get involved." I pointed my thumb toward her family room. "You have a son to consider."

"I'm not saying we need to creep around dark alleyways to find suspects." She topped off our glasses. "We just have to chat with people in our community who might know more about Russ than they think. It's like putting together a puzzle. A piece here, a piece there, until you see the whole picture."

"Don't you ever read mysteries? That's what the amateur sleuth always says, but in the end, their life is in danger."

"Yeah, but they always survive." Ashley waggled her perfectly sculpted eyebrows at me.

"Ha. It's all fiction. You can never predict what'll happen." I took a sip of the refreshing drink. "Besides, we both moved away and now we're outsiders. No one will confide in us."

She let out a long breath that ended with a sigh. "I don't know how to break it to you, but I'm not an outsider."

I shrugged. "You've been back long enough for them to forgive you for moving away? How long did it take?"

"It's not that." She glanced toward the living room. "The reason they accepted me back the second I drove into town is because my son is fatherless, thanks to his dad serving his country. They'll tell me anything. Face it. You need me."

"Oh, Ash. I'm so, so sorry." My eyes turned a little misty, so I took a chug of the sangria.

Mrs. Price brought in a small platter of juicy, barbecued ribs. Her ash-gray hair was short in a ragged sort of way, almost as if she had taken scissors to it herself. Her thin body didn't look strong enough to carry the small platter and her shoulders were hunched.

"Hunter, dinner's ready," Mrs. Price called out. "Hello, Carissa. It's been forever since I've seen you. I'm glad you joined us."

"Thanks for letting me intrude, Mrs. Price."

"Oh poo. You call me Fran. There's no need for formality around here." She placed the platter in the center of the table. Her pale blue eyes appeared almost sunken in, which made the bags beneath them all the more obvious. "I have watermelon slices and a green salad in the fridge. Ashley, can you put those on the table and wash Hunter's hands?"

"Sure, Mom."

I jumped up. "You get Hunter ready for dinner. I'll take care of the watermelon and salad. You don't have to wait on me. I remember how to make myself useful in the kitchen."

"You don't have to do that, hon." Fran motioned her daughter toward the fridge. "You're our guest."

Ashley and her mom froze in place as I opened the refrigerator. It surprised me when Ashley bolted from the room.

Fran turned her back on me and collected silverware from a drawer and plates from a cupboard, her shoulders even more hunched than when she'd brought the ribs in from the grill.

The refrigerator was almost bare. Slices of watermelon were stacked on a plate and a small green salad sat heaped in a bowl. There was a jar of peanut butter, a smidgen of jam, a loaf of bread, and a quart of milk. A few condiments were lined up on the bottom shelf. And a half-full pitcher of sangria. Had Ashley used up money they didn't have to entertain me? I had no business eating even a bite of their precious food, but I had no idea what to do without causing them extreme embarrassment.

I placed everything on the table and set Hunter's milk in front of him.

Ashley busied herself with getting her son settled in. She cut tiny bites of meat and watermelon into small cubes on his plate.

"I wan' wa'ermelon." His chubby fingers stretched for the bright red fruit. "And peana' bu'er sammich."

"Take a bite of meat and then you can have a sammich." Ashley coaxed a bite into his mouth, then handed him a small toddler's plastic fork to spear his watermelon.

Pink juice dripped from his chin as he gobbled up the fruit. "I wan' more."

"Eat another bite of meat first."

Fran gave me the platter of ribs. There was no longer a smile on her weary, weathered face.

I took one of the smallest pieces. "This smells delicious. I can't remember the last time I had barbecue."

"Your dad doesn't grill?" Fran passed the salad to me.

"Mom was our grill master. I never had time to learn." A lump formed in my throat. I should have spent more time at home instead of looking for excuses as to why I couldn't come for a visit. I should have asked Mom to teach me... before it was too late.

Hunter, his mouth half full, told his mom about his adventures with his gamma that afternoon.

Ashley fixed him a small peanut butter sammich then tried to lighten the mood by sharing humorous stories about people I remembered. She had slowed down on drinking the sangria and Fran barely touched hers.

Once Hunter ran back to his cartoon, Fran waved us away. "You girls go relax. I'll clean up."

"Mrs. Price, err, I mean Fran. You've done all the cooking. We'll wash the dishes and clean up."

"That's true, Mom. Go put your feet up. I know you're dying to finish your book."

"You girls are sweet. I might just do that, seeing how it's due back at the library tomorrow."

Ashley and I washed and dried in silence.

Once the kitchen was sparkling clean, my friend drained the last sangria from the pitcher into our glasses and motioned for me to sit at the kitchen table.

"I didn't want you to know how bad things have gotten, but you can see why I desperately need work." She twirled the stem of the wineglass in her hand and wouldn't meet my gaze. She sighed and squared her shoulders. "A couple of mom's friends will drop off some of their unsold farmers' market produce tomorrow. They sometimes add in eggs and milk for Hunter. At least we haven't starved yet."

"There's nothing to be ashamed of. Everyone goes through hard times." I didn't want to pry. "I'll give you an advance on your wages tomorrow."

"It wasn't supposed to turn out like this." She swiped at her eyes with the back of her hand. "Bruce and I never got married. I kept putting it off because, well, I saw what my dad did to my mom, and I never wanted to be in that position. I finally agreed that when he came back from deployment, we would have a wedding and start a family. My pregnancy was a big shock, but I was sure it would be okay. Bruce would come back and everything would be just like we'd planned. Except..."

I squeezed her hand. I couldn't even imagine what she had been dealing with while I'd been flying around in a private jet with Vince, drinking champagne, and being an unknowing partner in swindling the taxpayers out of more than a million dollars. I was ashamed.

"When he was killed, his parents received the death benefit. They wouldn't give their own grandchild even one penny. In fact, they claimed he wasn't Bruce's son." She sniffed. "I had to pay for a DNA test to prove it. At least Hunter gets a small stipend from the government every year until he's eighteen. How could they turn their backs on their own flesh and blood?"

"I'm so, so sorry, Ashley."

"Mom's been a great help supporting us. But her savings got wiped out from trying to recover after the fire and then she lost her job four months ago. She found a waitress job, but it's only Sunday nights and sometimes special events as they need her. It doesn't pay much. We've gone from barely hanging on to we're about to lose everything."

"What can I do to help?" My little shop wouldn't solve their financial troubles. There had to be a way to fix it, but I just didn't see how.

"Having a job to put food on the table is a huge relief." She stood, grabbed a tissue, and dabbed at her eyes.

Hunter ran into the kitchen and wrapped his chubby arms around his mother's legs. "I wanna cookie."

Ashley ruffled his thick hair and opened a cupboard. A lone box of animal crackers sat on the shelf. She handed her son a cookie, who fisted it and ran back to the family room. After wiping her eyes, she inhaled deeply, and then returned to sit at the table. She wouldn't meet my gaze.

CHAPTER EIGHTEEN

In an obvious attempt to divert my attention from her bare cupboards, Ashley changed the subject. "A developer is pressuring Mom to sell our five acres. He's offering below-market value, but it'll hold us over for a while until we get back on our feet."

There it was again. A developer swooping in to buy up acreage from people in dire financial difficulties.

"Did you hear about Seth North having to sell some acres to a developer?"

"Yes, that's how Golden State Developers contacted us. Our property is adjacent to Seth's, or I guess it's now the developer's property." She swirled the ice cubes in her goblet. "Selling is our only option at this point."

"Has your land been rezoned yet? It would surprise me if the city agrees to any development."

"All we've been told is Golden State said they were working on it. It's why they can't give us full market value." She shrugged. "I guess we can try to hang on until they get approval to rezone and see if they'll pay more for the land.

But I'm afraid the bank won't give us the time to wait and we risk losing everything."

I found it strange that a development company would fork over so much money for land, even at below-market value, without knowing whether they would be able to build. Did the company's management know something that the public didn't? My curiosity was on full alert.

"Who's in charge of the company's acquisitions?"

"Hey, Mom," Ashley called out, "what's the name of the guy who wants to buy the orchard?"

There was silence for a few moments, then Fran poked her head through the kitchen entry. "Grant McIntyre from Golden State Developers. Why do you ask?"

"I'm curious." I waved my hand in the air. "This is the second time today I've heard about a developer buying up land. Isn't the city anti-development?"

"They have a ban on chain stores coming in, but from what I can tell, this is supposed to be high-end housing with mixed retail projects." Fran scrunched her brow. "There are a lot of folks in town ready to read me the riot act because I'm considering it. I'm sick and tired of their judgment when they can't be bothered to care about the circumstances we've found ourselves in."

"I'm not passing judgment, Mrs. Price." The formality from my childhood years was hard to break, especially given the duress the woman was exhibiting. "I'm sure it will work out. I was just curious."

Fran chewed on her lower lip, then sighed. "Sorry. I didn't mean to take it out on you. It's been stressful enough without the comments people make about me."

Hunter called out, so Fran hurried back to the little boy.

This family would depend on the paycheck I provided, so

it was more important than ever to get my shop open. While tourists would bring in a lot of the income, I counted on locals embracing and supporting my shop. But, at this point, they wouldn't. Not while they thought I was a murderer. I had to fix it so I could provide steady employment for Ashley. I kept my voice low so Hunter wouldn't overhear. "Aside from Jasper, the mayor, and Seth, who else had issues with Russ?"

Ashley snorted. "You need to keep his mother on your list of suspects."

I shook my head. "I just don't see it."

"Think about it. Was your front door or Victoria's door still locked when you showed up?"

"Mine was. I didn't check Mystic's door, but I'm sure the police did."

"Ask your dad about the details." She stood and filled two glasses with water, then handed one to me. "If both doors were locked, then Victoria is the only one with a key to lock up after she left."

Oh, no...so does my dad. I shivered. I wouldn't allow myself to entertain my suspicions, even for a millisecond. "I'm not sure how much my dad knows. Detective Miller swooped in and virtually kicked him off the case."

"You should ask Detective Hottie. I'd bet he'd confide in you."

It was my turn to snort. "No way. According to Dad, I'm his number one suspect."

CHAPTER NINETEEN

After an uncomfortable night tossing and turning on their sagging couch, I left at the crack of dawn to return to my dad's and get ready for work. The scent of dark, faintly bitter coffee greeted me when I stepped into the house. I hoped he'd made a full pot. I would need a lot of caffeine today.

"Morning, Dad." I grabbed a mug and filled it.

He looked me over. "Morning, Cari-girl. Rough night?"

I looked at my rumpled clothes and groaned at a reddish-purple stain where I'd splashed some sangria. "Some couches aren't made to be slept on, but it was better than driving home so late."

"Glad you remembered my advice." He took a sip of coffee. "Rumors are spreading that Fran and her family are going through a tough time. What's going on?"

I filled him in on their circumstances.

"Look in the pantry and box up any food you think they'll eat." His cheeks reddened, and he cleared his throat. "I guess quite a few women in town don't think I know how to grocery shop or plan meals. They're always dropping off pasta kits and pre-packaged stuff. I haven't known what to do with any of it."

"They're probably hoping you'll fix it and invite them over for dinner."

The tips of his ears started to flame. "That's ridiculous."

"I saw Mayor Torres leave here awfully early yesterday morning."

"Is that right?" He raised an eyebrow.

"Uh-huh." I waggled my eyebrows. We were both adults, after all. "Anything you need to tell me?"

"Yeah." He wiggled his eyebrows back at me. "It's none of your business."

"Daaadddd..."

He pointed his finger at me. "I don't go poking my nose into whether or not Jasper's finally asked you out. Right?"

My ears quickly matched the shade my father's had turned. "I have no idea what you're talking about."

"Ha. You've both been tiptoeing around each other for the last couple of months."

"No, we haven't." Small towns...some things never changed. "You're trying to change the subject. What's going on with Mayor Torres? You have to realize gossip is flying all over the place."

My dad turned pale. "What gossip?"

I did another eyebrow waggle, but this time, Dad didn't even smirk. Instead, he crossed his arms in front of his chest. His biceps bulged.

"I'm serious. It's imperative you tell me what's being said."

"Okaayyy...let's see. You've been seen dining with an auburn-haired woman. Um, Dillon said you'd gone out with his mom."

His pale face turned red, and he sputtered, opened his

mouth, closed it, and opened it again. "H-how did you happen to meet Dillon?"

"He's my new employee." I sat back and crossed my legs, swinging the top one back and forth. "He's a great kid."

This time, his mouth gaped wide open.

I was in awe. I'd never had this effect on my dad before.

"It's okay, Dad. We barely talked about you and Sandy." I leaned in toward the big man sitting across from me, hoping I was too old for my dad to ground me. "Dillon just found it odd I wasn't aware you were dating his mom."

He jumped up as if a hot iron had been placed on the seat. "Look at the time. I'd better get ready for work. It'll be another busy day jumping at Harvey's beck and call."

I did a mental forehead slap. I should have been asking for insider investigation information—not teasing him about his dating life. "About that, um, investigation...my shop door was locked, but how about Mystic's front door? Is that how the, ah, killer got in?"

Dad examined my face with hooded eyes. "You're not poking your nose in where it doesn't belong, are you?"

"No! I'm just curious. Ashley and I were talking about it last night and it puzzled me."

"You shouldn't be discussing this with civilians. Best leave it to the authorities." He patted my hand and winked. "But, off the record, both doors were locked."

Jasper's bakery was hopping by the time I made my way in. I took my place in line and pretended to eye the siren call of the pastry-filled glass case. Ashley was right. Once he noticed me, his gaze flitted to me frequently as the line inched forward. I guess I wasn't as covert as I'd planned because as soon as we made eye contact, he gave me a huge grin and a wave. Except, he forgot to put down the croissant he'd been holding when he waved, and it flew halfway across the room. Fortunately, it missed hitting anyone. Several patrons chuckled when they turned to see what had distracted the baker. My face burned and probably matched the same shade of red as Jasper's.

I was desperate to turn around and flee to the solitude of my shop, but I held my head high and waited in line. When I reached the counter, Jasper had his hand in the pastry case and was hovering over the chocolate roll.

"Wait!" My voice was overly loud and my face heated again. "I've decided to try something different today. What do you recommend that is more, um, fruit-filled?"

His green eyes twinkled in the overhead spotlight as he plucked a mouthwatering, jewel-toned treat from the case. "I have a phyllo tartlet with a layer of honey-sweetened cheesecake topped with blueberries and strawberries. I used apricot jam for the glaze. Will that work?"

"Sounds delicious. I'll take it." I inhaled the aroma the petite pastry box exuded when he handed it over. The strawberries were fragrant with their ripeness. I handed over my credit card and took the coffee he had poured.

His fingers brushed mine when he returned my credit card. It seemed time had slowed, but then he was back to being the busy patisserie owner, already talking to the customer who stood behind me. I often wondered why he didn't have his hired help working the front counter during the busy morning crunch, but now I realized he was a charmer. The townspeople knew him and he chatted with them, which kept them coming back day in and day out.

I carried the box and coffee down the street to my shop. I juggled to keep from dropping them as I inserted the key into the lock and opened the door. Unease settled in my stomach as the image of finding Russ flitted through my head. The air smelled of disinfectant. After making sure I locked the front door, I set the box and coffee on the counter and gingerly walked to the back room.

Everything appeared to be in order, aside from one missing copper still. I powered up the laptop in my office and grabbed my tartlet. While I snacked, I ordered a new still. It would take three weeks for the new still to arrive. So much for having the Celebration Blend for the grand opening. I'd plan a month-versary celebration instead.

A soft knock at the door made me jump, and I knocked the empty coffee cup over onto the middle of the keyboard. I tossed the empty containers into the trash and looked toward the front door.

Detective Miller stood with his hands cupped around the sides of his eyes as he peered into my shop.

I tried to calm the butterflies that started flying around my stomach.

Was he here because he had good news, or was he going to attempt to get me to incriminate myself? Or worse, arrest me? Dad's words about his charm about getting nuns to confess whirled around my brain.

My hands shook as I unlocked the front door. I reminded myself I would call our attorney if things became uncomfortable.

"Good morning, Detective Miller." I'd opened the door about six inches. He didn't need to feel welcome.

"May I come in?" He gestured at the opening. "There are a few things I'd like to clarify with you."

Uh-oh. That didn't sound like he was here for a friendly call. "I guess."

He followed me into the shop, and we both perched ourselves on barstools at the countertop. Detective Miller took two sheets of paper from a manila folder he carried and set them in front of me. "Can you review your statements and verify that the information is correct? If so, sign and date at the bottom of each page."

I took the papers and started reading without asking if he'd like any tea or coffee. I didn't want to give him the impression it was okay to linger longer than necessary. My dad's warnings were foremost on my mind. The printed report of my statement the other morning appeared to be complete and error-free.

I read over the papers and got the feeling he was studying me. But I never caught him looking directly at me, and it made me nervous.

I signed each page and slid them across the counter.

"Thanks for dropping these by." I gestured around the shop. "As you can imagine, I have quite a bit of work to do before I open."

"Not a problem. I needed to ask you a few more questions, anyway." He flashed me a bright white smile with teeth that had obviously been professionally straightened and whitened.

A shiver slithered up my back. I pressed my lips together and nodded. I had no choice but to comply.

"I'd like you to tell me again about your relationship with Russ." He narrowed his eyes. "Isn't it true you were lovers?"

"Ew. No way." Where in the heck did that rumor come from?

"But I have several confirmed reports that they overheard a lovers' quarrel between you two." He tapped the end of his pen on the marble counter.

"Who said that? What are their names?"

"I can't reveal my sources."

"Let me guess. It was an anonymous tip." Someone in this town had it in for me. What had I done to deserve their wrath?

"I won't confirm it was or wasn't." Detective Miller pursed his lips. "Tell me about your arguments."

I took a deep breath and told myself I wasn't admitting to anything criminal. "It's no secret Russ didn't want my shop to open. He was afraid I'd take business away from Mystic Valley Candles."

"And would you have cut into their profits?"

"No. Not at all. Victoria and I are planning to collaborate on combining some of our products to bring in new clients. Being shop neighbors will be a win-win for both of us."

He practically snorted. "I doubt you'll get any collaboration from Ms. Lewellyn. She's blaming you for her son's death."

I froze. "Wait. What?"

She'd been devastated over her son's death when she'd rushed into my shop and saw his body, but I'd assumed she'd lashed out at me in her grief. But to make an official accusation against me was unfathomable.

"It's ridiculous. She's grieving and isn't thinking straight."

"She's got quite a lot to say about you, Ms. Carmichael. And then there's the small problem of your fingerprints being the only ones on the murder weapon." He flashed me that white smile again. This time I didn't fall for that smile. He looked like a predatory shark with those teeth. "Why don't you tell me your version?"

I fiddled with my phone and then gazed at his light-blue eyes. "I'd rather have my attorney present to discuss anything further with you."

He raised his hands, palms facing up, and shrugged his shoulders. "It's your prerogative, Ms. Carmichael. But if that's the case, I'd rather take you down to the station and continue our interview there."

"Are you arresting me?"

"Do I need to arrest you?" A slow grin spread across his face. "No, it's a mere formality. If you want an attorney, let's continue this in a formal setting."

He waited by the front door while I placed a call to my dad's attorney. The receptionist put me on hold for several minutes before promising Alfred Sanchez was available to assist me.

"My attorney will meet me at your office in an hour. Can I clear a few things up and meet you both, then?"

"Whatever is convenient for you, Ms. Carmichael."

I didn't like the way he kept saying my name. There was a snippy undertone. Like he was reminding me, or was it himself, that I was Robert Carmichael's daughter. Guess I'd have to leave it up to the attorney to straighten him out. "All right. I'll be there in an hour."

I watched him drive off, then sent Mari a text to let her know I wouldn't be at the shop. I also sent my dad a text alerting him that I'd called the attorney. I'd leave things open with Ashley. I shouldn't be at the police station for more than a couple of hours.

Hopefully.

Five minutes later, tires screeched as a car came to a sudden halt in front of my shop. I jumped when someone yanked my door open and sent the bells jangling. It was my dad.

"What did Harvey say? He's not accusing you, is he?" Dad's face was beet-red, and I was surprised smoke wasn't billowing from his ears. He was so angry. Just like in the cartoons.

"No. It's nothing like that." I shouldn't have told my dad I'd called the attorney. Except, if he found out while I was in the middle of my supposed interview, it wouldn't have been pretty. "I was told Victoria has accused me of killing Russ."

"That's ridiculous." He glared at the closed door between the two shops. "She knows you had nothing to do with it."

"There's also the small problem of my fingerprints being the only ones on the, ah, murder weapon."

"Oh, Cari-girl." He straightened his shoulders. "Alfred's a good attorney and will know when to bring in someone with more criminal defense experience."

Oh boy. I hoped it didn't come to that. I wanted to believe I'd be in the clear within an hour or two. "Thanks, Dad."

"Do you want me to go with you to the station?"

"No. That's unnecessary."

He looked about as relieved as I felt. Given his background with Detective Miller, I thought we were both afraid he'd get into some sort of altercation.

"Can I ask your honest opinion?" I didn't wait for a response. "Do you think Victoria has it in her to kill her own son? Could he have pushed her over the edge by ruining her financially?"

He ran his hands through his still-thick hair. "I don't see premeditated murder. An unfortunate accident might have happened if she were angry enough, but no, she wouldn't have murdered him."

"She warned me Russ might try to sabotage my shop.

Perhaps she found him here and picked up the still to get his attention when he wouldn't listen to her and one thing led to another." I mused for a moment. "Is it possible she dropped the still, and he slipped in the oil and hit his head?"

"I'll look at the reports and see if that's a possibility." He kissed the top of my head. "Call me the second you're done with Harvey. And listen to your attorney's advice."

CHAPTER TWENTY

While we'd waited at the front of the station for the detective to show up, I'd learned that Alfred Sanchez had gone to school with my mom at the local high school. Despite being in his early fifties, he had a full head of thick, black hair and not one wrinkle or laugh line on his mahogany-toned face. He shared a few memories of my mother, but when my eyes filled with tears that threatened to spill, he turned to other topics.

"Don't answer any questions whatsoever unless I approve."

I nodded and wondered for the millionth time if a day would ever come when I wouldn't miss my mother as much as I did.

Detective Miller led the way to a nondescript beige interrogation room. Alfred followed on my heels. We were offered chairs at a battered metal table after declining cups of ten-hour-old battery acid coffee.

Detective Miller outlined the facts. He was forthcoming and, to be honest, charming, and I decided I'd misread his intent when he questioned me at the shop. Or else my dad had read him the riot act, and he'd reassessed his intentions.

The men chatted amiably for a few minutes, with my attorney asking a question every now and again.

I got my hopes up that it had all been a mistake and I'd get to leave soon.

Except, of course, that wasn't what happened.

"Ms. Carmichael, we need to document your version of the multiple verbal arguments you got into with the deceased." The detective glared at me. "We have several eyewitnesses who can attest to the facts."

"Detective? Would you give me a moment to confer with my client?" Alfred's voice was calm. "Even though I've known both of her parents for decades, I've only just met her."

"Of course. Take as much time as you need." He stared at me. "I'm not here to harass Ms. Carmichael, no matter what she might have told you."

Was this guy passive aggressive or what? Still, I saw no point in poking the hornets' nest, so to speak, so I held my sarcasm in. "Thank you."

Once the door was firmly closed, Alfred turned toward me and his black brows arched over his coal-black eyes. "Now, young lady, tell me what bee got into his bonnet?"

Apparently, we were both on the stinging insect idiom wavelength. As quickly as possible, I told my attorney about Russ's threats, and his repeated arguments with his mom, and yes, I'd stuck my nose in and told him off a time or two. But, for the life of me, I had no idea who overheard those arguments, except for Victoria. I mentioned the fingerprints on my still. There was no denying that concrete evidence.

When I ran out of facts and speculations to share with

him, he outlined what I should tell the detective before he summoned him back into the room.

"So, Ms. Carmichael, what will your attorney allow you to tell me about my case as it pertains to your repeated altercations with the victim?"

I rolled my eyes. *Seriously? Well, two can play this game.* "On multiple occasions, of which I don't have specifics because I had no idea I'd be in this position, Russ harangued his mother over finances and the way she ran the shop. He became so verbally abusive, it was obvious I needed to step in and defend Victoria on three or four occasions. He then turned his verbal abuse toward me, but I ignored it and returned to my shop."

"Isn't it true you told him, and I quote, 'You'd better watch it because karma's going to catch up with you and it won't be pretty?' Would you care to explain that?"

I glanced at Alfred, who nodded. "I probably said something like that. What I did not say is I wanted him deceased. I'd never wish that on anyone. No matter how disagreeable they might be."

"Maybe you're too smart, being the police chief's daughter, to come right out and threaten harm."

I saw a hint of malice beneath the smirk that crossed his lips. Was he trying to hide something by throwing suspicion on me? At this point, nothing was too far-fetched, and I'd rather the killer be someone who wasn't nice instead of someone I knew and might even like or admire. I finally admitted to myself that the killer was most likely someone in the community and not a random drifter. The two locked doors to our shops proved it.

Alfred interjected. "You're speculating and badgering my client. We're willing to provide facts so the perpetrator can be caught and brought to justice. If you want to play games, then we're done here."

"Your client's fingerprints were the only ones found on her still. That, combined with the fact that the two front doors to both shops were still locked when you found the deceased, indicates someone with a key was the perpetrator." This time, he didn't try to hide his smirk. "That leaves you, Ms. Carmichael. Two indisputable facts."

"Victoria Lewellyn has keys to her shop and she might have worn gloves." There. I told him.

"Ms. Lewellyn is a frail woman. Who would ever think she'd be capable of smashing her only child's head in?" Detective Miller crossed his arms. "No one would believe that."

I crossed my arms to mimic him. "Let's talk about the fingerprints on the still. Why, being the chief's daughter, would I not have wiped it completely clean of my prints? Someone obviously wore gloves and left the prints there to throw suspicion on me."

"All conjecture. Your conspirator theory doesn't support the facts." Detective Miller leaned forward. "We'll find more evidence that'll implicate you and then, boom, you'll be back in jail for good. Right where you belong."

The venom in his words made me reel back.

A calloused hand on my arm held me in my chair. Alfred gave a small shake of his head as if warning me not to respond. "Detective, it's clear your personal feelings are coloring your investigation. This interview is over. I'll be in contact with your supervisors."

CHAPTER TWENTY-ONE

We stepped out of the police station, and I squinted from the bright sunlight. It was hard to believe life went on around me when my own was falling to pieces right in front of my very eyes.

Alfred turned to face me. "Tell me about the detective. Why does he seem to have a vendetta against you?"

"I don't think it's against me personally. It's against my dad, and I'm the means to get to him."

"What's he have against Robert?"

"He wants my dad's job." Those words didn't ring true. There was something else going on besides the chief's job. I worried my San Francisco scandal had me seeing conspiracies in everything now. But still, something was fishy.

"Then we'd better make darn certain he doesn't manufacture any evidence to get you convicted. Oak Creek doesn't need someone like him as the chief of police." He gave an exaggerated shudder. "I'll make some phone calls and talk to his supervisor. Perhaps they can rein him in."

His words warmed me. He didn't think I was guilty of the heinous murder. On the walk back to my shop, I replayed the detective's accusations over and over in my head. I stopped mid-step and was almost knocked over by a group of power-walking, stroller-pushing moms, all dressed in brightly colored leggings and activewear. They glared as they huffed past me while two toddlers waved from their toy-strewn strollers.

I resumed walking and thought about what had almost caused me bodily harm when it had stopped me in my tracks.

Detective Miller had said I'd go back to jail for good—where I belonged. That made me wonder if he, or one of his acquaintances, had a connection to the bribery scandal in San Francisco.

I had tried to tell myself it was a victimless crime. Politicians and developers had taken taxpayer money, but no individuals had been hurt by their actions. What if that wasn't the case? My conspiracy theories were out of control.

After I locked the shop door behind me, I sent Mari a text to tell her I'd finished with my so-called interview. With fresh tea brewed and a cup sitting in front of me, I began the arduous task of opening cardboard boxes and shelving the vials of precious essential oils. Organizing wouldn't have been so bad, but I had to check the amounts received against the amounts I ordered and paid for. Basically, it was an inventory audit while I arranged the stock on the shelves. It wasn't something I enjoyed.

A knock at the front door announced Mari's arrival. She had a small copper still nestled in a cardboard box. I opened the door and lifted the box from her wiry arms. Even though she was in her seventies, she was stronger than me and more than capable of carting the still around, but it didn't seem right to let her continue to carry the heavy box.

"Where did you find this?" I set the box on the marble counter.

"I remembered a friend who'd toyed around with distilling their own hooch once upon a time. He gave it up after almost getting caught a few years ago." Her eyes sparkled. "It's been hidden in his garage all this time, and it took some elbow grease to get rid of the grime. He said we were more than welcome to keep it."

I took the still out of the box and examined it. There were a few scratches and a couple of minor dents, but other than that, it looked perfect. It was smaller than my confiscated still, so I'd keep my order intact and use both once the larger one arrived. "I can't thank you enough. What do I owe you, or your friend?"

She waved me off. "Nothing. His only required payment is that I have to cook dinner for him one night."

I lifted an eyebrow. An old friend who wanted Mari to cook for him? Was there a romance brewing? "I'd be happy to buy a bottle of gin—or whatever his poison is—to thank this mystery man."

She noticed my interest and guffawed. "I'm too old for that kind of nonsense. Ira's an old friend who likes a home-cooked meal once in a while."

"Uh-huh. Why am I just now hearing about this 'old friend,' who just so happens to live in this area?"

"Who says he lives in this area?" She picked up the still and walked to the distilling room. "Come on. Let's see if we can get another batch of the Celebration Blend going."

We spent the next couple of hours reviewing our last set of notes. I measured the dried herbs, flowers, and Pixie citrus peels I wanted to use, then fired up the still. I would need to distill each ingredient separately and then blend the resulting essential oils to create the perfect fragrance.

"How did the 'interview' go with your friend? Ashley, right?" Mari curved two fingers and wiggled them twice.

"Yes, that's her name. She's perfect for the shop, and I know you're both going to love each other." I carefully placed a lid back on the coriander seed container. "She's a single mom and is struggling financially right now. I'm so glad I listened to my intuition and offered her the job. Just like you did with me."

"And it was the best decision I've ever made." She reached over and hugged me.

"It was the best thing that could have happened to me, too." I blew out a noisy breath. "I made another hasty decision that I'm a bit uneasy about, though."

Mari patiently waited while I collected my thoughts.

"I hired someone else. A young guy, Dillon's his name, to work part-time. He seems like the perfect fit."

"Then what's bothering you, darlin'?"

"First off, I don't have an operational shop, so there isn't any income to pay either employee. And second, my dad is dating Dillon's mom. Talk about awkward should things go wrong between our parents."

"But you felt that you should hire Dillon after interviewing him?"

"I'm not so sure. It just happened."

"Then it was meant to be. As far as Robert and this woman dating and making you feel uncomfortable, don't borrow trouble. Let them take care of their relationship and do everything you can to build a trusted friendship with Dillon."

"How did you get to be so wise?" I wiped down the tabletop with a clean cloth, then sat in a wood chair. I patted the chair next to me. "Maybe you can help me figure out how to stay calm over the way Detective Miller is treating me?"

She sat down and kept her eyes fixed on my face. "What's happened?"

"He insisted I go to the station for questioning, so I had to get Dad's attorney to meet me there." My jaws clenched and my heart raced.

She set the vial of lavender oil in front of me. "You can't control the detective, but you can control your reaction. Use the essential oils and massage to calm yourself and then you'll be better equipped to think clearly."

I applied a few drops of lavender oil, mixed with avocado oil, and massaged the mixture into my wrists and temples. "But that wasn't the worst of it. Detective Miller accused me of killing Russ and said he'd find the proof to put me back in jail where I belong!"

She hissed a couple of times then placed a few dried lavender buds, chamomile petals, and orange peels inside a small muslin pouch.

"What are you going to do with those?"

"There's a certain detective who seems to have anger management issues. I'll mix up a little concoction that might help."

Mari had been called a witch a time or two. If knowing the right kinds of nature's bounty to use for physical and emotional ailments made her a witch, then she was.

My ex-boyfriend, Vincent, had called her one, but he hadn't meant it as a compliment. Mari hadn't approved of him, especially after he blamed me for his downfall and threatened to get even. Greed had been the basis of his downfall, along with his inability to take responsibility for his own actions. I had nothing to do with karma catching up to him.

"How are you going to get him to use it?" Call me skeptical, but I didn't see that man going along with her recommendations.

"I'll have a nice visit with him tomorrow morning and, well, leave it to me. The less you know, the better."

My cell phone chimed with a text from Ashley.

> I'm in front of your shop. Can you let me in?

I thumbed a reply.

> Be right there.

I rushed to let her in.

Her eyes were rimmed with red and she held a tissue.

I motioned her inside, then re-locked the door. "What's wrong?"

CHAPTER TWENTY-TWO

"The developer is pressuring Mom to accept a rock-bottom price right now." She shook her head and wiped her nose. "We can't afford to take that little money, and we can't afford not to sell."

"There's got to be something we can do." I guided her to sit on one of the padded bar stools as Mari entered the room.

"Good afternoon. You must be Ashley. I've heard so much about you." She bent down and rummaged through a few drawers, then straightened up and placed three vials on the countertop. Next, she poured a teeny amount of sweet almond oil into a tiny glass bowl, and then added two drops from each vial. A lovely citrus fragrance filled the air.

I was instantly transported back to my grandmother's kitchen when I was a small child. A red-checked tablecloth had covered her square kitchen table, and white melamine bread plates sat in front of the four chairs. She had me climb onto a chair and helped guide my hands as we sliced huge pink grapefruits in half with her large butcher knife. The fragrance from the sliced grapefruit peels tickled my nose with each slice of the knife. She then allowed me to sprinkle mounds of white sugar over each half.

The memory flitted away as new scents from Mari's oils replaced the grapefruit. Mari had explained to me that our olfactory sense was the only one that provided straight passage to the brain, instead of connecting first to nerve endings. It was one reason scents could trigger such powerful memories, even more than visual prompts.

"It's nice to meet you." Ashley appeared mesmerized by Mari's wrinkled, sun-spotted hands. "What are you mixing up?"

"Grapefruit, bergamot, and sandalwood essential oils, with sweet almond oil to make it gentler on your skin."

"My skin?" Ashley glanced at me and lifted her eyebrows.

Mari picked up the small bowl and jerked her head toward the soft seat at the side of the room. "Come sit over here and remove your shoes."

"I don't think..."

"Come, child. If you're going to be Carissa's right-hand woman, you need to believe this is more than simply a paycheck."

Ashley looked at me again.

I nodded and used my hands to wave her to the low chair.

She sat as directed, and soon her feet were wrapped in warm, wet towels. Lavender wafted up from the towels and blended with the grapefruit fragrance still lingering in the air. I hadn't warmed up lavender-scented water, and I hadn't seen Mari do it. Perhaps she was a witch because the stress fell from Ashley's shoulders like she had shed a sweater.

Once the towels began to cool, Mari slipped them off

and moved a low ottoman beneath Ashley's feet. She began to slowly work her oil mixture into the soles of my friend's feet and massage in long, deep strokes.

Ashley closed her eyes and rested her head against the back of the chair. A single tear trickled from the corner of her eye and down her cheek.

"Breathe in the fragrance of grapefruit and breathe out the worries that plague your mind." Mari's voice was low and melodic. "Let the sandalwood ease the anxieties that weigh you down. Allow the bergamot to bring back your memories of joy and dispel the sadness that whirls around you."

This nut-brown elderly woman had done the same type of ministration for me so many times during those dark days after being arrested. I wouldn't have survived if it hadn't been for Mari. She'd been there to front the bail money and had held my hand when I had to call my dad to tell him just how bad it was. And she was there to offer a solution when I fled the city and slunk back to Oak Creek. I was grateful she extended the same care to Ashley. She had trained me how to do the same, but somehow, I didn't have her magical touch for knowing exactly what to do and what to say.

"Cari, this gift will come to you when you stop doubting yourself. You must put San Francisco in the past and let it stay there." Her voice was barely above a whisper.

I turned to smile at her, despite my disbelief in her words, and saw Ashley had fallen asleep. It was what she needed. I gathered the wet towels and took them to our laundry room.

Mari followed and washed her hands in the farmhouse-style sink. She hugged my shoulders. "I'll make her some tea when she wakes. I meant what I said. Let your mind relax over the past. You need it not only for yourself, but so you'll be stronger to help your friends through their darkest times. Trust me, it will get darker before dawn comes."

Ashley stretched her arms over her head and yawned.

I hurried back and sat in the chair next to her.

"I'm so sorry. I don't know why I broke down like that."

"It's all right. You've had a lot of stress piled up on you. It was bound to happen."

She carried a mug of tea and handed it to Ashley. The herbal fragrance of apples and hay in the chamomile blend, along with faint undertones of spicy ginger, filled the air. "Drink this. I added a touch of honey."

"Thank you. And thank you for the foot massage. I've never had anything so relaxing in my entire life." She took a tentative sip of tea. When she found it wasn't too hot, she took a larger swallow.

"You've been carrying too much stress for too long." Mari pointed at Ashley's neck. "I'm surprised your shoulders and neck aren't stiff."

"How do you know they're not?"

Mari laughed, her quiet voice tinkling like a bell. "Your body connects through meridians. I would have been able to feel it in the pressure points on your feet. Have you been having stomach aches recently?"

Ashley's eyes widened, and she nodded.

"Did you experience any tenderness in a particular spot while I massaged?"

She pointed to a spot on her left foot, about an inch below the ball of her foot. "It didn't hurt too much, so I guess tender would be a good word for it."

"I'll give you a tincture of ginger. Add a teaspoon to a cup of chamomile tea every morning." Mari tapped the spot on Ashley's foot. "You can also help with the symptoms by applying light pressure and massaging this spot in small circles."

"Thank you. Stress has always given me an upset stomach, but this has been the worst." Her eyes teared up again. "It's been one thing after another, with no end in sight."

I rummaged through one of the product drawers and pulled out a small rollerball tube. It contained a blend of peppermint, fennel, chamomile, and black pepper essential oils, along with local organic grapeseed oil, to create the appropriate saturation for applying directly onto the skin. I handed Ashley the tube.

"Rub this over your stomach twice a day for a week and massage until it's absorbed into your skin. It should relieve some of your tummy discomfort."

"Thank you. I'm going to try all of these things." She tucked the tube into the pocket of her purse sitting on the floor next to the chair.

I hadn't had a chance to tell Mari about the tragedies that had befallen Ashley and her mom, but I was certain she'd picked up on the sorrow Ashley had experienced. "Things may seem hopeless, but we'll figure this out together."

"This job is a lot of help, but unless something changes, I don't see how we can afford to keep living here."

I made a mental note to give Ashley an advance on her wages and take her to Dad's house to clean out his pantry.

Mari stood. "I've got an appointment I need to get to, but we'll talk more about this later."

"Thank you, Mari, for everything." Ashley rose and bent down to hug the elderly woman. "When I walked in here, I was ready to murder Grant McIntyre."

CHAPTER TWENTY-THREE

With the front door locked after Mari departed, Ashley stretched her arms over her head for a moment, then sank back into the chair. "That was amazing. I feel so much better. Does Mari still own her San Francisco shop?"

"No. She wanted to retire a few months ago and talked me into buying her inventory. It seemed like the right thing to do with my grandmother's legacy." I shrugged. "I think it was her way of jolting me out of my pity party and forcing me to get my life back on track."

"That was fortuitous timing." She gazed around the shop. "How did she end up here in Oak Creek?"

"She has too much energy to be retired." I laughed. "She got bored and showed up to help set the shop up a month ago. I hope she puts permanent roots here and stays. Honestly, I think our town's artistic and free spirits appeal to her and she's already made a ton of friends."

She flashed a bashful smile. "I feel like she's already a great friend, so I imagine she makes friends no matter where she's at."

I heartily agreed. "Do you feel calm enough to talk about what happened with the developer?"

She gestured at the boxes I had piled around the room, some with their lids gaping wide open. "I'll tell you later. You're not paying me to sit around and mope."

Ashley was quick to pick up what I had in mind for stocking the shelves. She also came up with a good idea to apply labels to the edge of the shelving so we could quickly pull product when needed, instead of inspecting the tiny labels on the vials. Until the still functioned full-time, I had a reliable, high-quality vendor who supplied me with organic essential oils bottled and ready to sell.

While she organized the vials, I ran down the street to our local general store, Summers, which had been a fixture in our town since the late eighteen hundreds. Since its humble beginnings as a small hardware store, it had blossomed and grown into an emporium. A sales clerk greeted me when I entered and directed me to the office supply section, where I found a label maker. As I stood in line to make my purchase, I couldn't help but notice the sideways glances patrons threw my way or the whispers that floated on the chilled air. Words like murder, jail, and chief's daughter seemed like they would be my lifetime companions in this town.

I hustled back to my shop and let myself in. "Here you go."

Ashley took the label maker and started cranking out labels. In the short time I'd been gone, she had unpacked two boxes and made neat rows of opaque vials on the product shelves.

"You're quick." I bent down and collapsed the empty boxes. "I worry too much about how to organize while I'm unpacking. It would have taken me hours to do this."

"I've had a lot of practice. Is this the first time you've worked retail?"

"I worked in Mari's shop, but she never had me set up the inventory. I was sales and the reflexologist, and eventually, she suggested I start my own reflexology business on the side."

Ashley's eyebrows rose. "So that's how..."

"Yes, that's how my snake of an ex got me involved in the payoff courier business." I cleared my throat. "I honestly didn't realize he was using me."

"Do you mind if I ask exactly how it worked?" She looked embarrassed. A faint tinge of pink showed up on her cheeks and she wouldn't meet my gaze. "I know you're innocent, but how did you not realize you were transporting documents and cash between clients?"

And that was the crux of why most people assumed I was guilty. No one could comprehend that I wasn't aware of what I was doing.

I sighed. "Vincent, the snake, made a huge deal about supporting my new business. I had planned on sharing space in Mari's shop and continuing to help her on the retail side, but he was very insistent that I branch out and separate from her."

"He sounds controlling." She pushed a strand of blonde hair away from her face. "Was he abusive?"

I shook my head. "Not in the physical sense, so I didn't recognize him for what he was. But you're right. He was controlling. When I finally gave in and ended my employment and connection with Mari, Vincent gave me a traveling case to use for clients and explained how I didn't need to own or work in a shop. He even had ten client appointments all lined up for me."

"Sounds like the perfect job and boyfriend." She gave a half-smile. "Except it wasn't, was it?"

"You're right. He had the traveling case made with beautiful burgundy-colored leather, but the sides were hard and didn't bend or bow. It was custom-made and expensive—Vincent made sure I saw the receipt. And I'll admit, I was terrified I'd ruin it. There were all sorts of compartments, including a large insulated and waterproof compartment to hold warm, lavender-infused wet towels to use for my clients." I used my hands to show her the dimensions of the case, about the size of an airplane carry-on. My case even had wheels and a handle to pull. Just like luggage.

"What I *didn't* see was the hidden compartment on the bottom that opened with a special magnetic key that, of course, all his clients had. When I left to wash my hands before and after the appointment, my client would insert whatever it was into the case. My next client would retrieve whatever had been hidden and add whatever needed to be passed on to Vincent, who coordinated the whole courier schedule."

"Wow. That was an elaborate scheme, but clever."

"Tell me about it." My shoulders sagged. To this day, I had never determined whether Vincent had actually loved me or if he had chosen me because I'd been a gullible young woman he could easily manipulate.

"Don't pay any attention to the gossipers. Something new will come along and the San Francisco scandal will be old news."

Unfortunately, something new had come along—in the form of Russ's murder. It only made the gossipers' tongues wag faster since I'd found him dead, in my shop, with my fingerprints all over the murder weapon.

"Are you going to offer reflexology services here?" Ashley's voice cut through my dark thoughts.

"That's the plan. I've arranged a small treatment room in the back, but I want to get the retail side going before I accept clients." What I didn't tell her was I'd lost my touch after San Francisco. Sure, I could go through the motions, but Mari was right. It wasn't good enough. When we set up the treatment room, I insisted that a hot water sink basin be included. I'd never allow a client to be out of my sight again. But even with those safeguards in place, my fear and humiliation kept me from finding my touch.

"Will you train me?" She suddenly seemed self-conscious. "I mean, if there's some downtime in between customers. I don't want to take business away from you."

"That's a great idea." Why hadn't I considered it before? It would also give her another source of income, should she move elsewhere. "I can teach you, but I'll want you to attend some professional classes for training before you work with clients. You don't have to get a license in California. However, I would strongly advise you to try to get your certification. I'll find the information and we can figure out some way to make it work, since I'm sure you'll need to go to Ventura for the classes."

"Oh. I didn't realize there was that much to learn. I thought it was mostly just rubbing feet with a blend of oils." Her smile fell, and she lowered her eyes. "I won't be able to afford classes."

"Don't worry about the classes yet." I smiled at her and looked at her long, strong fingers. "Mari taught me, and I'll teach you. You'll be good at it."

After I turned the still burner off to allow the oils to cool and separate from the hydrosol, I followed her lead on the unpacking. It didn't take long to unpack the boxes I'd been procrastinating over the previous week. We chatted, but every time I tried to bring the conversation back to Grant McIntyre, Ashley redirected us to another topic. I got the hint and stopped trying to pry. If my friend wouldn't tell me what was going on, perhaps I should go to the source himself. I had my grandmother's property to dangle in front of him.

I also realized I needed to talk to more people about Russ and find out who else might have wanted him dead. A little on the shy side, I'd learned to be a conversationalist after working as a reflexologist. People confided in me all the time, so I hoped that would continue when I talked to those who might know something to help me find the killer.

My phone chimed with a text from my dad.

4:30 OK to visit the shelter?

I sent him a thumbs-up emoji back.

"My dad's coming by at four thirty and I have an errand to run. Do you mind reorganizing some of the product I unpacked last week?" I showed her the cabinet in the treatment room. "And please do me a favor and open every drawer and cupboard and organize however you decide."

"Are you sure? This is your shop." Ashley bit her lower lip. "I should wait until you're here to change anything."

"You've proven you know what needs to be done, and it's obvious I have no idea." I kicked myself for not paying closer attention to the inventory while I worked for Mari. "Look around and if you see a way that we can improve the retail side, make a list and we can talk about it tomorrow."

Ashley got to work, and I grabbed my purse and headed

out the door. Mystic Valley Candles' door was closed and someone had taped a paper sign to the glass.

Closed due to a family emergency
Will reopen Monday

CHAPTER TWENTY-FOUR

My heart went out to Victoria, but I thought it best to not contact her until I'd proven my innocence. I pulled up the address on my cell phone for Golden State Developer's office and walked toward my destination.

A faint buzz sounded when I opened the door of the older wood-framed house. When I stepped into the reception area, the stench of dust and neglect, with undertones of bologna, hit my nose. Rickety bamboo-framed chairs with frayed rose-colored seat pads, which all looked stained, lined the sides of one wall. A beat-up metal desk sat next to a dark, narrow hallway that appeared to lead toward the back of the single-story home-turned-business.

"I'll be with you in a minute." A raspy male voice called from the back of the house. It made me think he was a smoker.

"No worries." I glanced at the questionable chair pads and continued standing. I walked over to the desk, but there weren't any papers lying on top and the computer monitor was black.

"Sorry about that." The man's voice made me jump. "I'm Grant McIntyre. How can I help you?"

"Nice to meet you." I reached out and gave his extended hand a brief shake. "I'm Carissa Carmichael."

"How can I assist you, Ms. Carmichael?" Grant's hair was grayed at the temples of his thinning, blond hair, which he'd slicked back with a greasy hair product. He pushed black-framed glasses back onto his aquiline nose with a well-manicured index finger, but it wasn't enough to hide his eye twitch upon hearing my name.

"I've been told you're buying some orchard properties east of town. I was wondering if you were still in the market. I'm thinking about selling."

"It depends on where it's located and the acreage." Grant licked his lips. It reminded me of a lizard. He tried to smooth the wrinkles out in his khaki slacks with the palms of his hands, and his pant cuffs were frayed. His scuffed black shoes were dusty. I wondered if he'd been tramping through orchards looking for another steal.

"My grandmother left me four acres off of Lemon Grove Road, parallel to Kumquat Street. Are you familiar with that location?" I had always wondered about the names of the roads since there wasn't a citrus orchard in sight. Avocados were king.

"I know where it is. White adobe farmhouse on an avocado orchard?" He waved me toward a chair. "Have a seat and let me take down your information. It might dove-tail nicely with our other acquisitions."

I wasn't sure how the wobbly chairs could support my weight, much less Grant's. I didn't want to sit, but I wasn't sure how to decline. Instead, I perched gingerly on the edge of the cushion and hoped I wouldn't fall. "Can you tell me what your plans are for the land you're purchasing?"

Grant tilted his head to the side and his black eyes, magnified by his glasses, blinked rapidly. "Does it matter what our plans are?"

"Rumors fly around a town like this, and it made me curious."

"I'm sure you'd like to add to those rumors." His voice held a sharp tone as he stood. "I don't think the chief of police's daughter is interested in selling her family's home. I think you're poking your nose in where it doesn't belong."

"That's not it at all." I sprang from the chair. "I really am looking to sell and move into town. It's too isolated out there for me."

"When you've placed an offer on a house in town, come back and talk to me. Until then, mind your own business."

And with that, he ushered me out of his office and locked the door behind me. My conversation hadn't gone as I'd hoped, but I was certain Grant McIntyre was hiding something he didn't want to get back to the chief of police.

The mayor was next on my list, so I headed to City Hall.

A gravel walkway meandered beneath canopies of ancient gnarled oaks and led to a Spanish-style house with an arched portico. This was home to City Hall. While I walked, I made a list of several questions I wanted to ask. That had been my mistake with the developer. I hadn't been prepared.

A woman in her sixties, if I had to guess, sat at a polished mahogany desk just outside the mayor's office. I glanced at the nameplate on the front edge of the desk as I approached the unsmiling, ramrod-straight, deeply wrinkled woman.

"Excuse me, Ms. Babcock. I was wondering if I might have a word with Mayor Torres."

She scowled.

"Can I set up an appointment when she's available?"

"What's the purpose of your appointment?" Her helmeted salt-and-pepper hair didn't move even a millimeter when she shook her head. "She's a busy woman and doesn't have time for non-city business."

I glanced at my dusty yoga pants and wrinkled T-shirt. Perhaps I should have dressed more appropriately. "I'd like to talk to her about Golden State Developers."

She waved her liver-spotted hand, shooing me away. "That's for the City Council. Go talk to them."

"Wouldn't Mayor Torres have some kind of information about a developer who comes into town and starts buying up orchards at a discounted rate?" I narrowed my eyes on her. "Or perhaps you're familiar with the situation and can let me, as a resident of Oak Creek Valley, know what's going on."

She shook her head vigorously, and her dangly purple crystal earrings brushed against her leathery cheeks. "No. You need to take that up with the council. Now, if you'll excuse me, I must get back to work."

When Irene Babcock stood and entered the mayor's office, I saw the mayor sitting at her desk before the battleax receptionist closed the door. I considered barging in but held myself back. My dad's position in town meant I had to remain circumspect. Plus, I didn't want to get on the bad side of the mayor or her gatekeeper while I was trying to get my business up and running. I wondered how much power they had to make a business owner miserable.

CHAPTER TWENTY-FIVE

I walked back to my shop, chewing my lower lip. My two attempts at finding information had been a bust. Neither the developer nor the mayor's office had been forthcoming on anything. It was almost like they were trying to hide something or divert my attention, which seemed suspicious.

My phone chimed with a text, pulling me from my worrying thoughts. I checked the screen and smiled when Jasper's name popped up.

> Would u have time for a drink tonite?
> Around 7?

I froze mid-step. *Is he asking me out on a date or is it only because he has new information for me?* I wasn't sure how worried I should be about his confrontation with Russ. Still, my dad didn't express any concerns when we talked about him. He would have warned me away from the baker if he thought there could be a potential issue, right?

> Sure. Where should we meet?

Jasper must've been glued to his cell because the reply was almost immediate.

> Margaritas at Paco's?

Thinking about Paco's tart sweet signature libation made my mouth water.

> I'll see you there.

I was glad he'd chosen a busy place. I would be surrounded by people in case he turned out to be sketchy.

When I entered my shop, Ashley danced around with a feather duster in her hand as she whisked it along the glass shelving and over the larger apothecary jars. Music played from her cell phone speaker. She smiled and her cheeks turned rosy-pink when she caught me watching her.

"I hope you don't mind the music. It makes me work faster." She waved the duster at me. "The glass shelves will need to be dusted more often than if they were wood. But the colorful reflection of the jars will make it worth the effort."

I looked around the shop. Several cardboard boxes had been broken down and neatly stacked by the door. Shelves had been reorganized with a combination of essential oil vials and tinted jars. But what made my heart flutter was the display she'd created on one of the corner tables. Various sizes and colors of apothecary jars were displayed alongside a variety of essential oil accessories and jewelry. She'd propped up a book on creating your own blends of aromatherapy, the colorful cover complementing the rest of the display. She had also unboxed two diffusers, one that operated with a power cord and another that used reeds with vials of essential oils next to them. I was certain our customers wouldn't be able to resist.

"I hope you realize how amazing you are." I stepped closer to the table. "This display is everything I had hoped it would be when I ordered the products. I just haven't found the time to put it all together."

"I thought we could vary the display table by season by changing out the colors, scents, and accessories." Ashley walked to the table and fingered the vial of oil. "I didn't open this before I talked to you, but using a diffuser to demonstrate your products might create additional sales."

"That's a great idea. Victoria also recommended using a fan to blow the scent out toward the sidewalk on busy days."

"The longer you're in business, the more you'll get a feel for what customers like." She peered at me and seemed almost shy. "I don't want to overstep any boundaries or rush you into purchasing more stock, but perhaps you should consider merchandise that ties in with the theme of whatever festival brings tourists to town, or at least keep to the theme of each season."

I nodded at each of her ideas. "Let me locate the product catalogs, and you can take a look. I'll get a list of the annual festivals from the Chamber of Commerce. I don't think we should go overboard, but a few pieces might generate interest. We can always special order if a customer has their heart set on something."

"If you're worried about overhead and storage, that might be the way to go."

"What do you mean?" I unscrewed the lid to the citrus and black pepper blend of essential oils and poured enough to cover the bottom of the reed diffuser. I rearranged the reeds and placed them back into the container.

"Purchase one of whatever you want to showcase for the

festival or season. Build a display around it and let customers special order it. You can use your display item year after year with no need to store large amounts of merchandise to meet the demand." She picked up the book and thumbed through it. "Books will be a big seller. This is the only one I found, but I assume there are several others on the market to choose from."

"You're absolutely right. I ordered quite a few books, but they're at my house. I'll bring them in tomorrow."

Mari's shop had been small and situated in a neighborhood frequented by locals versus tourists. Her biggest draw had been her reflexology, and she sold essential oils as a side. My shop was in a prime tourist area, and I needed to remember that.

Ashley walked me around the shop and showed me what she had done. We talked about ways to make the product easily accessible. She flipped through several artistic photos of apothecary jars, along with one of the display tables she'd taken with her cell phone.

I gave her approval to upload to the shop's Facebook and Instagram pages, and we talked about scheduling posts. I was getting more and more impressed by her intuitive feel for organizing and marketing skills. I gave a sigh of relief that I'd made the right decision to hire her when I did.

CHAPTER TWENTY-SIX

"Grab your purse and drive me to my dad's house. He wants his pantry cleaned out of all the stuff some of the local ladies have given him." I picked up my phone and sent a quick text to him, asking him to meet me there.

Ashley lifted her eyebrows. "What do you mean? Why would people be giving him stuff?"

I laughed and rolled my eyes. "Apparently, single women are trying to get his attention by dropping off baskets of food and meal kits. I think they're hoping to entice him to ask them out on a date or over for dinner."

"Seriously? Wouldn't it work better if they invited him for dinner?"

"They probably tried that route and when it didn't work, they brought the food to him." I locked the door behind us as we stepped onto the sidewalk. "He said you should take whatever you want."

She came to a dead stop, and her lips started to quiver. "No. I can't accept charity."

"Trust me, it's not charity. My dad doesn't want the clutter in his pantry and he won't use it." I took hold of her elbow and pulled her toward the side street where she'd parked her car. "He's the pickiest eater I've ever seen. His idea of gourmet food is beans and franks. None of the food they dropped off appeals to him. If you don't want whatever is there, you can at least help me box it up and we can drop it off at the food bank."

"I don't know…"

"Truly, you're doing us both a favor by taking it off his hands." I turned and looked at her, tilting my head. "Have you heard anything about my dad dating the new sheriff's deputy? I think her name is Sandy."

"Is she the bicycle cop? Petite with auburn hair?"

"I'm not sure. Someone told me he was seeing a woman who'd recently moved to town with her son."

"That must be her. She's cute." She turned toward her car. "Are you okay with that?"

I shrugged. "Sure. I want him to be happy, and I guess it makes sense he would be more comfortable around a law enforcement type."

"But?"

"I feel odd that there's another kid involved in the equation." I wasn't sure why I worried, since my dad hadn't even acknowledged it. Then again, Dillon obviously had been told something was going on. I needed the full story, too.

"Maybe it was just a date or two." She stopped in the middle of the sidewalk. "But why would she move here if nothing came of it? Wouldn't that be awkward?"

I nodded. "I need to be honest with you. I interviewed her teenage son, Dillon, for a position. He's the one who told me they were dating."

Her eyes went wide and her mouth dropped at the corners.

I jumped in before she could say anything. "I still need

you to work full-time during the week. I had set up the interview before your application came in. Since he's a college kid, I thought I'd meet with him anyway for part-time work."

"If you need to cut my hours, I understand." She gestured back to the shop. "You might not need as much help as you think."

"Please don't worry. You'll get all the hours you need, and Dillon will fill in on the weekends. Don't you remember the tourist crowds over Easter break? Summer will be like that, and we'll need all the help we can get." I started walking again. "Come on, let's go clean out my dad's pantry."

"So you're okay knowing your dad is dating another woman whose son you just hired?" She shook her head. "Small towns...doesn't get much crazier than that."

"He's a great kid and if his mother is even half as nice, I'm happy for my dad."

"What does he say about our new bicycle cop?"

"He won't say a peep."

While we rummaged through the mostly unwrapped culinary gift baskets stacked in my dad's walk-in pantry, I told Ashley about my visits to the developer's office and City Hall. "It's almost like they're both hiding something. Aside from what you and your mom have experienced with Grant, what other rumors are going around in regards to other people getting railroaded into selling their property?"

"Only Seth North selling some acres last year. But if you drive out east of town, it looks like several parcels aren't being taken care of and the trees are dying." Ashley picked up three boxes of couscous and put them in a brown paper bag. "It makes me wonder if the owners sold to Grant and he's letting the produce trees die before he bulldozes it down."

"I'll take a drive and write down the locations, then visit City Hall and see if I can find out the owners."

"Go about a mile past my house and turn left on Silverwood. You can't miss it."

"Do you feel up to telling me what upset you earlier today?"

"I probably overreacted. It was part anger and part sadness, knowing we're going to lose our property." She wrinkled her nose. "Grant showed up first thing this morning and told us he was changing his offering price to thirty percent less than he originally offered. He said something about market values. Blah, blah, blah. I think he found out how desperate we are."

"Can you sell the land to him at that price?"

"Not at all. The only option will be bankruptcy, and we'll be left without a roof over our heads." Her face turned a splotchy red. "My mom has worked hard her entire life. She's mortified about failing on her loan, and I'm angry this person is trying to take advantage of her situation."

"No wonder you're upset." My mind whirled, wondering what I could do to help her out. I couldn't think of anything. "What are you going to do?"

"I have no idea. Mom's planning to discuss it with a local real estate agent and see if they can come up with a solution."

"I hope they figure something out." I really wished I could come up with something that would help my friend and her family.

She spun around and almost knocked over one of the dozen jars of red pasta sauce sitting on the pantry shelf.

"Oops. Trust me, this food will see us through for a couple of months. You have no idea how much I appreciate it."

"Let me find a cardboard box for the sauce." I gestured at the six bottles of local organic olive oil and six bottles of balsamic vinegar. "I'll take three bottles of the olive oil to use in my shop. You can have the rest."

"I'll take two of each. That'll last us at least a year or more. Seriously, these women need to be a little more creative than this if they want to get his attention." She reached for a package of gourmet orecchiette pasta. "There must be fifteen packages and look at all these varieties of sauce."

"Take them all. Dad isn't a fan of it. He's a meat and potatoes kind of guy."

We uncovered a couple of baskets containing fajita and margarita fixings, minus the meat and vegetables. "Take this. The next time I come over, I can help you drink the margaritas."

"No. You should keep this."

"I don't need it, and I'd rather you keep it for another girls' night in." I pointed at my dad's built-in liquor cabinet inside the pantry. "Besides, we have more booze than we could possibly consume. Most of it is gifts from people who didn't know what to give him. I guess, when in doubt, give a bottle of whiskey or vodka to the chief of police."

She gave me a sideways glance. "If you're sure your dad doesn't mind."

"Trust me, you're doing us both a favor." My dad's gravelly voice filled the pantry, and both Ashley and I jumped.

My hand flew to my heart as if I could quiet the pounding. "I didn't hear you come in. You didn't have to sneak up on us."

"I didn't sneak up on you." Dad grabbed one of the

grocery bags we had filled. "Is your car unlocked, Ashley? I'll start loading it up for you."

"Chief Carmichael, you don't have to do that."

"Call me Robert. There's no need to be so formal when I'm not on the job." He chuckled. "I'm happy to do my part. I was thinking the pasta and sauce had turned into rabbits, it was multiplying so fast."

I laughed at his description. "The only way you'll slow this down is to make certain everyone knows you're off the market."

His face reddened, and he grumped as he picked up the paper sack. "I'll be back for more."

Ashley elbowed my side. "I see what you mean about him not wanting to talk about his dating life. But I'm pretty sure he's involved with the bicycle cop, or someone else. Did you see him blush? It's adorable."

I started piling homemade canned food and boxes of fancy crackers into a cardboard box, while Ashley and I chattered. The assortment of jarred homemade pickles, vegetables, fruits, and jams, each labeled with the contents, use by date, and the creator astounded me. I was glad they wouldn't go to waste. My dad needed to put a stop to the unrelenting baskets of food left on his doorstep.

Dad stuck his head into the pantry. "Hand me a couple of those bags. I might as well give you some cheeses and salami cluttering my refrigerator. I'd be headed for cardiac arrest if I ate all of it."

"You truly don't need to do that. I feel guilty enough as it is taking all of this."

"If you don't take it, then it'll end up in the trash. You wouldn't want that to happen, would you?" Dad snapped open a bag.

"No, sir." Ashley walked over and hugged my dad. "Thank you."

He blushed. "No need to get mushy. Glad someone can take this stuff off my hands."

"As Carissa said, there's a way to get the food gifts to stop."

Dad grumped again and bent into the refrigerator.

It wasn't long before the three of us finished and loaded everything into Ashley's car. She gave each of us a tearful hug and climbed into her old Honda. Right before she drove away, I tucked an envelope containing an advance on her wages into her purse and hoped she'd be able to sleep without worry tonight.

Once she left, my dad grabbed his keys. "Come on. Let's get to the shelter before they close."

CHAPTER TWENTY-SEVEN

We headed west down the central road for a couple of miles. Dad turned onto a side street that fronted a Spanish-style strip mall that had been around since the nineteen fifties. Despite its age, the buildings had been well kept. He drove behind the strip mall and an older brick building, squat and rectangular, came into view. A sign in front proclaimed it to be Oak Creek Animal Shelter. He parked in the gravel driveway that ran parallel to the shelter. When I opened the car door, dogs barked and a large bird squawked from inside the boxy building.

A bronze bell jangled when we opened the door, and we made our way into the waiting room. A chest-high wooden counter, painted bright yellow, separated the waiting room from the door leading toward the sound of barking. Farm-style benches, painted the same cheery yellow as the counter, lined the room that had been wallpapered with paw prints in every color of the rainbow. Large framed photos of an assortment of animals hung from the wall, and my eyes almost crossed at the busyness of the decor.

A middle-aged woman came into the room from the hallway behind the desk. "Hi, Chief. What can I do for you?"

"Hey, Yasmine. My daughter is interested in adopting a dog." He gestured toward me. "This is Carissa. Carissa, meet Yasmine."

She wiped her hands on well-worn jeans and extended her right hand. "I just washed my hands, but they're still a little damp. Didn't want you to think it's from one of the animals."

I took her extended hand and shook it. "It's nice to meet you. Do you have any medium-sized dogs available?"

"C'mon back. I have a few that might interest you."

We followed her down a brightly lit corridor to a door at the end. Large, floor-to-ceiling kennels lined the walkway on both sides. Several were empty. Some held playful kittens and dozing cats. She led us through another doorway, where more enclosures lined the corridor. The yipping and barking increased as we entered, and several dogs stuck their snouts through the chain link of the cages.

She came to a stop in front of the farthest enclosure and opened a small gate leading to the pen. A medium-sized apricot-colored dog lay on her side. The dog lifted her head to look at us, then laid it back down and sighed. It took everything I had not to rush to pick up one of the four puppies nursing on the tired mother. They ranged in color from apricot, like the mom, to brown, to spotted white and black, to pure chocolate.

"The puppies are four weeks old. They'll be ready for adoption in another four weeks."

"Why do they look so different?" I was puzzled. It looked like they came from different mothers.

"Someone found the mother on the street and brought

her in. She was about a month pregnant when we got her, so it's hard telling how long she'd been on her own. Most likely, there are different fathers for each of the pups."

I grimaced. "Poor thing."

"She was super hungry and flea-ridden, but it didn't take long for her to get healthy."

"Do you think there was any damage to the puppies from the mother living on the street?" my dad asked.

"I don't think so. They're meeting the milestones we expect, and the vet says they're all healthy and thriving."

One by one, the puppies unlatched from their mother and tumbled over each other in clumsy play.

"Go ahead and play with them." Yasmine motioned me into the pen. "If you don't want the responsibility of a puppy, I have other mature dogs you can look at, but they're all fairly large. We're guessing that, with the size of the mother, they'll stay in the medium range."

I walked in and sat on the clean concrete floor. It didn't take long for the four puppies to come inspect me. The apricot-colored puppy wiggled up onto my legs, and then crawled up to my chest. It gazed at me with chocolate-brown eyes before nuzzling my arm where I had dabbed a bit of Pixie citrus essential oil that morning. She sniffed, then nestled herself into the crook of my arm with her nose close to the citrus scent and fell asleep.

"I think she's adopted you, Carissa." She stroked the head of the mother dog.

"She's so snuggly," I murmured into the puppy's fur. "Have you named her yet?"

"No. We leave that to the new family unless they don't find a home right away. Then we name them and post their photos to the shelter's website."

My dad, ever the practical one, interjected, "Do you know what kind of mix she is?"

"The mom seems to be some kind of terrier and spaniel mix. She's very friendly and has responded well to both my female and male volunteers." Yasmine shook her head and pointed to the puppy in my arms. "Unfortunately, without doing a doggie DNA test, we can't even guess what the pup's father is. He was probably on the shorter size, maybe even a dachshund, given how short this pup is compared to her siblings."

"It doesn't matter. This is the one." I looked at my dad. "I think I'll name her Pixie. Her coloring is kind of orange, and she seems to love my citrus essential oil."

"Wonderful! I'll start the paperwork." She gave the mother dog one last pet, then strode to the entrance. "Do you want to stay here while I work on it?"

I nodded. "Thanks. She's sleeping and I don't want to disturb her."

She laughed. "I'll bring the forms back to you when they're ready to sign. It won't take long. Once you're done, I need to close up for the night."

"The animals are left here by themselves?" I worried they would get lonely.

"Someone will come in to check on the animals for a couple of hours later tonight, and I'll be back here by six every morning." She rubbed her cheek. "Funding is limited, and I'm the only full-time staff member. Most of our help comes from volunteers, so I can't ask them to work in the middle of the night."

Dad shook his head. "The city budget is overwhelmed, so I'm glad they continue to support your operation as much as they can."

"Every bit helps, but I'm not sure what we'd do without the donations and volunteers who give of their time."

Yasmine was true to her word, and it didn't take long for her to bring the forms back to me for my signature. I placed the sleeping pup back by her mother and dug into my purse for my credit card.

"Your dad already paid. I'll call you to schedule your adoption day but, in the meantime, feel free to drop by as often as you want to play with her."

I gave my new puppy one final caress then walked out to find my dad. He was already sitting in his pickup truck, country western tunes playing on the radio.

"Thanks for paying the fees. Let me know how much and I'll reimburse you."

He waved off my offer. "Consider it an early birthday present."

"You realize my birthday isn't for another six months, don't you?"

He chuckled. "Of course I know when your birthday is. But Pixie is a gift that will keep giving love year after year, so there's no reason not to make her an early present."

"Thanks, Dad." I leaned over and gave his cheek a kiss. "Wanna take a drive east and check out some dying orchards before an early dinner?"

CHAPTER TWENTY-EIGHT

"What would you find so interesting about these orchards?"

"I think there's something odd going on with Golden State Developers. They seem to swoop in on folks who have fallen on hard times and pressure them to sell at prices the owners really can't afford."

Dad started the engine and headed east on the main thoroughfare. "What are you hoping to find?"

"I want to find the owners and see if they were pressured into selling."

"While it may be morally sketchy to do that, it's not illegal." Dad rubbed the red birthmark that sat just below his right ear. "I have to ask again, what do you hope to find?"

"I think there's got to be a connection between Russ's murder and Grant."

He was silent for several minutes. I knew better than to interrupt while he thought.

Finally, he broke the silence. "I agree there's something fishy going on, but I'm not sure there's a connection to the murder. I'll help you find the addresses, but you'll need to check with the owners or previous owners yourself. I can't have anyone complaining I'm wasting the taxpayers' hard-earned money on something that's not a crime. Plus, I don't need Harvey to think I'm interfering with his investigation."

"Thanks, Dad. Ashley said once we go past her house for about a mile, turn left onto Silverwood and we'll see the orchards." With everything going on, I had shoved Detective Miller from my mind. It was less stressful that way.

"I recall seeing it a while back and wondered why the owners were letting it die."

"Doesn't it seem strange Grant would be trying to buy property that far away from Seth and Fran's land?" I gazed out the window at the passing tangerine, olive, and avocado orchards. "Have you heard what he's planning on doing with it?"

"No, and the mayor and City Council aren't talking either." He slowed the truck as we approached a stop sign at an intersection.

"Shouldn't it be public record?"

"From what Mayor Torres is saying, the developer doesn't have to file anything until they're ready to request permits."

I glanced at my dad and took a deep breath. He wasn't going to be happy thinking I was interfering with an investigation. "I, um, tried to see Mayor Torres earlier today and find out about the land sales and development. I'm still curious why she was at our house so early Sunday morning too, but her gatekeeper basically threw me out and I didn't have a chance to talk to the mayor."

It was a good thing he hadn't gotten back up to speed after the stop sign because his head whipped around to look at me and as a result, he yanked the steering wheel to the right and the truck's wheels slipped onto the soft dirt of the shoulder. We narrowly missed driving into the irrigation runoff ditch before he corrected his path and pulled us back onto the asphalt.

Dad swiped his hand across his forehead. "Young lady, can you save your remarks for when we're not in a moving vehicle?"

I'll admit, my heart was pounding, and my hand had turned bone-white from gripping the armrest of the truck. "Sorry about that. The conversation was on a roll and I thought I'd just throw out my train of thought."

He grunted. We drove along in silence until the first dying trees appeared. It was a heartbreaking sight. Row after row of twelve-foot-tall mature avocado trees had brown leaves drooping from dead limbs, while the ground was littered with avocados and dead leaves. Dad pulled over on the wide gravel shoulder and cut the engine.

"This has been going on for a while," I muttered.

"The heat wave this past week made it worse."

"You'd think whoever owns this would have harvested the fruit before letting the trees die." I shook my head at the colossal waste of food that could have been put to good use feeding the needy.

My dad pulled his laptop from the narrow space behind our seats and logged on to the city's account. He typed in our location and drummed his fingers against the steering wheel while we waited to access the records. He wouldn't meet my gaze, so I assumed he was trying to not chew me out over my attempt to interview the mayor.

Dad pulled reading glasses from his pocket and peered at the screen, tapped a few keys, then leaned in closer to the screen. "Huh. Whaddaya know. It looks like Victoria and Russ Lewellyn used to be joint owners until Golden State Developers bought the parcel four months ago."

"Isn't that interesting?" I nudged his arm with my

elbow. "Looks like I'm a chip off the old block, after all. You know, instinct for crime and all that."

My dad grimaced. I probably shouldn't have reminded him of "the crime" I'd been involved in before.

"I appreciate your help, but I'm worried about you getting hurt. Given my position, I can't condone you questioning the mayor, or anyone else for that matter. But, whatever you do, promise me you'll be careful."

"I'll be careful." I hoped I could keep my promise to my dad.

CHAPTER TWENTY-NINE

I thought about my meeting with Jasper tonight and I decided I'd better tell my dad. "By the way, what do you think about Jasper?"

He raised his eyebrows at me. "He seems like a responsible, hardworking business owner. Why?"

"Rumor has it he might have gotten into an altercation with the victim."

"Oh, yeah. The cockroaches." Dad pursed his lips and pushed his glasses to the top of his head. "If I'd been in his shoes, I might have done more than threaten Russ. I hate to speak ill of the dead, but that man went out of his way to cause trouble."

"So you don't think he tried to get revenge for what Russ did?"

"Personally, I don't think he did, but Jasper's still an official suspect. And you didn't learn that from me." He turned to look at me. "Why are you asking about Jasper?"

"He asked me to meet him for drinks tonight at Paco's." My face heated up and the tips of my ears burned.

My dad's loud guffaws filled the cabin of the small truck.

"It's not funny. I don't know why you're laughing." I crossed my arms in front of my chest, and then looked at my watch. Five thirty. I hoped there was enough time to pick up the box of books, get home, fix a quick dinner, change, and freshen my makeup. Not that I was trying to make an impression on the baker. "Can we stop by the farmhouse on the way home? I need to pick up some books."

"Sure." He swiped his pale lashes with his fists. "It's about time that boy asked you out."

"Are you sure he's not involved in the murder?"

My dad was a good cop, but even the best could be fooled sometimes.

He stopped laughing. "He has a decent alibi, but it's not airtight. Enjoy your date without feeling you need to interrogate the poor love-sick guy. Just don't go off with him by yourself. Stay around the crowd."

"What do you mean? What's his alibi?" *Love-sick? What was that all about?*

"Security video shows him locking up the patisserie, walking up the flight of stairs to his apartment above the shop, and not coming down until three-thirty the next morning. He went straight into the patisserie and didn't leave until we showed up with sirens blaring when you called emergency services."

"Wait a minute. There are security cameras in the arcade?" *Why didn't I know about that?* "Did you check the recordings for my shop to find out who might have entered with Russ?"

"Jasper installed the cameras himself after the incident with the cockroaches. He figured it would deter him from any further harassment." Dad shook his head. "I wish I could have taken Russ in and charged him with something, but there wasn't any proof he was the culprit."

"That makes sense, but too bad the rest of the arcade doesn't have security cameras."

"I agree, but there's never been much crime to warrant the expense."

"Back to Jasper. Is it possible he snuck out without being seen?" Relief started to creep in, but I wanted to be certain.

"That's where the alibi is a little iffy. There aren't any security cameras on the courtyard side, so it's possible he might have gone in and out the back." He stroked his emerging stubble. "I've spent a lot of time with Jasper since he came to town, and he seems to be a good guy. Even their altercation wasn't something I worried about at the time. Heck, Russ's own mother threatened to kill him a time or two."

"So you're sure it's safe to meet him for drinks?"

"Yep, as long as you don't drink and drive. Nor should you walk home alone in the dark. Take Lyft or you can call me for a ride."

With Jasper cleared by my dad, it was time to force Victoria to talk to me. Even if she was an innocent, grieving mother, she might know something that would help the investigation.

"Okay. I'll call Lyft."

Dad chuckled again. "I'd insist on coming to pick you up, but I don't want to scare the poor guy off."

"How do you know Jasper has, um, feelings for me?"

"It's my job to know these things."

Great. What chance did I have when my dad was the chief of police in a very small town? "Okay. If you can rib me, why don't you tell me about Mayor Torres? Why was she at your house so early on Sunday morning? Is it romance or about the murder?"

It was my dad's turn for his face to redden. "You're not going to drop that, are you?"

"Nope."

He heaved a sigh and shifted in his seat to turn toward me. "This goes no further than between you and me."

"Scout's honor." I held up two fingers.

"Russ was blackmailing the mayor and there is not, nor ever has been, a romantic connection between us."

I waited at least ninety seconds and my dad still didn't say another peep. He only looked over my shoulder and gazed at the dead orchard. "What? That's it? C'mon Dad, you gotta give me the details."

"That's all she told me, along with her alibi for the night he was killed." He scratched along his jawline, his five-o'clock shadow grayer than the red it had been when my mom was alive.

"And what did she say?"

"No one can accuse you of being a complacent pushover." He shook his head. "She was with a male friend all night but would prefer I don't contact him unless absolutely necessary. She's afraid it will jeopardize her position."

My dad squirmed.

I pushed him toward full disclosure. "I pinky promise I won't tell another living soul. Who is this mysterious friend?"

He rolled his eyes at me. "I shouldn't be telling you this, but if I don't, you'll probably trail her until you find out. Grant McIntyre."

My eyes bugged out. Mayor Torres was an attractive woman. Grant? He was slime. "Ewww...why would she?"

He shrugged. "Who can explain matters of the heart?"

"Still, ewwww." I tapped my index finger on my lower lip. "Is it possible he's using her to get approval to develop the land?"

"That's exactly why she wants to keep their, ah, friendship quiet. Beatriz has assured me she won't pressure the council to vote in favor, and she'll excuse herself from the vote once he submits plans."

"So she says now that there's a murder investigation. Did she tell you why Russ was blackmailing her?" Was it possible the mayor and the developer murdered Russ together? I wondered if that scenario had even been considered.

"It's obvious. He found out about her relationship with Grant." Dad turned back to face the steering wheel and started the truck. "Let's get you home so you can get dolled up for your date."

"Daaaddd. It's not a date. He might have some information on who else wanted to kill Russ."

"That's a new way to a man's heart. Margaritas and murder."

CHAPTER THIRTY

Jasper had a pitcher of margaritas, a basket of tortilla chips, and fresh guacamole on the table by the time I got there. He looked relaxed in a white T-shirt and jean shorts. A glint of red in his two-day stubble made him seem rugged and even dreamier. When I reached the table, he jumped up and gave me a peck on my cheek before pulling my chair out for me.

"Thanks, Jasper." Perhaps this was more than a chance to talk about murder. I told myself to not get my hopes up, but my heart wouldn't listen.

His hands shook slightly when he handed me a menu. He had to clear his throat twice. "Would you like dinner or some appetizers?"

While I had hurriedly fixed my dad a Cobb salad for dinner, I hadn't taken the time to eat. Instead, I'd dolled up, as my dad had put it, taking time to flatiron my curly hair and apply foundation to cover the generous sprinkling of ginger freckles that covered my nose. I'd also applied more than a quick swipe of mascara to my curly eyelashes, along with eyeliner, so my chocolate-brown eyes popped. My white embroidered peasant blouse showed off my olive-toned skin, while the burnt-orange linen skirt minimized my addiction to Jasper's chocolate rolls. My stomach growled and my mouth watered as the scent of browning onions, garlic, and grilled meat wafted from the kitchen. "Have you eaten yet?"

"No. I spent part of the evening prepping for tomorrow, so I don't need to get up so early to start the baking. If you like, we can split the nacho appetizer and then order whatever you'd like for dinner." He glanced from his open menu to my face. "Unless there's something else you'd rather order for a starter."

I was glad I hadn't eaten dinner with my dad. The nacho platter was large enough to share for dinner without ordering anything else. "That sounds great, although I'm not sure I can eat an entire entrée after the nachos. Would you like to split an order of fajitas, too?"

His face relaxed. "That sounds good."

"How about chicken nachos and beef fajitas? That way we get a little of both kinds of meat." I set the menu on the table. "Would you rather get shrimp? They're tasty too."

He shook his head and held his index fingers up in the sign of the cross. "No shellfish for me. I'm super allergic. If you'd rather eat shrimp, we can order separately."

"The beef is fine." I filled my margarita glass and took a sip. The frosty concoction filled my mouth and slipped down my throat. "Have you always been allergic?"

"My mom had me tested when I was five after my dad died from anaphylactic shock after chowing down on deep-fried shrimp at an all-you-can-eat buffet in Vegas."

"Oh, Jasper. I'm so sorry about your father." I had struggled with the death of my mother as an adult. I couldn't imagine how hard it would be for a young child to lose their parent.

He shrugged. "The worst part is my dad was supposed to be at a conference in Kansas City. But he was in Vegas cavorting with his secretary. It was quite a shock for my mom, and she's never forgiven him, even though he's been long gone."

"No doubt." I reached out and gave his hand a quick squeeze. "I'm still sorry. Kids shouldn't have to carry around that kind of burden. Did your mom ever remarry?"

"No. She took over my dad's insurance business and turned it into a successful company. That became her life, and she always hoped I'd take over." He gave a low laugh that I almost didn't hear over the din of the dining room. "She argued with me about going to pastry school and tried to get me to change my mind, but once she tasted my chocolate rolls, she paid my full tuition plus room and board."

"Ah, she's a woman after my own heart."

"Well, she hasn't swooned over them quite like you." He gave me an impish grin.

My face heated, and I was glad I had worn my heavy-duty foundation. I was saved from having to answer when the waitress came to take our orders. I let out a gasp when I looked up to order and saw it was my high school frenemy, Lacie Simmons. *What is she doing here?* I glared at her, and she glared right back at me.

"Hi, Lacie." Jasper glanced from my face to hers and back to me. "Do you know each other?"

"We went to high school together, but this is the first time we've run into each other since graduation. Welcome back, Carissa." She gave a light tinkling laugh, and she arched her eyebrows. "Bet your dad is soooo happy to have you home after another scandal."

I wanted to throw the bowl of guacamole into that smug face. I tried to keep my expression still so she wouldn't know how much she'd hurt me both in the past and now. I looked her up and down. She was still trim and cute, with long blonde hair pulled up into a messy bun. "Nice to see you. How long have you worked at Paco's? Weren't you running your husband's office? What was his name?"

"Brett. You know darn well it was Brett." She fidgeted with her pen and order pad. "We divorced a few years ago."

"Ah. So you guys split up." *No surprise there.*

Brett had been my boyfriend during our senior year of high school. Lacie was more interested in the chase and the theft of her "friends'" boyfriends. It never took her long to tire of them after she started dating them. Except, in Brett's case, she'd married him right after graduation. Perhaps it was because he came from money and had a nice career waiting for him. I realized I was being catty, but I'd suppressed a lot of anger at someone I had once considered my friend.

Their marriage was one of the many reasons I'd fled to San Francisco at the first opportunity. "And now you're working here? How nice."

Lacie narrowed her eyes at me, then switched on her megawatt smile and turned to Jasper. "Are you ready to order yet? I hope you liked the margaritas. I had the bartender put a couple of shots of Grand Marnier in just for you."

"It's great. Thanks." Jasper handed Lacie our menus and gave her our order, making sure she would alert the chef to his shellfish allergies.

She flounced away as she swayed her curvy hips accentuated by her short black skirt. *Why do I let her fluster me so easily?*

He raised his margarita glass and clinked it to mine before taking a sip. "I take it there's some bad blood between you two. I'm sorry she had to be our server."

I shook my head. "It's fine. I didn't realize she worked here. It caught me by surprise."

"Let me guess. She was your friend, but then stole Brett from you."

"That's what happened, although that wasn't the worst of it."

He raised his eyebrows. "Oh?"

I huffed. I didn't want to talk about it, but if I didn't, I'd stew all night long. "During Christmas break our senior year, Lacie threw a party. My dad was chief of police back then as well, and I tried to live up to his standards and rules because I didn't want to jeopardize his job. Anyway, she pressured me to drink a couple of wine coolers, which wouldn't have been a big deal. Someone, she swore it wasn't her, put some kind of drug in them. I ended up getting arrested after trying to drive home and crashed into a tree. I wish I remembered that part. I blacked out."

"I can see how that's unforgivable. You're lucky you didn't kill yourself or injure someone else."

"Exactly. Anyway, between the boyfriend and that party, I've tried to avoid her at all costs." I rubbed my face, then sighed when I remembered I had makeup on. *Great. I probably smeared it. I hope I don't look like a clown.* "It was hard on my parents, but eventually the attorney got the charges dropped when some kids came forward and said someone had drugged me without my knowledge. They never admitted who it was, but I felt like the entire town never believed me or the kids who stood up for me. I moved to San Francisco the day after graduation."

"For what it's worth, she's paid her dues. She's had a

pretty tough life, so hopefully she's learned her lesson and changed." Jasper's green eyes glittered in the flickering votive candle sitting on the scarred wooden table. "But let's change the subject. Is there any new information about the murder investigation?"

Not for a minute did I believe Lacie had changed, but I decided not to dwell on it. Instead, I gave him a quick overview of what I'd found out while keeping my pinky promise to my dad about not sharing the mayor's secret. I also didn't confront him about his altercation with Russ. If Detective Miller or my dad thought he needed further investigating, I'd leave it up to them. "How about you? Any new rumors floating around town about who else might have wanted to commit murder?"

He turned his head and stared at the colorful Spanish-tiled bar, where a beefy gray-haired man sat on a stool, his back toward us.

"Is everything okay?" I asked when Jasper scowled.

He seemed to come out of his funk and gave his head a quick shake. "Sorry. That's Seth North over at the bar. Did you question him yet?"

"No. You don't seem to like him much."

He waved his hand as if to dismiss my question. "It doesn't matter. You should talk to him."

"Is it possible he might be involved? Russ's supposed theft at North Valley Trading Company happened last year. Would Seth wait that long for revenge?"

Jasper shrugged. "It wouldn't hurt to chat. Maybe he was waiting for the right place and time."

"And my shop just happened to be it? Lucky me." I stood, ready to walk over to the bar and introduce myself.

CHAPTER THIRTY-ONE

Lacie placed a sizzling platter of nachos in front of Jasper, her sapphire-blue gaze locked on his face. She completely ignored me.

"Let me know if I can get you anything else, Jasper. Your fajitas will be out in about twenty minutes." Her voice was breathy and low. "And the chef said not to worry about any shellfish cross-contamination. He's experienced with food allergies."

"Thanks, Lacie. We're good for now." Jasper looked at me. "Let's eat before it gets cold."

Once the waitress was out of earshot, he leaned toward me. "I can invite Seth to join us for nachos and you can grill him while we eat."

"Are you sure? I noticed you scowling at him. Besides, is he acquainted with you enough to feel comfortable joining us?" My hands started sweating. It was one thing to question a person on my own. It was an entirely different thing to make a fool of myself in front of Jasper. And truth be told, I had been looking forward to getting to know the baker better.

"I'll offer to buy him a round or two. Everyone knows he would never pass up free booze, no matter who's offering to pay." He stood. "And like I said before, my issues with him don't matter. I'll be back in a sec."

As he walked toward Seth, I noticed a soaring bird tattoo on his left calf. With each step and flex of the muscle, the bird looked like it flapped its wings. While I admired the artistry, it was nothing compared to the baker's well-toned backside. I wondered if he sampled his own bakery products and if he did, how he'd managed to stay so fit. Jasper placed a hand on Seth's shoulder and, with his free hand, gestured toward our table. Seth turned and nodded when he saw me. He picked up his bottle of beer and walked over to our table.

"Evening, Ms. Carmichael." Seth dipped his chin toward me as he grabbed a free chair from an empty table next to ours. "Thanks for the invite."

"No problem. And please, call me Carissa."

His slate-colored eyes were heavily framed with deep crow's feet, and his gaze traveled over my face and down to my chest. "Ah, the prodigal daughter returns home to the chief of police."

He gave me a creepy-crawly sensation, and I crossed my arms in front of me while I tried to think of a response to his insult.

Before I could say a word, Jasper clasped Seth's forearm so tightly, that the beer almost slipped from the older man's grasp. "There's no need to be insultin' to the lady. We are tryin' to be neighborly, seein' you were sittin' there alone with your *cerveza*."

Two things jumped out at me. First, Jasper's Texan accent had turned very pronounced and two, Seth's face had turned an angry red, which made his thick, white eyebrows stand out.

"Now, boys, let's settle down. There's a lot of catching up I want to do and I'd like to become reacquainted with the people of Oak Creek since I plan on putting down roots here." I tried to channel my soothing reflexology voice, the one that lulled people into quiet naps. "That's why I invited you to sit with us. I understand you own the largest recreational equipment store in town."

My tone must've worked because Jasper released his grip and the color of Seth's face returned to normal.

"Yes, ma'am. North Valley Trading Company has been in my family for over ninety years."

"That's quite an accomplishment, especially with the difficulties of the economy." I took a sip of my now-melted margarita, then gestured at the men to help themselves to the nachos. "I'm sure your family has some fascinating stories to tell about the famous and infamous people coming into town."

"That they do." Seth sat straighter and puffed out his chest. "When my father was alive, we were invited to all the movie sets and wrap parties in the valley. I was even an extra a few times as a young boy. 'Course we were the only shop the studios considered whenever they needed on-site recreational equipment."

"What a wonderful heritage. I hope your father preserved photos and memorabilia of those events." I was laying it on thick, but Seth seemed to need his family's business complimented and admired.

"The family's rec room is devoted to all that. In fact, the Board of Trustees have asked us to loan several framed photos and artifacts to the museum next year to showcase the movie industry's involvement in our valley over the last century."

"I'll be sure to visit when the exhibit is up." I watched my so-called date from the corner of my eye. He had calmed down, but he wasn't happy. "Jasper, have you had a chance to watch a movie shoot since coming here?"

"I've provided pastries for movie set breakfasts a couple of times, but so far there hasn't been time to hang out while they're shooting." He had a wistful look. "I don't have enough employees yet to take off for long."

Seth opened his mouth, but before he had a chance to insert another snide remark, I jumped in. "We must do something about that. Most of the time it's a lot of boring, standing-around-waiting-for-nothing time, but when you see the stars in action, it's magic. Right?"

Seth nodded. "One of my fondest memories is watching them film Lee Majors in The Six Million Dollar Man. It was my first role as an extra. 'Course, now it's kinda cheesy, but back in the seventies, it was thrilling to a ten-year-old kid."

"I remember my dad watching some reruns of that show." As a teen, I had teased him about how ridiculous it was compared to the hot shows at the time, but that hadn't deterred him from watching it every chance he could.

We sat in silence for a few minutes while we polished off the remaining nachos and guacamole. My stomach churned at the thought of pushing Seth into revealing what happened to Russ, but I had to do it. "I'm sure you heard about me finding Russ Lewellyn in my shop."

"It's about the only thing this town's been talking about since it happened." He drained his beer, raised a hand over his head, and snapped his fingers three times.

Less than a minute later, the bartender placed a new

bottle of beer in front of him. Jasper indicated it should go on our tab.

He didn't bother to acknowledge the bartender or say thank you. Instead, he chugged half of it down. "I'm surprised you're not locked up, but then I guess it helps to be the chief's daughter. Apparently, some people *can* get away with murder."

Jasper growled and leaned forward, but I kicked his shin beneath the table and gave my head a slight shake. He didn't flinch, but Seth jumped, glared at me, and reached his hand down to rub his lower leg. *Oops. Wrong shin.*

"Why, Mr. North, funny you should say that. Just the other day someone told me Russ took you to the brink of bankruptcy and there wasn't a darn thing you could do about it except sell off some of your family's land. Rumor has it you threatened to kill him." I was making the threat part up, but after spending fifteen minutes with this pompous man, I was certain Seth hadn't bothered to reign in his wrath.

"The only thing I'll say about that is you'd better keep your nose out of what doesn't concern you, Carissa." He spat my name out like it was bitter.

"When you all but accuse me of murder, it becomes my business." I tried to keep my voice low since several restaurant patrons had turned to stare at us.

Lacie stood fifteen feet away, frozen in place, as she held a tray with our sizzling fajitas.

"Let me make it clear. I'm not accusing you, but I am trying to find out who is trying to frame me. I hoped you'd be open to sharing your ideas on who might have wanted to kill him."

Seth stood and his chair fell back with a clatter.

"There's not one person in town who isn't happy to see that man get his due."

CHAPTER THIRTY-TWO

He slammed the beer bottle onto the table, causing beer foam to shoot up and over the neck of the bottle. Its gold liquid puddled on the table. Seth strode away and, with an abrupt shove, pushed through the front door.

I exhaled the breath I'd been holding for the last minute. Jasper quickly mopped up the beer with the flimsy napkins he'd snatched from the stainless-steel dispenser that sat on the table, then rearranged the glasses and dishes. Lacie placed a cast iron griddle laden with charred tender steak, grilled onions, and red bell peppers on the table. She promised to return with tortillas, sour cream, cheese, beans, and rice. She no longer seemed eager to hang around and flirt with Jasper.

"Are you okay?" He touched my trembling hands, then took the pitcher of margaritas from my cold fingers and poured me a glass.

"I knew it wouldn't be easy to talk to him, but never in a million years did I dream he'd be so volatile." I sipped the tangy concoction and wondered if I should order a shot or two of tequila. "You must have known he was…"

"Arrogant? Pompous? A bully?" He gulped down his own margarita.

"I'm sorry I dragged you into this. I hope you don't lose business because of me."

"You didn't…"

We both turned quiet when Lacie brought out the accompanying dishes for our fajitas.

"Thank you. Sorry about the scene with Seth." Jasper pressed a twenty-dollar bill into her now-empty hand. "We should have taken it outside."

She shrugged and slipped the bill into the front pocket of her skirt. "It's not the first time he's acted up, and I'm sure it won't be the last. Enjoy your dinner, Jasper. Let me know if you need anything else."

I thanked her as well, and this time she looked at me, nodded, then turned on her heels and headed to the kitchen. We were quiet while we each built a fajita. I preferred mine with steamed corn tortillas, meat, grilled veggies, a scoop of *pico de gallo*, and a squeeze of fresh lime. I'd save the beans, cheese, and sour cream to use as a dip for the fresh basket of tortilla chips that came with our meal.

Jasper filled a flour tortilla with meat, a smear of beans, and added guacamole, sour cream, and loads of cheese on top. He sprinkled several healthy drops of bottled hot sauce over the top before taking a bite. He closed his eyes as he chewed. I took a bite of my fajita and savored the tender, juicy meat and the caramelized flavors of the onions and peppers.

"This is the best. Every time I come here, I intend to order something new, but I'm afraid I'll miss the fajitas if I do."

"I'm the same way." I took another nibble. "Although, if you like tamales, they make the best I've ever had in a restaurant. They're almost better than my mom made. Her mama and *abuela* taught her as a young child in Mexico and tamales have been our Christmas dinner tradition since before I was born. My *abuela* taught me to make them, but it's been easier to order from Paco's."

His eyes opened wide. "You make homemade tamales?"

"Yep, since I was old enough to climb onto a chair to reach the counter."

He tilted his head and looked over my hair, face, and arms, then slowly smiled. "With a last name like Carmichael, I'd assumed you were just a tanned Scottish girl, more prone to making scones."

I laughed, glad he was trying to lighten the mood after the intense confrontation with Seth. "Oak Creek is quite the melting pot. I'm a little of this and a bit of that on my dad's side. And you're right, there's some Scot. On my mom's side, we're mostly Latino. How about you?"

"I'm one hundred percent Texan." He assembled another fajita.

"How can that be when you live in California? Shouldn't you consider yourself a Californian?"

He snorted, then grinned. "A Lone Star native is always a Lone Star citizen. They don't quite appreciate my patisserie the way Oak Creek residents do, so I'm hoping to stay here for good."

"I'm glad to hear that." We chatted about our childhoods and found we'd both grown up riding horses. I'd spent a lot of my youth on horseback, riding the trails in the Topatopa Mountains that ringed our valley, while Jasper had spent his time riding horses on the open plains. It surprised me to learn that he and my dad had spent many hours riding together and even camping in the mountains. I wondered why my dad hadn't mentioned it to me.

"Since my assistant chef quit to stay home with her baby, I don't ride like I used to. I miss it."

"Are you interviewing for the position? It can't be good to work seven days a week." I sat back and wished my skirt had an expandable waistband.

"I've had a couple of people apply, but they weren't a good fit."

I was curious about the type of man he was. He'd been quick to grab Seth's arm and express anger when he'd jumped to my defense after I'd first been insulted. He'd also gotten into an altercation with Russ over the health department inspection. Still, I didn't see him getting so angry he'd bash another man over the head in my shop and try to frame me for it. Seth, on the other hand, seemed more than capable of murder. His anger simmered constantly. He was predisposed to blame me for the murder, without even knowing me or my situation, and he obviously had issues with the chief of police.

Before I had a chance to ask him about his search for another assistant chef, my phone chimed with a text. It was from my dad.

On way to pick u up. Harvey is threatening
to arrest u. I called atty.

CHAPTER THIRTY-THREE

"No." The word slipped from my mouth before I could stop it. My head spun, and I gulped down the glass of ice water sitting next to the empty pitcher that had held the margaritas. How much had I drank?

"What's wrong?" He stared at my shaking hand as the condensation-wet water glass slipped from my fingers.

"My dad is picking me up in a few minutes. Detective Miller needs to interrogate me tonight."

"But it's after nine. Couldn't he wait until tomorrow morning?" Jasper swore beneath his breath. "I'll go with you."

"There's no need. My dad will be here soon and my attorney is on his way." I fumbled for my wallet and opened it. "Besides, you don't want that detective setting his sights on you. How much do I owe you for dinner?"

"It's my treat." He gave me a strange look and rubbed his jaw. "Are you implying I'm a suspect?"

"No. Not at all." My voice shook. I started talking fast, my words barely coherent. "It's just the detective thinks everyone's a suspect, and then there's the problem with not having a video camera at the back of your building, and I heard about the health inspection and the fight you had with Russ. But I'm sure you're innocent."

My words hung in the air as Jasper looked at me in disbelief. Finally, he stood, pulled out his wallet, and flicked two fifty-dollar bills on the table. "This should more than cover the meal and tip. I thought our dinner was the beginning of a friendship, if not more. I didn't expect you to interrogate me to find out if I was a murderer."

"No, that's not it at all. Please believe me." My eyes stung when I realized I was talking to his backside, which was already halfway to the front door. As he walked out, my dad walked in. They exchanged a few words, and Jasper pointed his thumb in my direction. But he never looked back at me.

"Hey, kiddo." Dad plopped down in Jasper's vacated seat. He picked up a tortilla chip and dipped it in the *salsa verde*. "Sorry to interrupt your date. Jasper seemed kind of tense. Everything go okay?"

"No. I blew it."

"It can't be all that bad. What happened?" He dipped another chip, this time in the *salsa roja*, and popped it into his mouth. "I wonder if Paco will share his recipe for this. I could eat this on just about everything."

"I can't talk about it now. Why does the detective need to see me tonight? Couldn't he at least wait until tomorrow morning?" My voice sounded tired, resigned to the fact I'd just lost a good friend who might have turned into something more. Plus, I wouldn't be able to go to the patisserie for chocolate rolls anymore. I'd never be able to show my face there ever again.

"I'm not sure, Cari-girl." He heaved a loud sigh. "It's probably some kind of power game. He's kept himself scarce the last couple of days but still has dispatch sending me on wild goose chases."

"I'm sorry I got you involved in this, Dad." I wanted to take my too-tight skirt off, put on flannel jammies, fill a diffuser with lavender oil, curl into a ball, and sleep until all this went away. But that wouldn't happen. "I got into it with Seth North tonight. He's one nasty man. I'm sure our argument will be all over town by tomorrow morning."

"He wasn't always so bad. Almost losing the business was hard on him. Then his wife divorced him within a few months after that and took money he needed to save his family's property. That's when he went over the edge. I think he's an alcoholic, but not one business in town will refuse to serve him drinks. His drinking hasn't helped his financial stability, even after selling the orchards, which has made him even more erratic." He popped another chip into his mouth and eyed the empty margarita pitcher. "If you helped drink all that, you'd better keep your mouth closed and let Alfred do the talking. He should be at the station by now."

"I'm more than happy to leave it up to him. My lips are sealed, except for my name, rank, and serial number."

We stood to leave, and he gave me a hug. "We'll get through this."

Once again, I was taken into the interrogation room with my attorney.

Detective Miller strode into the room, a look of triumph on his face like he'd won the jackpot at the Chumash casino near Santa Barbara. He slapped two large, color-print photos of a man's hairy leg in front of me. A large bruise and a bloody gash were centered on the shinbone. "Ms. Carmichael, Seth North showed up here claiming you assaulted him and demanded we arrest you. Did you cause this injury?"

I looked at the detective and back at the photos. I'd accidentally kicked him beneath the table, but it had been barely a tap. "No."

He picked the photos up and strode toward the door. "Wait here."

My attorney looked at me over the rim of his bifocals perched on the end of his narrow nose. "Why don't you tell me about these accusations while we're waiting?"

I filled him in about my conversation with Seth North and how I'd accidentally kicked him instead of Jasper. "It was more of a nudge and not a real kick. Besides, even if I'd been trying to hurt him, my sandals are soft leather. I couldn't have done that."

The minutes ticked away and turned into a half hour while I talked.

Alfred scooted his chair away from the table and looked at my feet. "Are those the sandals you nudged him with?"

"Yes." I slid my chair out and unbuckled the strap to the sandal. I lifted it from my foot and handed it to the attorney. "See? The leather sole is entirely flexible and the edges are rounded."

He nodded as the door to the interview room flew open. Detective Miller scowled. "You'd better not be tampering with evidence."

"What evidence? There isn't any blood, and besides, it's too soft to have done that kind of damage." I held my sandal up and remembered something. "Seth was wearing blue jeans. I couldn't have injured him wearing these."

"We'll see about that. I need to take them in for evidence." He placed a plastic bag in front of me.

"Look at the gash on his leg and tell me *this* did that kind of injury." I held up my sandal. "Why is he lying?"

"I have two witnesses who confirm you instigated a verbal confrontation with Mr. North. Shortly after, he was seen by numerous witnesses hobbling out of the restaurant." The detective crossed his arms.

So that's what he was doing when he left the room for so long. Obtaining the names of people who'd been in the restaurant while Seth threw his tantrum. I was certain one of those witnesses was Lacie. But would Jasper have thrown me under the bus? Could he have been that angry with me or was he trying to keep the suspicion on me instead of the focus turning to him?

"He's the one who started yelling at me. He faked that limp." Although, to be honest, I hadn't watched him after he headed toward the exit. I huffed a breath out, bent down, unbuckled my second sandal, and placed it in the bag with the first. "Fine. But I want these back sooner than later."

"There's still his accusation of harassment against you." Detective Miller loomed over me. "I'm entirely within my rights to arrest you and hold you for twenty-four hours while we wait for the lab results on your shoes."

CHAPTER THIRTY-FOUR

My head spun and my vision blurred around the edges.

My attorney raised his hand. "I'd proceed with caution if I were you, detective. It's obvious Mr. North is throwing malicious, unwarranted accusations at my client, and you don't need to be seen as falsely accusing Ms. Carmichael based on personal enmity."

"You can't hide behind your father forever, Ms. Carmichael. You're free to go. For now."

Pain pricked my bare feet as the small pebbles, embedded in the concrete sidewalk, pressed into my soles with each step. I hobbled behind Alfred as he led the way to his car. My dad had asked him to bring me home, and I wasn't about to argue.

On the short drive home, I wondered why Seth would accuse me of something I didn't do. Was he trying to scare me away from asking questions? Did he have something to hide?

Alfred stopped the car in my dad's driveway and put it into park. "I'm not sure what you've gotten yourself mixed up in, but it might be a good idea to lie low for a while. I'll talk to your dad about hiring a P.I. to look into Seth North and Detective Miller."

"I'll talk to him tomorrow morning. I don't want him to spend any more money on trying to defend or protect me, and he won't let me pay for it." He'd made so many sacrifices to extricate me from the San Francisco scandal. He didn't need to do it again, no matter what he said.

"Let me know, and I'll set up a meeting."

After I thanked Alfred for coming to my rescue so late at night, I let myself into the house and found a note from my dad saying he'd been called out to a fatal car accident and would be away for most of the night. His note puzzled me since accidents weren't usually his responsibility. Depending on where the accident occurred, either the California Highway Patrol or the sheriff's department responded. I said a quick prayer for those involved, then went to the kitchen and filled a foot basin with hot water and several drops of Frankincense oil. I sat in my grandmother's rocking chair, immersed my aching feet into the water, and closed my eyes to relax and inhale the slightly sweet, slightly woodsy fragrant aroma.

I woke an hour later with chilled feet and drool that had dripped halfway down my chin. As I toweled off my feet, the rustling of leaves and snapping of twigs reached my ears. The side yard window of the kitchen had large, four-foot-tall hydrangea bushes growing beneath the window frame. It sounded like something or someone had shaken the bushes. I reached over and flipped the light switch off and waited for my eyes to adjust to the darkness.

When I didn't hear any new sounds, I took slow, cautious steps toward the window, trying to tell myself it was an animal or the wind that had caused the sound.

Except, it wasn't windy, and it had to have been a large critter to have made that loud of a noise. I was halfway to the window when the glass exploded and something heavy fell to the hardwood flooring. The initial crash sent me diving for the ground. I covered my face with my hands as the tinkling glass hit the floor.

The screech of the backyard gate's hinges echoed in the night air.

Had the intruder run away?

I crab-walked to where I'd left my cell phone and crawled to the stairway.

The graveyard shift 9-1-1 operator answered my frantic call. "What's your emergency?"

"Toby? This is Carissa Carmichael."

"Carissa, are you okay?"

"Someone just threw an object through my dad's side window and shattered the glass. Chief Carmichael is at the scene of the fatality, so I'm by myself." I tried to provide as much information as I could without letting my voice quiver or break. It was an almost impossible task.

"Are you injured? Is the intruder still there?"

"No, and I feel reasonably safe." I moved up the stairs to my dad's bedroom and keyed in the code to his gun safe. I might not have practiced shooting within the last several years, but I could handle a gun if I needed to protect myself. "I have my dad's shotgun. I'll lock myself in the bathroom, so let me know when a black-and-white is here and I'll disarm.

"Do you want me to stay on the line with you?"

"No. I'll be fine. What's the ETA of the unit?"

Toby clicked some keys, and the radio squawked in the background. "Less than three minutes."

"Okay. Have the officers call my cell or you can call me when they arrive."

He chuckled. "Honey, you'll hear the cavalry arrive with their sirens going full-on. No one messes with the chief's daughter."

"Thanks, Toby." I disconnected and went to my bedroom to slip on sturdy shoes before I locked myself in the connecting bathroom. The last thing I needed was stitches from a glass cut. It wasn't long before the sound of wailing sirens interrupted the silence. When they reached the front of the house, I slipped from the bathroom and locked the shotgun back into the cabinet. After turning on all the house lights, I made my way to the front door. I placed my hands on top of my head and stepped onto the front porch.

"Carissa, are you all right?" Bryon held his gun in a tight grip and pointed it toward the house. "Is anyone else here?"

"I'm fine. I'm pretty sure they ran out the back gate right after they threw the object into the house." I brought my hands down and wrapped them around my middle. Not only was the night air chilly, but my body was finally reacting to the threat.

Two more officers exited their squad car.

Bryon motioned them forward. "Ms. Carmichael says she heard the perp run through the backyard gate. Check it out."

"I didn't look at what they threw through the window. It's in the kitchen."

Despite the late hour, Bryon looked immaculate, with sharply creased slacks and his uniform shirt didn't have a wrinkle in sight. The glare from the headlights coming from the two patrol cars made his gray eyes look extra-large behind his glasses. He pulled on gloves and told me to wait while he checked the house to make sure it was safe. I didn't listen and followed in right behind him, ignoring the loud sigh that escaped his lips.

Once we reached the kitchen, he knelt down next to the softball-sized object. Now that the lights were on and I wasn't panicking, I saw white paper with printing had been wrapped around the object. He used the tip of a pen to peel the paper away. Beneath the paper was a large, gray rock, similar to what was found all over the mountains surrounding our valley.

He used his gloved hands to smooth the paper flat. In big, bold letters, someone had left me another warning.

KILLERS BELONG IN JAIL
NOT OAK CREEK

"Not this again." I buried my face in the palm of my hands. "Why is someone blaming me for Russ's death?"

He pulled a plastic evidence bag from his pocket and placed both the rock and the note in it. "Can you think of anyone who's targeting you?"

Uh, yeah. The investigating detective. But I couldn't say that to anyone but my dad. I shook my head and shivered. "What scares me is that this person must've known I was here all by myself. Someone's watching me."

"I had Toby contact Chief Carmichael. He said he'd be home as soon as he can." He tapped his fingers against the mag light hanging from his utility belt. "I'll wait in the car until your dad shows up."

"Thanks. You're more than welcome to wait inside." My dad and Bryon had been friends since he'd started working in Oak Creek Valley. He'd been a part of our barbecues, picnics, and camping trips before I'd moved away, so I knew him well.

"I have some calls I need to make. Thanks though." He motioned toward the shattered window. "Go ahead and clean up the glass. I'll text you the name of an emergency glass repair company, and hopefully, they'll be able to replace the window within the next few hours."

Once he returned to his car, I grabbed a broom and dustpan. I had just started to scoop up the largest chunks of glass when my cell chimed with the glass repair company information. While I made the call, I heated water and fixed a cup of soothing lemon balm tea sweetened with local orange blossom honey. The dispatcher said it was a busy night, but they'd have someone at our house by eight the next morning.

I sat at the kitchen table and sipped the tea, willing my heart to stop pounding and my mind to calm down. It seemed obvious my questions were making someone very nervous, and I needed to figure it out before the violence escalated. After washing and drying the teacup, I cleaned up the glass. I allowed my thoughts to go over everything I'd learned so far as I swept the glass into a dustbin and mopped the floor.

By the time I had wiped the last shard up, I was exhausted. I dropped onto the overstuffed couch and closed my eyes while I waited for my dad. It was nearly two in the morning before his key turned in the lock and Bryon drove away. From the entryway light, I could see his hunched shoulders as he walked toward the stairway. He looked as tired as I felt.

"Hi, Dad. I'm still awake."

He turned and walked into the family room and collapsed into his recliner. "You didn't need to wait up for me. Bryon filled me in and said you'd scheduled the glass repair."

"I don't think I could've slept." I stretched my arms over my head and yawned. "Can I get you something to eat or drink?"

"Naw. I'm fine, just beat." He closed his eyes and exhaled.

"Why were you called out to the accident scene?"

"It was a hit and run. Grant McIntyre was killed tonight."

"But..." I had wanted the developer to be the killer. "What happened?"

"He was on the back road heading to Ventura. It looks like someone pushed his car off the road and down a steep ravine." Dad's mouth pressed into a grim line. "He wasn't wearing a seat belt, the fool. He might have survived otherwise."

"And there's no idea who hit him? Will you be able to find out?"

"Hard to tell. It happened out in the middle of nowhere, so there aren't any security cameras. If the perp is local, then they'd know which back roads to take to avoid being spotted." He pointed toward the kitchen. "And with this threat against you, it makes me wonder if it isn't all connected."

I shivered. "It doesn't make much sense to me. Why kill Grant and only try to scare me?"

"Like I said, if Grant had been wearing his seat belt, he might still be alive. I think whoever did it only meant to scare him." He sighed and tapped his fingers against his dark blue pants. "I had to break the news to Beatriz. She's pretty broken up. Maybe you can take her some flowers or a casserole or something in the morning. Whatever you think is best."

"Sure. I'll figure something out."

"Go on up to bed. I'll sleep here on the couch until the window gets repaired."

"They'll be here by eight." I yawned again. "Would you like me to bring you a blanket and pillow?"

"No thanks. I'll be fine."

CHAPTER THIRTY-FIVE

The invigorating aroma of coffee drew me to the kitchen a little before seven. My dad was showered and dressed, and while there were dark smudges beneath his eyes from fatigue, he looked wide awake. I, on the other hand, looked like something a cat would drag in. My eyes were bloodshot, my raven-black hair was frizzy, and my skin looked sallow. He poured a mug of coffee, liberally doused it with milk, and handed it to me without a word. Instead of sipping, I gulped it down and then poured another cup.

"How many pots of coffee did you drink this morning to look so awake?" I sipped my second cup of coffee this time.

"This is only my second cup." He raised it to me. "I've had a lot of practice with this job and being sleep-deprived. Surviving is all about mental attitude."

That or men didn't need to rely on conditioner, flat irons, or makeup to look presentable. When the doorbell rang, my dad answered it and let the glass repairman in. I excused myself and went to finish getting ready for my day. I thought I'd have enough time to stop by the deli and pick up a main course dish for the mayor, and I decided I would do the same for Victoria. I hadn't extended formal condolences to her after Russ's death, and this would be the perfect excuse to chat with her. I'd also ask Ashley to go to the patisserie to buy something sweet for the two women. I was sure I was persona non grata at the bakery after last night.

With two containers of minestrone and two freshly baked baguettes from the deli in hand, I drove to my shop. Ashley was waiting for me in the parking lot. Unlike myself, she looked well-rested.

"Sorry I'm late. I hope you didn't have to wait long. The line at the deli was longer than I expected." I gave her the paper bag while I inserted the key into the lock.

"No problem. There's not much chance of me getting any extra sleep with a two-year-old in the house." She peered inside the bag and frowned. "You bought baguettes from the deli? What if Jasper finds out? He'll think you're a traitor."

With this town's gossip mill, he'd probably heard about it already. I locked the door once we were inside. "It's a long story, and I'll tell you about it later. Right now, I need you to buy two boxes of a half-dozen assorted cookies each at the patisserie."

Her frown deepened. "And you're not going down there because?"

"I promise to tell you about it when you get back. Just pretend you're buying the cookies for yourself. If Jasper says anything, tell him you haven't seen me yet this morning." I held out a twenty-dollar bill.

"Oh dear. This can't be good." She took the money and left without another word.

Usually, tea was the only thing I brewed at the shop, but today was a coffee kind of day. I dug through a few boxes until I found the single-use coffee maker with the container of pods. It would have to do since I'd been cut off from Jasper's enticing brew. I sighed, knowing I'd eventually have to make amends for hurting him.

It seemed to take forever for her to return, bearing the familiar pink bakery boxes with the patisserie's seal on the top. She balanced two large cups of coffee in a cardboard carrier.

"Bless you, my friend." I grabbed the coffee from her before even one precious drop could spill. "How much do I owe you? I don't think I gave you enough cash."

She handed me a five-dollar bill and raised her eyebrows. "Coffee's on the house."

My cheeks warmed, and I hoped it meant Jasper realized how sorry I was and accepted that perhaps he'd overreacted. "That's sweet of Jasper."

"Oh, it wasn't from Jasper. I didn't see him."

"Then who?"

"You'll never guess." Ashley waited a moment.

I shrugged.

"Do you remember Lacie from high school?"

I groaned. "Please tell me the coffee's not from her."

"Why? I thought you two were friends." Ashley pointed at the disposable coffee cup I held. "She said to make sure I told you this was from her. See? She put a smiley face and heart on it for you."

"Are you telling me Lacie is working at the patisserie?" I shuddered. It hadn't taken her long to worm herself into his life.

"She told me she was the new manager."

I shuddered again. Without a doubt, whatever was in the to-go cup wasn't going to be good. I tentatively peeled back the plastic lid and ran to the bathroom while I tried not to gag and tried not to spill even a drop of the nasty concoction.

I poured half the contents into the toilet, flushing as I did so. It was coffee all right with a little extra gift. It looked like it had been boiled, grounds and all, overnight until nothing but burnt sludge remained. To make it even more repellent, she'd placed a dead cockroach on top of the gunk.

Lacie had to have planned this. Jasper would never allow anything that vile in his shop, no matter how angry he might have been with me. Where was he when she created this horrible cup for me? Or had he been in on the plan? My eyes stung, and I blinked to chase away the tears that threatened to form.

"What's wrong?" Ashley stood in the doorway. "Was it too hot? Mine is perfect."

I motioned her inside the bathroom as I poured the remaining sludge into the toilet. Another cockroach slipped out and floated on top of the water.

"Ewww. How did she manage to..." She looked from the toilet to me and then to the cup with its heart and smiley face. "I guess you weren't such good friends."

"Definitely frenemies." I tossed the cup into the recycle bin, sat at the counter, and told her about my disastrous date. After telling her about the shattered window and Grant McIntyre's death, I rested my head on the counter. "How am I going to fix things with Jasper? I really liked him and now Lacie is going to ruin everything."

She was uncharacteristically quiet. Her face was pale and two splotches of red blazed on her cheeks.

"Are you okay?" I reached over and touched her hand. It was cold.

She shook her head. "If Grant is dead, there's no one to buy our property. The bank will foreclose on us."

"There has to be something we can do. Did your mom talk to the bank? Can't they give her some leeway because of the fire?"

"They have no heart. We'll be homeless."

"I won't let that happen. I'll talk to my dad and see if he has any ideas." I was ashamed about complaining about my nonexistent romantic life. It was nothing compared to what Ashley and her family faced. "Just because Grant is out of the picture doesn't mean the development company will pull out of its plans. They've bought land already and they'll want to put it to use."

"You might be right. The timing couldn't have been worse, even though we were angry about his lower offer." She sniffed and rubbed her eyes. "I'm sorry about your date with Jasper."

I waved away her concern. "It's nothing. I have you to make the run for chocolate rolls and coffee for me now. I don't dare set foot in the patisserie, with Lacie working there."

She gave me a half-hearted smile. "What do you want me to work on this morning?"

"I've been giving your idea of a soft opening some thought. Do you think we can swing it for Friday and our grand opening on Saturday?" I'd considered pushing it back another week but decided it was time to take the plunge. "I'll see if Dillon can come in for a couple of hours Friday afternoon and again on the weekend in case we run into any issues and need an extra set of hands."

"That's smart. Better too much help than not enough starting out."

I had thought the same thing, although part of me worried no one would step foot in my shop and I'd be a total failure. "Can you work on getting the word out and run it through the town's gossip mill? I'll forward the grand opening brochures I created and you can post them to our social media sites and hand out the printed copies around town."

"Sounds like a good plan."

"One last thing. Can you call Jasper and see if he can make the cookies for Saturday's grand opening? If he's not there, don't tell Lacie why you're calling. She'd sabotage the order somehow."

"Sure." Ashley whipped her cell phone out from her back pocket and called the number I gave her. "Hi. Can I speak with Jasper?"

A muffled female voice came through the phone.

"Can you tell me when he'll be in or where I can find him?" She held her index finger up and circled it around her ear while rolling her eyes. "Thanks. You've been a big help...not."

"What was that all about?"

"When Jasper finds out how she's treating his customers, he'll kick her to the curb in no time at all. What a rude woman."

"You'd think she would have outgrown that behavior since high school, but I think she's only gotten worse. What did she say?"

"She's running the shop for the time being, and if I don't want to work with her, then I can take my business elsewhere."

"She didn't actually say that. Did she?"

"Verbatim. And she wouldn't tell me where Jasper is or when he'll be back." Ashley let out a low whistle. "He'll be lucky to have any of his customers or part-time employees left once she's done with it."

"I'll come up with a backup plan for refreshments for

the opening." I pulled out a notebook and started a list. "As soon as I talk to Dillon, I need to run the cookies and soup over to the mayor. I'll take the other set to Victoria later this afternoon."

"Are you having a potluck brunch or something?" Ashley's eyebrows drew together.

"I didn't tell you about Beatriz and Grant McIntyre. They were seeing each other, and she's devastated by his death. My dad had to tell her and he asked me to take her some food."

Her eyes widened. "Ewww. How could she? I'm sorry he died, but he's kinda slimy. She's way out of his league, anyway."

"That's pretty much what I said too." Belatedly, I realized I'd broken my pinky-promise to my dad to not share that information. "You have to promise not to tell anyone about it, though. It might be important to the investigation."

Ashley lifted her eyebrows and her mouth formed a perfect little "o." She held up her pinky. "The secret is safe with me."

CHAPTER THIRTY-SIX

I linked my pinky with hers for a brief moment then left Ashley working on the laptop. I sent Dillon a quick text.

> Hey Dillon, it's Carissa. I'm having a soft opening on Fri with grand opening on Sat. Would you like to work a few hours each day? Or whenever you're avail.

It didn't take long for dots to appear on my screen, so I waited for his response.

> Yes! What time should I be there?

I paused, trying to picture how the workflow would go and when he'd be most helpful.

> Does 2pm work for you both days?

A thumbs-up emoji flashed on my screen.

Once I'd nestled the soup, baguette, and cookies in a gift bag, I drove to the mayor's house. It was a small, adobe-style bungalow painted a terracotta brown. A large variety of succulents dotted the yard, and a few looked like they were about to flower. I walked up the Spanish-tiled walkway and banged the iron ring that served as a knocker on the ornate, heavy wood door. Beatriz Torres opened the door. Her weary eyes squinted at me as if trying to figure out why I was standing there.

"My dad and I want to express our condolences." I thrust the bag at her. "I brought soup, bread, and cookies for you. Please let us know if there's anything else we can do."

"No one was supposed to know about us." The mayor glared at me now. "Robert promised he wouldn't tell anyone."

"I saw you at our house early Sunday morning. It wasn't his fault."

She glanced up and down the street, then motioned for me to follow her into the house. The interior design was in keeping with the exterior Spanish style—heavy, dark furniture, terracotta tiles for the flooring, and dark wrought iron accessories. She steered me through the living room and out French doors that led to a fenced-in garden. The focal point of the outdoor space was a three-tiered fountain that bubbled water. It cascaded and splashed into a round basin lined with colorful, artistically crafted mosaic tiles.

Beatriz sank onto one of the patio chairs and placed the gift bag on the table.

I sat down across from her.

"Tell me what you're doing here, Ms. Carmichael. I'm well aware the food is only a pretext for your visit."

"I swear my dad asked me to offer our condolences. He was sorry to see you so distraught when he talked to you last night."

In the bright morning light, I studied the mayor's face.

Fine lines surrounded her full lips tinted with coral-colored lipstick, and she'd applied a heavy layer of mascara to her eyelashes. Her eyes looked tired. It didn't appear she'd been crying recently. Or perhaps I was an ugly crier and Beatriz avoided the red-rimmed, puffy eyes that happened to me.

"That's very nice, but a card would have sufficed." She crossed her arms in front of her ample chest. "You have a reputation for being a busybody, poking into other people's business and affairs. Your father had no right to talk to you about me."

I couldn't promise I would keep her affair with the developer secret, since I'd already told Ashley. "You may have wanted to keep your relationship private, but with his death and everything going on with his land acquisitions, I'd think you would want to cooperate with law enforcement to help find whoever did this."

"What have you heard about it? What are the police saying?" She leaned in toward me.

"Nothing so far. There weren't any security cameras, so they have no leads." I was sure my dad had shared everything when he broke the news to the mayor the night before. "What will happen to Grant's company and his development plans? Will they continue?"

"My assistant made it more than clear when you barged into my office that I won't discuss Grant or his company." The mayor stared at me with her large brown eyes. "Do I make myself clear?"

"Yes, but..." I swallowed hard. "Do you have any idea who might have wanted to kill Grant?"

"It was an unfortunate accident, plain and simple. I told that fool a million times to wear his seat belt when he drove, but he never listened to me. Don't let your imagination run away with you, Ms. Carmichael." Beatriz stood. "Now, if you'll excuse me, I need to get ready for a council meeting."

I drove back to my shop, disappointed she hadn't been more forthcoming. I supposed I had been unrealistic, thinking she'd have some insight about who might have killed Grant. Not for a moment did I believe it was an accident.

After parking my car, I remembered the box of books in the trunk. As I walked toward the patisserie, I tried to be inconspicuous and blend in with a small group of tourists who ambled past the row of shops. It was hard to accomplish while I carried the box, but it was the best I could do. It would be beyond embarrassing if Jasper or Lacie saw me peeking in as I passed the patisserie on the way to my shop. Earlier, I'd taken the long way around the back of the arcade building to reach my shop in order to avoid going past the patisserie. However, the weight of the heavy box of books in my arms made me take the shortest route possible.

The patisserie was almost empty, something I'd never seen in the months since I'd returned to town. Jasper was nowhere in sight. Lacie, on the other hand, stood at the counter glaring at the unfortunate customer who appeared to be trying to decide what to order. She must have said something mean because his head snapped up and he turned around and headed for the exit without purchasing anything.

I managed to make it back to the shop without Lacie noticing me and without dropping the heavy box containing the aromatherapy books. Ashley excitedly showed me the social media posts she'd put up, and I was pleased we were already getting positive comments and likes.

I placed a few of the books around the shop, then stored the rest in my office. Next, I put together the raffle gift basket containing a variety of aromatherapy accessories and a certificate for a thirty-minute reflexology appointment. For every twenty dollars of merchandise a customer bought over the coming week, they'd get one raffle ticket. I'd draw the winning ticket a week from Sunday, and if the winner wasn't local, ship the items to them. It would be up to them to make it back to town to claim the reflexology appointment. I hoped it would generate a few more sales and excitement for our products.

CHAPTER THIRTY-SEVEN

Once Ashley returned from distributing flyers, we finished unpacking a few of the remaining boxes, and I showed her how to bottle and label the vials of my Celebration Blend.

She inhaled the scent and handed me the rose-colored vial. "I'll be your first sale. I'll take a bottle of this."

"It's on the house." I handed the vial back to her. "Try it out tonight, so you'll be able to recommend it over the coming week."

"Are you sure?"

"Absolutely. I need my team to believe in our products." I held out one of the product information cards I'd printed out with ten common ailments and the essential oils that could be beneficial. "Memorize this list and experiment with samples on yourself. I'll have a few stacks of these cards around the shop for people to help themselves to. I also have several resource books in my office we can refer to for a wide range of ailments, or customers can browse through the sample books set out."

"You've thought of everything. How to help headaches, abrasions, sore throats, coughs, earaches, chapped skin, hiccups, insect bites, indigestion, and sinus issues." She examined the glossy card. "I'm glad to see you've got a disclaimer that we're not medical personnel and to consult a professional doctor if necessary."

"Mari told me to include that on every piece of paper that leaves the shop. It will even print out on the receipt."

A light knock sounded on the front glass door. My dad held up two takeout bags from the Thai restaurant a half mile up the road.

I opened the door and the tantalizing savory aromas of garlic, ginger, and Thai red curry followed him in.

"I brought an early lunch for you both. Hope you like shrimp pad Thai and red curry chicken." He opened the bags and set containers, paper plates, and plastic utensils on the counter.

My mouth watered. "Thanks, Dad. Time got away from me and I didn't realize it was lunchtime."

"Thanks, Chief Carmichael." Ashley's gaze flitted between the food and my dad. "Um, how much do I owe you for lunch?"

"Absolutely nothing. I needed to get away from the station, and bringing lunch over was a good excuse."

"Thank you. It smells delicious." Ashley opened the plastic sleeves covering the forks, spoons, and napkins.

I divided the food between the three plates, and then looked at Ashley. "There's a bottle of iced tea in the refrigerator. Can you grab it along with three glasses?"

It didn't take long for the three of us to dig into the tangy rice noodles with jumbo shrimp and the succulent chicken enrobed with a coconut milk-enriched curry sauce. Once my stomach was full, I turned toward my dad, his comment about needing to be away from the station finally registering.

"What's going on at the station besides Detective Miller dreaming up new ways to harass me?"

"He's been interrogating Jasper since six-thirty this morning."

"Oh, no!" No wonder he wasn't at his bakery. "Why would he do that? I thought you said Jasper couldn't have killed Russ."

The chief rubbed his face, and his frown deepened. "This has more to do with Grant McIntyre's death. Someone saw Jasper's white truck heading out of town at a high speed shortly after he left Paco's. His truck seems to be missing this morning, and there's white paint on the back panel of Grant's car."

"He was upset when he left me last night, but I don't see him being so irresponsible as to leave the scene of an accident. What does he say about it?" My stomach churned, so I pushed my plate away. Had I angered him so much he'd made a fatal error and killed Grant? I thought guiltily of the pitcher of margaritas we'd shared. He shouldn't have been driving.

"He claims he hasn't driven his truck for several days and the last time he saw it, it had been parked two blocks from his bakery."

That was one of the problems living in downtown Oak Creek Valley. There wasn't enough parking, and while Jasper lived over his bakery, the city allowed no overnight parking in the arcade's limited space. Most downtown residents often had to hunt for parallel parking spaces blocks from where they lived since most of the homes had been built in the early twentieth century. I guessed the town's founding fathers didn't foresee households having a car for every adult in residence, and most homes didn't have garages or large enough driveways to accommodate vehicles.

"Wouldn't the security cameras in front of his bakery show when he came back from our dinner?"

"That's the problem. He didn't come back until four this morning to open the bakery."

"How does he explain that?" I frowned.

Jasper was reliable, especially when it involved his patisserie.

"He said he was upset, so he went for a long walk east of town. On his way back home, a friend saw him and offered him a ride. He ended up having a couple of beers and sleeping at the friend's house." My dad looked uncomfortable and wouldn't meet my eyes.

"And the friend will corroborate that?"

"Um, yeah. Except, it doesn't do much good because she didn't pick him up until after midnight. The accident occurred earlier than that." He hung his head. "I know you'll ask, so I'll just tell you. He stayed with Lacie."

I stiffened. No wonder she was the one working at the shop. Had he been simply toying with my emotions? Was his hopes of friendship and perhaps something more just a lie?

Ashley sucked in a mouthful of air, then had a coughing fit. I could barely understand what she was trying to say in between the coughing she struggled to control. "Sorry. I inhaled a piece of rice and there must've been a chili that went down too."

I filled her glass with more tea and patted her back.

My dad bent in front of her face. "Can you breathe?"

She nodded and coughed more.

"Good. I was afraid I'd have to do the Heimlich maneuver." He sat back down. "I've had to perform it twice. It scared me to death."

"But you're well-trained and saved their lives, didn't

you?" I nudged him with my elbow. "You shouldn't worry about having to do it again."

"You never know if it'll work or if I'll crack their ribs or something." The chief shuddered. "It gives me the heebie-jeebies thinking about it. You gals need to take a CPR and first-aid class soon in case one of your clients has a medical emergency."

I pulled out a pad of paper and added it to my list of things to do. It seemed like I'd never get any of it done.

Ashley finally got the coughing under control and wiped her watering eyes. She took another sip of tea. "Sorry about that. A piece of chili got stuck on the back of my throat. Carissa, I can't believe Jasper would get involved with Lacie. She probably drugged his beer, and he passed out. Besides, once he sees what she's done to all his customers, he won't want anything to do with her. She's not going to be any competition for you."

I shrugged. The only thing that mattered was relieving my guilt that I might have caused Jasper to get behind the wheel of his truck and, as a result, killed Grant. I needed to find out what happened because my instincts told me it was related to Russ's murder.

"What's she done with his customers?" Dad stacked the paper plates and put them into the trash can. "All she had to do was sell his pastries."

"Most people don't appreciate their desserts being served with a side of snark or snarled at while they're trying to decide," she answered. "I'm surprised she hasn't gotten fired from Paco's yet."

"She's probably on her best behavior when the boss is watching." My dad wiped the counter down with a clean napkin.

"It's more like the boss is willing to overlook just about

anything when she wears her short skirts." She snorted. "Don't worry. He was desperate for help this morning and she happened to be in the right place at the right time. I can't see him interested in her."

I couldn't help but worry. Lacie had been at the right place at the right time, and I was nowhere in sight.

My dad looked around the shop. "Are you ready to open on Friday?"

I hadn't told him much about it after his previous comment about my smelly woo-woo business. "Ready as I'll ever be. The only thing left to do is to figure out some kind of refreshment since Jasper's mad at me and being interrogated. I can't ask Lacie to whip up a huge batch of cookies. That'd be a disaster."

"How about a popcorn machine?" Dad asked. "We did one for the station's family picnic, and guests can serve themselves."

"We can buy a few gallons of lemonade to serve, as well." Ashley grabbed a pen and a sheet of notepaper. "Tell me what we need and I'll make it happen."

"The only problem with a popcorn machine is the aroma will cover up the scents of my essential oils." While I liked the idea, I wasn't about to let something like that undermine the focus of my shop's products.

"I have an idea. We can use the popcorn machine as a serving prop and buy pre-popped popcorn to fill it. That'll keep the smell to a minimum." Ashley's eyes danced. "I found really cute red and white popcorn containers at a party store in Ventura. They weren't very expensive, either."

"Do you have time to pick up the supplies?" I grabbed my purse and extracted the company credit card from my wallet. I handed it to her. "You can fill your car up with gas while you're at it."

"Sure. Let me call my mom and tell her where I'm going, and then I'll be on my way."

"I'll make a list of what I think we'll need and where to purchase the items." I turned toward my dad. "Where can I get a popcorn machine?"

"That's easy. Bryon owns one. I'll call and see when he can drop it off." Dad winked at me. "I'm sure he'll give you the friends and family discount, too."

Once my dad and Ashley were out the door, I walked around the shop, making sure I hadn't overlooked anything for the opening. I was as ready as I'd ever be. Butterflies flitted in my stomach. It wasn't the thought of the opening; it was the realization I couldn't put off going to see Victoria any longer. My work here was mostly done, at least until Ashley returned, so I couldn't procrastinate on visiting the grieving mother.

When I rang the doorbell of the rundown bungalow Victoria had shared with Russ, I half expected no one to answer the door. The faded and splintered green wood door flung open, and the stench of cigarette smoke and stale tobacco assaulted my nose. Victoria's gray eyes were red-rimmed and her thin, chapped lips were turned down at the corners. She wore a washed-out floral bathrobe that had turned a dingy gray. It did nothing for her crêpey skin, which held a tinge of yellow. It looked like she had aged at least twenty years since I'd seen her a few days before, and I wondered if she was sick.

Holding up the bag of soup, baguettes, and cookies, I cleared my throat. "I wanted to drop by and offer my sincere condolences. I truly am sorry for your loss."

Victoria looked at the bag and then at me. "I'm not sure

why you'd care. Russ wasn't nothing but trouble for your shop."

I exhaled the breath I'd been holding, half expecting her to accuse me of being a killer. "He didn't deserve to die."

She nodded and opened the rusty screen door. It squeaked on its rusty hinges and the sound sent a shiver up my spine. She took the offered bag.

Smoke wafted from the house, and despite my desperate need for answers, I didn't want to step foot inside, but there wasn't any other choice. "May I come in and talk with you for a moment?"

"That young detective told me you were a nosy busybody and I shouldn't talk to you." She inclined her head toward the inside of her house. "He's trying hard to convince me you're guilty. C'mon in."

CHAPTER THIRTY-EIGHT

I fumed as I followed Victoria into the gloomy interior of her home. *Why is Detective Miller so focused on me?*

She dropped the bag on a cluttered kitchen counter, and then led the way into her family room. The drawn curtains made the room dark, and the only light came from an ancient box television that sat on a small wood table. An old black-and-white movie played, and the volume was turned all the way down. I gingerly sat on the edge of a couch that displayed several stains of nondescript origin. A white cat jumped up beside me and rubbed its face against my arm.

"You can push him off if he bothers you." She picked up a second cat, this one black as coal, and sat in a recliner. The cracked leather, or maybe it was fake leather, had been repaired with duct tape. "Now, tell me why you've decided to pay a condolence visit all of a sudden."

"I, uh, wouldn't say it was all that sudden." The words tried to gush out of my mouth, but I bit them back. I didn't want to make her angry with me all over again. Instead, I stroked the purring cat and tried to calm down. "I thought you might need some time to grieve and, you know, let some of the gossip settle down."

I'd almost said die down but, at the last second, realized that'd be a huge mistake.

Her laugh sounded almost like a bark before it turned into a hacking cough.

"Are you okay? Can I get you a glass of water or something?"

She waved off my concerns. "Naw. I should've given up the cigarettes years ago, but I didn't. Now it's catching up with me."

"Are you seeing a doctor?"

"Yep. They tell me it won't be long before I'll need to cart an oxygen tank around." She hacked again and grabbed a pack of cigarettes. Victoria must've seen me cringe because she fingered the package and set it back down on the side table sitting next to her recliner.

"I'm so sorry. Is there anything I can do to help?"

"Thanks, but it won't be necessary. I'm thinking about closing shop and moving to Phoenix to be with my sister. There's nothing to keep me here any longer."

Silence fell between us. I wasn't sure I should keep saying I was sorry. Victoria's gaze kept flicking to her cigarettes. I gestured toward the pack, hoping if she lit up, she might relax and become more open about her son. "Go ahead. I don't mind."

"You sure?"

I nodded and watched her trembling fingers as they clasped the white tube and placed it in her mouth. A quick flick of her lighter and soon there was an orange glow at the tip and a trail of white smoke curled its way up to the yellowed ceiling. I waited for her to take a few puffs.

"I hate to barge in on you, but Detective Miller seems to have focused on me instead of looking at other possibilities."

"He does seem fixated on you." She blew out a ring of smoke. "He also seems to have a habit of sticking his nose in people's financial troubles, where it doesn't belong."

I leaned forward. "Can you give me specifics? Anything that might help keep his focus off from me?"

"He only asked about you and your daddy. Like if you'd been a troublemaker in school and he wanted to hear all the gossip about your problems up north." She flicked ash into an overflowing bowl. "When I tried to tell him about the threatening calls Russ had received a few weeks ago, that detective couldn't have cared less."

"Someone was threatening him? Do you have any idea who it was?"

Had Detective Miller even followed up on getting ahold of his phone records to look into it? I'd have to ask my dad.

Victoria shook her head. "My son wouldn't say."

"Was it a man or a woman calling him?"

"A man. He wouldn't talk to me about it." She took a drag on her cigarette, and I waited in silence. "Only reason I know is he got a call while he was here for dinner one night. I had chicken and dumplings, so he ate with me. That didn't happen often. He might've lived here, but he wasn't around that much. What were we talking about?"

"Russ received a threatening call while you had dinner together."

"Oh, yeah. Just as I sat down across from him, I heard a man say 'or else' before my son went white as a sheet, and then he turned red and stomped out of the house. He wouldn't tell me what it was about when I asked him later."

"I've been told that, ah, Russ got into a few pickles around town over the last few years."

She rolled her eyes. "My son was no saint, but he didn't do a thing to deserve to be killed in cold blood."

"I agree and want the murderer brought to justice. I hope you realize I had nothing to do with it, even though someone is making it look like I did."

"You wouldn't be sitting here in one piece if I thought you killed my son." She calmly gazed at me and lifted an eyebrow.

Whoa. That was an aggressive statement. Was Victoria capable of violence? Could she have accidentally killed her son? I swallowed hard and pressed her. "I'm glad you believe me. Do you have any idea who might have taken your son from you?"

"Like I said, he might have gotten into a few situations over the last couple of years, but I can't see those scrapes being worth killing over."

"You said something about Detective Miller sticking his nose in other people's financial troubles. Did he do that to you?"

Victoria's gaze shifted to the side before she stubbed out the cigarette butt and extracted another. She took a moment looking at the white tube, then lit it with a quick flick of her lighter. "It was in the past, but I s'pose if he harassed me, then it's likely he's harassed other people."

"What do you mean? Was it over Russ and any, err, indiscretions he might have had?"

She waved her hand and my gaze tracked the swirling smoke that wafted from the cigarette. "Nope. Let's just say the detective was very persuasive in talking me into selling our small orchard at below-market value."

"Why would he do that? Why would you accept those terms?"

"I have no idea why the man got involved in convincing

me to sell. Russ was livid when he found out, but he was the reason I had to find a buyer in the first place. Little good that did."

"I heard Russ bled you dry and you're almost in financial ruin."

Despite looking frail and elderly, Victoria moved deceptively fast. One second she sat in her recliner, puffing her cigarette, the next second she loomed over me, her eyes wild and her nicotine-stained teeth inches from my face. Her clawed fingers encircled my wrist. "Look here, girlie, I won't put up with your insinuations that I might have hurt my son. My only son. Now get your heinie out of here before I do something we'll both regret."

The second she stepped away from me, I didn't have to be told twice to leave. Once in the fresh air, I turned toward her and touched the palms of my hands together in front of my chest. "I'm sorry. I didn't mean to imply you had anything to do with it, and I know you're grieving. I'm trying to understand who did this to you, and I overstepped the boundary. I hope you can forgive me."

The door slammed in my face. I turned and walked back to my shop, while my face burned from the memory of upsetting the bereaved mother. It bothered me that I'd made so many people angry with my questions, and I'd have happily let the detective do his job of solving the murder. Except, as Victoria pointed out, he had it in for me and wasn't following up on finding any other suspects. Plus, I found it odd she'd said Detective Miller harassed her into selling their orchard. How did he fit into the picture? Could he have been associated with Grant McIntyre? I had no choice but to press forward, no matter whose toes I stepped on.

I decided a few well-placed bouquets of fresh flowers

would brighten the shop for the opening, so I stopped by Misty's Blooms. It was a couple doors away from Jasper's patisserie, and an armful of flowers would be the perfect cover to sneak a peek through his windows as I made my way back to the Aromatherapy Apothecary.

CHAPTER THIRTY-NINE

As I pushed through the glass door and into the florist's shop, a bell tinkled, announcing my arrival. The owner, Misty Bowman, was bent over a large pot as she tried to pour potting mix into the bottom from a huge sack almost as big as she was. She was middle-aged but seemed to do everything she could to slow down the aging process. Bright pink streaked her blonde hair, which she wore short and spiky. It accentuated her delicate face and made her china-blue eyes look large and round. She was almost five feet tall and slender enough to wear low-slung blue jeans that exposed a pierced navel when she turned to greet me.

"Hey, Carissa. I've been meaning to stop by and say welcome to the neighborhood." She wiped her dusty hands on her jeans and reached out to shake my hand. Her grasp was firm.

"Thanks. I should have called you a couple of days ago, but I just now realized we could use some fresh flowers for our opening. Can you put together an assortment for me? I'd also like a small condolence bouquet delivered to

Victoria Lewellyn." It was the least I could do after I upset her so much.

"Sure. Come to the back and I'll show you what I have." She wove her way around plastic buckets filled with water and others that contained moss and stones. "Ashley dropped off some fliers, and I taped one in the front window."

"Thank you. I appreciate it." I hated to admit I hadn't noticed. Instead, I'd been craning my neck to see if I could catch a glimpse of Jasper. I hadn't. "I'll take some of your business cards to set out alongside the flower arrangements."

"That's kind of you." She led the way into a large storage cooler in the back. The concrete floor was wet in spots thanks to the strategically placed water spigots and drainage holes. She gestured toward a row of white ten-gallon buckets on the far wall. A wildly colorful assortment of blooms was held in place, their stems submerged in water. "These just came in at o' dark-thirty today. They should stay fresh for at least nine or ten days, if you treat them right. If you're looking for a bargain, I can sell you a couple of bouquets of my older flowers, but they'll only last four or five days."

"How about I take two bouquets of your fresh flowers and one bouquet of your discounted blooms for our opening?" I figured if we could get through the weekend with all three bouquets intact, that would be more than sufficient. "I'll leave it up to you to put something nice together for Victoria."

"Do you have any specific flowers you want or don't want?"

"I'd rather have fragrance-free flowers or at least blooms with a light fragrance." I didn't want the arrangements to compete with the scents of my essential oils. "I'll leave it up to your expert opinion on what's best."

We spent several minutes discussing where I wanted to display the flowers and what types of vases she would loan me. It didn't take long for our conversation to turn to Russ's murder. Her opinion of him matched what others had mentioned so many times before. It wasn't a surprise that someone finally killed him. He had courted conflict and went out of his way to harass those he came in contact with. Misty and her shop hadn't been spared the nastiness Russ dished out either, and she'd seen him mistreat Victoria many times.

"Do you have any idea why Russ treated people that way?" I couldn't imagine living a life that made everyone miserable around me, including my own mother.

"I'm sure some people could make excuses that he had an alcoholic father who ruined his childhood, but I don't think that's entirely it. Some folks are born with a mean streak, and Russ was one of those people."

"Poor Victoria. She must've suffered living with that kind of husband and a miserable son. What happened to Russ's father?"

Misty pursed her lips and was silent for a moment. "Funny thing was, he just up and disappeared about ten years ago. No one's heard from him since."

"What? How can that be?"

"Victoria told people he'd run off with a new girlfriend, but as far as I can recall, he never came back. Some of his drinking buddies asked after him for a time, but people eventually forgot about him."

"Was he ever reported missing?"

Misty shrugged. "She said it wasn't the first time he'd taken off, and she was certain he'd been seeing a new woman. At that point in their marriage, I don't think she really cared if he ever showed up again."

Somehow, I thought there'd be some kind of legal implication with not reporting him missing. I'd have to ask my dad. He might even know what became of Mr. Lewellyn. Given both Victoria and Russ's tempers, I wondered if one or both of them had something to do with Mr. Lewellyn's disappearance. I shook my head to dispel my musings. I didn't need another mystery. There was enough on my plate as it was. "Can you think of anyone who hated Russ enough that they'd murder him?"

"No. The detective asked me that, but he was more focused on prying out gossip about you than listening to my list of people I've seen Russ get into altercations with."

Great. Detective Miller strikes again. "Yeah, he has it in for me. Aside from Jasper, Victoria, and Seth North, is there anyone else who's gotten into it with him?"

"Are you investigating?"

"With the detective focused on me, I have no choice. In case you're wondering, I'm one hundred percent innocent."

Misty laughed long and hard, and her gold navel ring bounced up and down, glittering in the lights. "Of course you are, Carissa. You've always been a good kid, despite the trouble that found you in San Francisco."

"Thanks. I appreciate that." I lowered my head. "You have no idea how many people hold that against me, even though I was clueless I'd been set up."

She patted my arm. "Back to your question. Russ almost got into a fistfight with that developer..."

"Grant McIntyre?"

Misty didn't act like she knew he'd been killed last night. I wasn't sure if it was public knowledge yet, so I bit my cheek to keep from spilling the news.

"Yeah. That's the one. And Mayor Torres. She wasn't a fan of Russ's, and they exchanged some nasty words a few weeks ago."

"What was it about?"

"I have no idea. Sorry." All during our conversation, she'd plucked blooms and greens from the buckets and placed them in an artful arrangement in a jade-colored vase. "Here's the first one. I'll drop off the other two arrangements tomorrow morning around eight-thirty and make sure I get Victoria's flowers delivered by tomorrow afternoon. I've got some deliveries to make in a few minutes, but I'll get your order done later this evening."

I handed her my personal credit card and made a mental note to order an extra company credit card. After thanking her for both the flowers and the information, I made my way toward my shop, passing Jasper's patisserie on the way. I held the arrangement up to shield part of my face as I walked past his front windows. I peered through the foliage and saw he was standing at the pastry counter. A look of hurt or it could've been dismay, colored his face as his eyes roamed his empty bakery. Lacie was nowhere in sight. I hurried past, not wanting Jasper to see me, but I couldn't help but wonder what my nemesis had told him about his lack of customers. Somehow, I was sure I'd be blamed.

After placing the floral arrangement on the counter, I walked around the shop to make sure everything was ready for opening on Friday. There wasn't one thing out of place, and I supposed I could have opened on Thursday. However, I felt more comfortable with an extra day to take care of any last-minute details and brew up another batch of lavender essential oil. I puttered around my distilling room and carefully measured out the ingredients I would need the following morning to start the still.

Ashley bounced in, carrying an armload of stuffed plastic sacks, bearing the party store's logo, just as I had finished wiping down the tabletop.

"You'll never believe what I found to go with the popcorn theme!" She dumped the bags on the counter and sniffed the bouquet. "These are pretty. Nice choice of non-fragrant flowers too."

"Misty put them together for me. She'll drop off another two arrangements tomorrow morning."

"Cool. Anyway, the party store not only had the popcorn tubs and matching napkins, but they had Mylar balloons shaped like flowers and potted plants." She glanced over at me. "I thought it would add a party atmosphere and fit with the theme of your shop. They gave me a business owner's discount, so I hope you don't mind buying a few extra props."

"You're right. The balloons will add to the festivities."

"Great. Then I hope you think my next idea is good, too." She looked relieved. "And if you don't, I can pay for it and use it for my mom's birthday party."

"I'm sure it's fine. You've come up with so many wonderful ideas. It'll be perfect."

"Well, you know how photo booths are so popular at parties and weddings? The party store had a garden party backdrop with coordinating photo booth props. Since almost everyone has cell phones these days, we don't even have to spring for a camera." She stopped talking as if she was waiting for my reaction.

"That's a great idea. It might bring in parents with kids, who otherwise might not consider checking us out."

"The backdrop has space to add in your shop's logo or

name to show up in the pics. I'll work on the graphics in the morning and attach it to the backdrop before we open."

"You've thought of everything." I reached over and gave her a hug. "That'll be great marketing when people share their photos on social media. Our name will be right there."

"That's what I thought too. We can take some photos of you, Dillon, and myself and post them to introduce the staff." She started unloading the popcorn containers and stacking them at the end of the counter. "When is the popcorn machine coming?"

"I haven't heard from my dad. I should probably send him a text to make sure he remembers." I grabbed my cell and thumbed a quick message.

When I didn't receive a reply right away, I figured he was busy. If we didn't get a popcorn machine by tomorrow evening, it wouldn't be the end of the world. We'd just use bowls to serve the snack.

Ashley and I walked to her car to collect the balloons and giant bags of popcorn she had purchased. She'd scored a close parking space, so I didn't even bother to lock the shop's door. Once we unloaded everything, we spent a half hour rearranging things to make space for the potential popcorn cart and a side table to stack serving boxes. I told Ashley to be there at ten the next morning to set up the photo booth backdrop and accessories and help me complete anything else that might need to be done for the opening.

After I locked the door behind us, we headed our separate ways, Ashley to see her son, and mom and me back to my dad's house. I walked in the opposite direction of my car and sped past the patisserie. It was a little stalkerish, but I wanted to find out what was going on with the baker. The usual brightly lit bakery was dark, and the door was shut tight. A closed sign sat propped up in the window. I glanced at my watch. Not even five yet, and Jasper had shuttered the shop. Was business that terrible or had the detective pulled him back in for more questioning? Another thing to ask my dad about.

I missed my farmhouse, but I wasn't about to go out there on my own. Once I got to my dad's house, I found it empty. He still hadn't returned my text, and I wondered if he was working late or if he was with Dillon's mom, enjoying a romantic afternoon and evening. I wanted him to be happy and have a companion, but the more involved he got, it kind of felt like a betrayal of my mother. Logically, I knew he wasn't betraying her or me, but my heart wanted to say he was.

I pushed the thought away, poured a glass of wine, and sat down on the comfy couch with a mystery novel. Within minutes, I was sound asleep.

CHAPTER FORTY

The light of the morning sun and the aroma of the coffee brewing woke me. I was still on the couch, but someone had draped an afghan over me, and the glass of wine was no longer on the coffee table. My book, with a bookmark peeking out from between the pages, had been placed on the table. It had been years since I'd slept so soundly. I stretched and rubbed a kink that threatened to tighten in my neck.

"Good morning, sleepyhead." My dad walked into the family room and sat on the edge of the coffee table. He handed me a mug of steaming hot caffeine with a liberal splash of milk stirred in.

"Thanks, Dad." I sat up and took a sip. "Have I told you lately how wonderful you are?"

"Aww shucks, Cari-girl, you're pretty great yourself." He looked at his watch. "I'm heading to Thousand Oaks this morning. I should be back in time for dinner."

"Will Bryon be able to drop off the popcorn machine today?"

"He said he'd send you a text when he got home after shift last night. You didn't get it?"

I fumbled around in the couch cushions until I found my cell phone. "It's dead. I'll charge it while I take a shower. Is everything okay with Jasper? He closed the patisserie early yesterday."

"Haven't heard anything, but then again, I wasn't around the station yesterday afternoon or evening."

I raised an eyebrow. "Oh?"

"I suppose you didn't get my text from last night, either." He rubbed his jaw and twisted his lips. "Sandy and I rode the horses up into the mountains. Didn't get back until late. You were sound asleep when I got home, so I thought you might have tried waiting up for me. I hope you weren't worried."

"No. I'm fine. To be honest, I fell asleep really early and slept the entire night." I gave him a wry smile. "I haven't done that since I was a teen."

"That's what a clean conscience and hard work will do for you." He patted my leg. "I left the bread and jam out for you. Do you want me to pop a couple of pieces into the toaster?"

"I'll fix it when I get out of the shower." I rubbed my neck and winced. "This couch isn't the best place to spend the night, and I'm hoping a hot shower will loosen up the knots."

"Do you want me to massage it for you?"

"Thanks, but there's no need. I'll apply chamomile and basil oils once I get out of the shower." I rolled my shoulders in circles, pulled my left foot onto the top of my right thigh, and angled the sole of my foot toward the ceiling. Applying pressure with my thumb, I walked it down the outer side edges of my big toe, then repeated it with each toe. "Ashley wants to learn reflexology, so today will be a good first introduction. I'll show her how to fix my stiff neck."

"Sandy's into aromatherapy and can't wait for your shop to open. Maybe I'll buy her a gift certificate for a session. She has a lot of lower back pain, especially after spending a full day on bike patrol."

Once again, I raised my eyebrows. Sandy must have been a good influence on my dad because he wasn't calling my career woo-woo stuff. "Tell her to call me and I'll schedule a session for her. It'll be on the house."

"I don't mind paying for it."

"It's the least I can do after all you've done for me." My eyes misted a bit. "I don't think I tell you often enough how much your support and belief mean to me."

"You mean the world to me, Cari-girl. I'd do anything to keep you safe."

"Let me schedule a session for you, too."

He scratched his ear and his cheeks flushed. "You'll have plenty of clients to keep you busy. I don't want to take up your time."

"You're afraid you might have to admit reflexology and the art of essential oils work." I teased him and lightly punched his shoulder. "Admit it, Dad, you don't want to have to say you were wrong, and I was right."

"I've never thought you were wrong. It's just, well..." He rolled his eyes and waved his hands in front of his body.

"Are you trying to say it's something for women and not men?"

"Maybe, but no, I don't think that's what my hesitation is. It just seems so New Age and out there."

"It's not New Age at all. In fact, it's been around for

almost forty-five hundred years. Both the Chinese and Egyptians used the practice for health and well-being, and a form of it was developed in the U.S. over a hundred years ago. I thought you knew that."

"Really? I had no idea." His knee bounced up and down a few beats. "Okay, when you get up and running, I'll schedule an appointment for myself."

"Do you have any specific pain and issues you want me to focus on?"

His face turned a deeper shade of red. "Well, um, I've been having some trouble with my knee. I'm worried I'm heading toward a knee replacement by the time I retire."

"You should have told me sooner. I could have been treating you all this time."

He shrugged. "Hard to believe a little rubbing can make it better."

"You'll never know until you try. Right?"

Dad laughed and then looked at his watch again. "I need to get going. Traffic down Highway 33 gets worse and worse every year."

"Before you go, can you tell me if you ever found out about the threatening phone calls Russ received?"

He shook his head. "Harvey caught me looking through the investigation files and read me the riot act. When I asked him about following up on the calls, he threatened me with demotion to foot patrol."

"Can he do that?" My temper burned at the thought of the detective disrespecting my dad that way.

"No. But he could start an Internal Affairs investigation, and that would be a nightmare. I did the only thing I could and backed off."

I gave my dad a long look. "What aren't you telling me?

There's more than overlooking Gram's little garden the detective is holding over your head."

Dad bent over and placed his face in his palms. "I'd rather not dredge it up, but you're right. Somehow Harvey's found out a few things about my past that I'd rather not have made public knowledge."

"Like what?" I prodded him with my index finger. "If he's threatening you, then I have a right to know what it entails. Maybe I can help."

He raised his head and gazed into my eyes. "There's nothing you can do. It's the past and can't be undone. And, in all honesty, I'd do it again to protect you."

"What do you mean, protect me?" I was puzzled. My dad was law-abiding, and I was certain he would never intentionally do anything illegal. "You need to tell me."

He didn't answer for a long time and the tick-tock of the clock on the mantle filled the space. The hands moved a couple of ticks before his voice broke the silence.

"I've never been as terrified as I was finding you unconscious behind the wheel of your car, smashed into a tree." He rubbed his jaw with a clenched fist. "I knew you weren't responsible for your condition, but couldn't prove it. No one would corroborate your convoluted story at first. After a couple of kids finally admitted you were drugged without your knowledge, I couldn't pry any names out of them. Their parents threatened lawsuits, so the department made me drop it."

"But the charges against me were dropped." And just like that, some of the puzzle pieces fell into place. "Except you either fixed some of the evidence against me or called in favors to stop the investigation. Am I right?"

Dad nodded. "The accident wasn't your fault, but there wasn't any proof to substantiate your innocence. I couldn't allow you to be convicted of the crime, so I did what was necessary."

I reached out and held his hand. "Detective Miller is now hanging that over your head."

"Yes. If I don't interfere with his so-called investigation, I think he'll let his suspicions drop. Right now, he's only hinting he knows something, but I don't think he can prove anything. I'm just worried if he drags Internal Affairs into the mess, my career will be over whether or not he has actual proof."

"I'm so sorry I brought this on you." My eyelashes became damp as I blinked back tears. It wasn't fair that a stupid prank by stupid kids could impact my dad's life like this.

"It wasn't your fault, Cari-girl." He squeezed my hand, then stood. "We'll get through this one way or another."

After my dad left, I plugged my phone in to charge and poured another cup of coffee. My heart pounded and my hands shook, thinking about Detective Miller. How could he be so arrogant and treat my dad that way? Was he trying to hide something by throwing suspicion on me or my dad?

My stomach rumbled, reminding me I hadn't eaten dinner the night before, so I rummaged through the refrigerator. I scrambled some cheesy eggs and piled the gooey curds and a ripe avocado from my orchard between two slices of whole grain toast. While I ate, I turned my barely charged phone on and scrolled through the messages I'd received while I slept.

An unknown number had sent a text message at ten last night. My screen showed a limited number of characters without swiping it open, and it was enough to make my hands tremble.

I'm watching u. Stop sn…

I swiped the message open to see if I could determine who sent it. Once I read the full message, I still didn't have a clue. A cold sweat bathed my back, and my hands shook so hard I almost dropped my phone.

> I'm watching u. Stop snooping or else u n
> yr dad will b sorry.

CHAPTER FORTY-ONE

I captured a screenshot of the text and forwarded it to my dad with a quick text. My phone rang a minute later.

"Are you okay? Do you have the doors locked?"

"Yes. Everything is fine. I think the person is just trying to creep me out and scare me away from asking questions." Just hearing my dad's strong voice calmed me down and helped me focus. My mind leaped to who might have sent me the text. Perhaps it could have even been Detective Miller, but I decided not to mention that to my dad. He had enough problems without me adding speculations.

"I'll turn around and come home. You shouldn't be by yourself."

"It's not necessary. Ashley's supposed to meet me at the shop at ten." The last thing I needed was for the chief of police to be breathing down my neck all day long. His tone told me he had slipped from dad-mode to cop-mode. And really, my hands had stopped shaking. Mostly. "We'll be fine."

"Forward the text to Bryon and I'll have him start a

search on the phone number used and see if he can track down the perp."

"The text just says it's an unknown number. There aren't even any random numbers assigned to it."

His heavy sigh came over the airwaves. "I still want him to take a look. He should drop the popcorn machine off around ten so he can check out your phone as well. Keep your doors locked and call me if anything happens. I'll have my phone on as long as I'm not in the courtroom."

After he disconnected the call, I typed an explanation and forwarded the text as he'd asked.

> The chief wanted me to forward the following text I got from a creeper. Unknown # but he thought you might be able to get it traced.

Three pulsing dots immediately appeared.

> Creeper is right! I'll see you later this morning and I'll take a look at your phone.

I nudged my cold egg sandwich around on the plate. I'd lost my appetite, and that snapped me out of the terror that had gripped me. A slow anger built that some unknown person or persons had stolen the lives of two people. It made me angry I couldn't live in my own home and had to rely on my father for safety. I listed all the things this person had done and I decided enough was enough. I wouldn't live in fear and behind locked doors any longer. My dad's warning about safety and how much he worried about me continued to echo in my head. I could be careful, but I didn't have to cave into the fear that person was trying to force upon me.

After the speediest shower I'd ever taken, while visions of the *Psycho* shower scene danced in my head, I dressed in yoga pants and a loose-knit tunic the color of sun-ripened apricots. Are these pants a little looser today? That thought cheered me. Perhaps I had been visiting Jasper's patisserie a little too often, and the break was doing me some good. Thinking of my forced diet made me think of exercise, and I decided I'd visit my new pup later today and play with her for a while. I wanted Pixie to get accustomed to me before she made the move to my house.

I finally made it to my shop after hyper-aware monitoring of my surroundings. Nothing looked strange, except for the emptiness of the patisserie. The closed sign was still up. That wasn't good. I was tempted to send him a text asking if he was okay. But if he was being questioned or held by Detective Miller, I didn't need to draw any additional attention to myself.

I called the patisserie's business line, hoping he would at least answer if he wasn't in custody. But the phone rang twice and went directly to voicemail, which said to leave a message, blah, blah, blah. I would have thought if he planned to close for a while, he would have given out some information on the recording, but he didn't. Despite our fallout from our attempted dinner date, I worried about Jasper and, truth be told, still had a crush on him. Yet another reason to be angry at the murderer.

When Ashley arrived, her knock on the front door made me jump from my skin.

I'd just started measuring ingredients to distill another batch of lavender and I almost bumped over a glass jar. I told myself I wouldn't be afraid any longer.

"I know I said I'd work on it this morning during business hours, but I was too excited thinking about the possibilities. I hope you like it." She bubbled with excitement as she handed me a letter-sized printout of the logo for the photo booth backdrop. "I have the digital file to take to the printer. They'll be able to print out a three-by-two-foot banner we can use to insert onto the backdrop."

My logo for Aromatherapy Apothecary was a sage-green colored circle with the name of the shop in the center, and the script font in dark olive. Watercolor drawings of apothecary jars and vials, of all sorts of shapes and sizes, along with drawings of herbs and flowers wagon-wheeled the central circle. She'd broken down the components and turned them into a rectangle, which better suited the photo booth backdrop. Written in dark olive-green font, Aromatherapy Apothecary was centered in a sage-colored rectangle, while leafy green herbs and flowers framed the rectangle. Our website address was near the top of the page in a font that matched the shop's name. She had also added the watercolor drawings of apothecary jars and vials along the sides, top and bottom, with more floral watercolor renderings in each of the corners. "This is amazing. Did my designer email the watercolor renderings to you?"

"I used some graphic software I like to play around with." Her face turned a dusky pink. "I hope I didn't do something wrong. Should I have gotten your designer's permission? Is the artwork copyrighted?"

"It's no problem at all. I bought the rights to use them however and whenever I want. I should have given you the digital files." I held the paper up. "You are one talented woman, Ashley. Why aren't you doing this as a career?"

"I thought I'd like to, but then Hunter came along. And, well, college has been out of the question." She smiled and hugged me. "I'm happy working here with you, and I can't wait to learn how to do reflexology."

I hugged her back. "Let's see if we can put your graphic design know-how to use. There'll be all sorts of labels you can create for the shop, along with brochures and cards. Maybe you can create notecards and I'll let you sell them on consignment? Give it some thought and let me know what you come up with."

Ashley bounced up and down. "I'm so excited. This will keep me up half the night thinking about ways to create."

I laughed at her enthusiasm and thanked my lucky stars we had crossed paths again. I handed the logo printout back to her. "It's perfect. Can you take it down to the printer?"

"You bet. I called them yesterday, and they told me it'll be ready by three this afternoon. That will give us time to hang it." She pointed at the wall. "You want to experiment with the height placement so the logo is prominent, without getting cut from the photos or hidden by someone's head."

"That's a good point. I don't think we can cover every scenario, but one way or the other, either the logo or website address will show up. We can't ask for better marketing than that." I fished inside my purse and extracted a key to the shop. "Here's a key for you in case I'm not here to let you in. After you deliver the graphic to the printers, go ahead and take a few hours off until it's ready to pick up. I'll meet you back here and we can hang it together and do any last-minute things for the opening."

After Ashley left, I went back to my distilling room. I rubbed my knotted shoulders and vowed I'd let Ashley practice reflexology on me this afternoon when she came back. As much as I loved having her around, I had to realize it was senseless to pay her for keeping me company now that the shop was ready to go. She would have the opportunity to work as many hours as she wanted once we opened. The fragrance of the herbs, citrus, and flowers calmed me... until someone banged on the front door.

CHAPTER FORTY-TWO

The cup of coriander seeds slipped from my hand, and I muttered a few choice words under my breath. The seeds scattered across the tabletop, and several rolled onto the floor. I scurried to the front door and peeked out. Mari's wrinkled brown face peered back at me.

"Oh, I'm so happy to see you." I opened the door wide enough for her to slip in, and I gave her a hug as she passed me.

She was dressed in a flowing Indian-inspired turquoise silk tunic top with white leggings. Her huarache sandals were tinted to match.

"Didn't I give you a key?"

"Yes, but I forgot it at home. I figured you'd be here, anyway." She set a yellow paper gift bag with lemon-colored tissue paper spilling from the top on the counter. "I brought you a little something for your opening tomorrow."

"You didn't have to do that, but thank you." I plucked a piece of tissue paper from the bag and rubbed it between my fingers. Lemon scent filled the air. "Can I open it now, or do I have to wait?"

"Open it now. I want to see what you think of it."

Once the mounds of lemony tissue paper were piled beside the bag, I pulled out a sealed plastic bag that contained what looked like tea leaves with citrus peels. A label bearing my shop's logo showed it was a Celebration Tea Blend. A fragrance similar to my Celebration essential oil blend wafted from the bag. I inhaled. "Where did you find this? I mean, how did you find this?"

She grinned. "A friend of mine runs the Tea Breeze shop in Santa Barbara. I told her about the essential oil blend you were trying to create and we thought it would be fun to create a tea blend using similar flavors."

"It smells amazing." I breathed in deeply again. "I'll go brew us a pot."

"No need." She pulled a small thermos from the straw carryall she used as a purse. "I have some ready to taste."

I retrieved two teacups from the back room, and Mari filled them with the hot amber liquid. Steam from the fragrant tea curled from the cups and filled the air, making my mouth water.

After taking a tentative sip to make sure I didn't burn my tongue, I sighed with contentment. "This is perfection. She captured just the right amount of citrus without overwhelming the other spices."

"I thought so too. It's one of the reasons I haven't been around much to help you out. It took longer than I expected to create the right blend."

"Do you think she would mind if we sold packets of the blend here? I'd pay her for the tea and give Tea Breeze credit, but I love the look of my logo on the package." I brushed my fingers across the scripted olive-green font.

"That's exactly what I had in mind." She fumbled

around inside her tote. "Here's Tanya's business card. Call her and she'll work something out for you."

I squeezed her thin arm. "Thank you. I feel like all the small details are finally falling into place and all that's left to do is open the door and let clients in."

The small woman slowly twirled around and looked at the completed setup. "It's gorgeous and you'll make it a huge success."

"I owe it all to you." And I truly meant it.

"Don't sell yourself short. I may have provided some inspiration, but Aromatherapy Apothecary is one hundred percent your vision and accomplishment."

My grin was huge. I was proud of myself, too.

A text pinged on my phone.

> I'm parked in front of your shop. Can you please open door so I can deliver popcorn machine without throwing my back out?

As I flung the door wide open, Bryon stood holding the red and white carnival-themed popcorn machine. I had envisioned something large, like what you saw at a movie theater or a street corner vendor, but this model was a small tabletop appliance. It was better than I had expected.

"I thought your popcorn machine was going to be huge!" I poked him in the arm as he walked past me. "This bitty thing isn't heavy enough to throw your back out."

He grunted, then flashed me a grin. "Just wait until you're my age."

Mari fussed with Bryon a bit over where it should be set up. She had him move the table and machine at least five times before it satisfied her. Once he showed us both how to turn on the lights and the heat lamps, Bryon held his hand out to me, palm up.

"How much do I owe you?" I grabbed my purse to retrieve my wallet.

"I need to take a look at your phone." He waved his fingers inward. "Chief's orders."

"I'll hand it over as long as you promise not to keep it."

"Let me see the text." He wiggled his fingers at me again.

"Fine, but I don't know why you need it. I already sent it to you." I entered my password, opened the text message, and placed the phone in his outstretched hand. "Please give it back to me. My business depends on it."

He took a screenshot, tapped the screen a couple of times, and took several more screenshots before texting the photos to himself. His cell phone pinged, and he pulled it from his pocket before handing me my phone.

"I'll take these photos to the techies, but I doubt they'll be able to determine who sent the text. It was probably from a burner phone."

"That's what I figured." I tucked my phone back into my purse before he could change his mind about confiscating it. "Will you let my dad know, or should I?"

"I'll let him know next time he checks in." He headed for the door.

"How much do I owe you for the use of the popcorn machine?"

"I'll bill you the friends and family special discounted rate payable in cookies."

"I'm happy to pay for the use." I worried someone might think I was taking advantage of him because I was the boss's daughter.

"Seriously, bake me a batch of cookies and I'll be a happy man."

"If you're sure..."

"Yep. That's all I want." He patted his stomach. "I don't need it, but I have a weakness for good cookies."

"Any special flavor?"

"Surprise me." Bryon's radio squawked and unintelligible words came out. "Gotta run. Good luck with your opening."

Before I could lock the door behind Bryon's disappearing backside, Mari grabbed her tote bag and rested her hand on mine. "I need to leave, too. You've done a marvelous job, darlin', and I know your shop will be a huge success."

"I meant what I said, Mari. This wouldn't have happened without you." My eyes stung as I remembered how this tiny woman had stood beside me throughout my journey, even when I had seemed to turn my back on her counsel.

She gave me a long hug, and when she released me and gazed into my eyes, I could see hers were bright with unshed tears as well. "I'll drop by when you open in the morning, but call me if you need an extra set of hands earlier than that."

With Mari on her way and the door securely locked, I cleaned up the spilled coriander seeds and started the distiller. While my hands measured out rosemary for the next batch I'd start distilling later, my mind whirled with the puzzle of who had killed Russ and Grant. Could it have been two separate crimes with two different killers? I was especially troubled that Detective Miller had threatened to demote my dad over trying to find Russ's phone records, even though he didn't have the authority to do so. Something didn't add up.

Even if Victoria slammed the door in my face, I needed to talk to her again about that threatening phone call Russ had received. I popped a vial of the Celebration Blend oil into a white bag displaying my shop's logo, then added a few sheets of sage green tissue paper.

I grabbed my purse and walked two blocks over to the chocolate shop, Sweet Surprises. When I pushed through the glass door, the blonde behind the counter removed her earbuds.

I placed an order for a dozen assorted chocolate truffles, half milk chocolate and the other half dark chocolate. Despite not being chatty, the teen, dressed in a cotton candy-pink polo shirt and white capris, was pleasant. She even offered to gift wrap the box when I mentioned I was purchasing them for a friend. I took her up on her offer.

Once I'd paid, I picked up the cotton candy-pink bag and walked toward Victoria's house. Just as I rounded the corner of her block, Detective Miller was climbing into his car in her driveway. I scrambled to the closest tree, prepared to hide should he drive toward me. Instead, he backed out of the driveway and turned in the opposite direction. Why was he visiting the grieving mother? Had he found new evidence or solved Russ's murder?

When I was sure Detective Miller wasn't coming back, I hurried to the front door and knocked.

The door flung open with a bang.

I jumped at the sudden noise.

A bony hand reached out and yanked me into the dark house.

CHAPTER FORTY-THREE

I stifled a screech when Victoria hissed in my ear. "That detective didn't see you come here, did he?"

I shook my head, and she released her grip on my arm. I rubbed where her fingers had dug into my skin. "Why was he here? And why don't you want him to know I came to visit?"

"I need a cigarette." She turned her back on me and walked toward the family room.

I followed. "Here are some chocolates and I thought you might enjoy my Celebration Blend of essential oils. I wanted to apologize again for my last visit." I placed the bags on the coffee table and glanced around the room. "Do you have a diffuser? If not, I'll bring you one."

She glared at me and lit a cigarette. Once she had inhaled and then exhaled a smoke ring, she gestured for me to sit down.

I did as directed. "Why was he here?"

"Same as you, I s'pose. You both want to blame me for my son's death." She stared at the glowing tip of the white tube held between her index and middle fingers, then picked up a glass tumbler with her empty hand and sipped the amber liquid.

"I wasn't blaming you." I tried to resist the urge to wave away the smoke that hovered in front of my face. "Isn't the detective certain *I* committed the crime? He's been trying to convince everyone I know that I'm guilty."

"He wants you to be guilty, but he also knows he can't alter the facts enough to get you convicted. I s'pose that's why he's looking for another easy target to pin the killing on." She stubbed the cigarette out and rubbed her eyes with balled-up fists. "Now, why don't you tell me why you're really here?" She took a healthy gulp from the tumbler.

This wasn't going as I had planned. Instead of me questioning Victoria, I was the one getting grilled. I didn't like it one bit. "I'm concerned about the threatening phone call Russ received during dinner. My dad's being shut out of the investigation, and we both think it's important. Except we can't access his phone records."

"So, I know something you and your hotshot daddy don't know," Victoria smirked. "How's it feel to be on the outside?"

My head swam. Her moods seemed to be all over the place and none of them were good. "I think the important thing is we both want the same thing. Russ's killer needs to be found and brought to justice."

"That's true, but what makes you so sure you or your daddy are the ones to do it?"

I shook my head, trying to clear the buzzing of the older woman's bitter words. "It doesn't matter who does it, as long as it's accomplished. We're both on the same side, and I think we both agree Detective Miller isn't doing what's necessary to solve the case."

She took another drink, then extracted another cigarette

from the almost-empty pack. She held it up in front of her face and rolled it between her fingers, slow and deliberate. She finally lit it, inhaled, and then blew the smoke toward me. "I get what you're sayin'."

When she didn't say anything for a full minute, I caved. "Do you have any idea who called Russ? Can you get hold of his cell phone records?"

There was that smirk again. "I can do better than that. I know for a fact who made that threatening call."

Again, nothing but silence. I inwardly groaned when I realized she wanted me to grovel for the information. Was her illness making her cantankerous, or was it the amber drink she kept sipping? Or was she playing this game to hide something from me? I wasn't happy, whatever her reasoning was. "I'm here to help you with no ulterior motives. Can you at least give me a hint about who it was?"

"Do you know why I don't want the detective to know you're visitin' me?"

"I don't know. Is it because he might think we conspired to kill your son together?"

She snorted. "Good gawd, girl, don't go puttin' that idea in his head or we might be sharin' a jail cell together."

Her pronunciations were getting sloppy, and I suspected it had something to do with the drink she sipped. "Why don't you tell me what you know so we can help you get closure?"

She rolled her eyes and tossed back the remaining drink. "I'm not terribly interested in helpin' you. I'll lose out on a bunch of money if I don't keep it a secret."

It seemed like the liquid she'd been imbibing was loosening her tongue. I finally grasped what Victoria probably didn't want me to know. She was blackmailing or planned to blackmail the caller. Could that be why Russ met his demise? Had he been blackmailing the same person?

"Do you think that's a good idea? He killed once. He'll probably kill again if he thinks you're going to spill his secret."

She looked at me and mimicked locking her lips with a key. Was she really not going to give me any other information?

She stubbed out the cigarette and crossed her arms in front of her chest. "I'm retiring and have a lot of medical bills ahead of me. My son, may he rot in peace, left me broke, so I have to do what I can to take care of myself."

"I understand, but if you don't provide the information you have, justice won't be served. Isn't it important to see justice done for your son?"

Victoria snorted. "Justice don' pay the bills. Besides, my son is gone and buried. He don' care about justice now and never did, even when he was livin'."

"Please call me if you change your mind or worry about your safety. Better yet, call the chief." I gave her one last long look before I admitted defeat. "There's a killer out there, and neither of us wants to see you come to harm."

With nothing to do until Ashley returned, I took a short walk while I tried to decipher everything Victoria had said —or hadn't said. I still couldn't figure out if it was the strong drink she'd been sipping on or if it was her illness that made her act so Jekyll and Hyde. It saddened me to see her health, both physical and mental, deteriorate like it had.

I headed toward the city's walking path that wove beneath ancient oaks and giant eucalyptus trees. When Southern California had a normal rainy season, a babbling brook ran beside the path until it dried up in mid-summer. I found the sound soothing, especially when I had a lot on my mind. While there were several homes and businesses skirting the area, somehow the city had made the asphalt-paved trail feel secluded and serene. Maybe it was the vast number of trees that lined the trail that blocked out most of the noise from traffic and hid the view of the various buildings in the area.

Once I reached the trail and headed eastward, I pulled my hair up into a messy bun to allow the faint breeze to cool off my hot neck. I skirted the pockets of sunlight that filtered through the trees and kept to the shade. I'd forgotten how hot it could be walking in the direct afternoon sun. A group of chattering elderly women power-walked past me, heading west. Without pausing for a breath, they waved to me and rushed on with their exercise.

I walked ten more minutes without seeing another soul, then turned around and headed back toward town. As I rounded a bend in the pathway, I stopped in my tracks.

Mayor Torres and Detective Miller stood in the middle of the trail about twenty yards ahead, their backs turned toward me. Their voices rose and fell, both angry. My feet tripped over each other as I bolted behind a massive oak tree. I must've disturbed a squirrel because a few acorns rained on my head and the rodent's chattering scold sounded loud in the quiet shade.

Beatriz and the detective fell silent, and it didn't take long for me to hear the clickety-click of the mayor's high heels and Detective Miller's hard-soled shoes moving toward me.

"Who's there? Come out where I can see you." His voice was harsh and commanding.

"I don't see anyone. Maybe it was a squirrel or something."

"I'm not taking any chances." His voice moved closer to my hiding place.

"You're being paranoid, Harvey."

I held my breath.

The squirrel above me chattered and rained down more acorns. It leaped to another branch, then scurried to the far side of the trunk of the tree and chattered at the pair. I heard more acorns hit the ground.

"See? It's just a squirrel. I need to get back to the office and out of these shoes. They're killing my feet."

"You should have worn sensible shoes." The detective's voice moved away from my tree and the mayor's shoes clickety-clacked as they walked back toward the trail's entrance to the street.

When I could no longer hear them, and the squirrel had decided I wasn't a threat and scurried off, I peeked around the tree to see what they were up to.

Even though they were too far away for me to hear what they were saying any longer, it was clear from their body language they weren't very happy with each other. He pointed his index finger at the mayor. He moved his hand so violently, back and forth, it almost looked like he was stabbing it at her. The mayor's fists were clenched into balls. In the blink of an eye, she reached up and shoved him in the chest. He stumbled back, caught his balance, then widened his stance and crossed his arms.

I couldn't believe what I was seeing, so I pulled my cell phone from my pocket, silenced the ringer, and took photos of the pair. I didn't know what Detective Miller said when he leaned in close to the mayor's face, but it must have been bad. Her shoulders slumped and, from my vantage point, it looked like it had taken all the fight out of her. She shook her head and wiped her palm across her cheek. He said something else, and I zoomed my cell camera in and snapped more photos. Beatriz slowly unzipped the top of her black cross-body bag, pulled out an envelope, and handed it to the detective. He grinned when he opened the envelope. He extracted a stack of green bills and fanned through them.

My camera captured it all.

I had to wait another five minutes before the coast was clear for me to exit my hiding place. As I walked back to my shop, I wondered why the mayor was paying the detective. Was he blackmailing her over her affair with Grant? Was she a victim? The exchange of cash wasn't a normal business transaction and was almost guaranteed to be illegal, no matter the reason. Maybe the mayor and I could help each other get out of the clutches of the detective intent on ruining my life.

When I arrived back at the shop, I sent the photos to my dad with a quick text telling him where I'd seen the pair together. After I turned off the heat to the distiller and checked the fragrance of the resulting oil and hydrosol, I glanced at the clock and realized I'd missed lunch. There wasn't even a crumb to eat in the shop, and Jasper's patisserie was still closed. I got in my car to head to my dad's house, then decided to swing by the mayor's office first. The photos I'd taken weighed on my mind.

Irene Babcock's desk was empty, and her computer screen was dark.

I tried the handle on the closed door of the mayor's office. It was locked. I knocked and waited half a minute, then banged on the door again. No one answered, so I left.

Back in my car, I headed to the mayor's house. I wasn't sure I should intrude, but then decided if I could collect any information on what I'd seen transpire between her and the detective, my dad could piece it all together and make sense of it. I hoped it would provide evidence Detective Miller needed to be relieved of his position.

There weren't any cars in the driveway, so I almost didn't stop. She most likely wasn't home, but it wouldn't hurt to check. I parked alongside the curb and made my way across the Spanish-tiled walkway to the front steps of the house.

The mayor's door swung open before I rang the bell.

CHAPTER FORTY-FOUR

"What do you want? Haven't you bothered me enough?" Beatriz's eyes were bloodshot, and the sharp fumes of tequila hit me with each word. Her hair looked like she had repeatedly raked her fingers through her mane, creating disheveled tangles. Instead of her usual high heels, she was barefoot, and her bright red toenail polish was chipped in several places. She wore yoga pants and a bleach-stained teal T-shirt. I'd never seen her dressed so casually. Her usually impeccable lipstick was half chewed off and her mascara and eyeliner were smudged at the outside corners of her eyes.

"Can I come in? There are a few things I'd like to talk to you about. It's best I did it in private."

She waved her hand for me to enter, and once I was inside the house, she slammed the front door before she locked it. I felt like a fly entering a spider's web. I half expected her to break out into a cackle, rub her hands together, and call me "my pretty." Maybe I shouldn't watch scary movies. I tried to remind myself this woman was probably as much of a victim as I was.

We sat down in the family room and she picked up a shot glass filled with gold liquid, tossed it back, then sucked on a lime wedge. She didn't offer me anything besides a glare.

"To what do I owe this intrusion?" Her angry words cut through the silence.

I was relieved she wasn't slurring. I had enough of that after talking to Victoria earlier.

"I had an interesting walk along the trail this afternoon."

Beatriz reached for the bottle of tequila and poured another shot. Her hands were shaking as she banged the bottle back onto the glass coffee table. She tossed the shot back with another lime wedge chaser.

When she said nothing, I pulled my cell phone out, opened the camera app, and scrolled through the photos. I found the one showing her handing the detective the envelope and turned my phone around so she could see it. "Would you like to talk about this transaction?"

"It's city business and doesn't concern you. We ran into each other while out for a walk, and I gave him some documents he'd been asking for."

"I'm on your side, so you don't need to be defensive." I wasn't going to point out that no one in their right mind would wear high heels on a trail walk. "Why give so much cash to Detective Miller? He seemed like he was gloating after you gave it to him."

I handed her my phone to show her the picture of Miller fanning the cash.

She shoved the phone back at me. "It's none of your business." She settled back onto the couch and stretched her arms over her head, revealing a large rip in the armpit of her T-shirt.

"The fact that he's trying to pin Russ's murder on me makes anything and everything he does my business." I paused for a moment to see if she'd explain. When she didn't, I pressed on. "There's something fishy going on. I think he's harassing you. Maybe even blackmailing you? I'm only trying to help."

"I don't need your help, and I'd appreciate it if you'd keep your nose out of my affairs."

My ears perked up. Was her use of 'affairs' a slip? "I think we need to talk about that affair, as in the romantic kind. What happened between you and Grant? How did you hook up with him?"

She waved her hand dismissively. "I've let that charade run on long enough. I wasn't involved with that self-absorbed man. He pursued me, but I'd never stoop that low."

"My dad said Grant was your alibi for the night Russ was killed. Was that a lie?"

"We were together for a while that night, but certainly not for a romantic liaison. The chief jumped to that conclusion, and I didn't correct his assumption."

"Why not? If you weren't having an affair, why would you be with Grant that night?" And why let my dad assume she was involved unless she was trying to hide something else?

"Because this godforsaken little town is driving me crazy with the gossiping, and I'm sick and tired of having to explain myself every time I turn around." Mayor Torres poured another shot and stared at the gold liquid she held. "I can't believe you'd come back here to live, no matter what happened in San Francisco. Anything would be better than this."

I ignored her comment about me. She was trying to get

me off the track and defensive. "If you weren't having an affair, why would you be with Grant that night?"

"That's none of your business." She tossed back the shot and bit into a lime wedge.

She was right. It wasn't any of my business unless it had something to do with the murders. "Fine. Have it your way. But I still need to know about the exchange of money between you and Detective Miller."

"You're getting tiresome. Just drop it." Her voice was low and quiet, the words slurring at the end. She rested her head on the back of the couch and closed her eyes. The tequila was finally doing its job.

I gave her a couple of minutes to relax, hoping she would be more apt to share her secrets with me.

It didn't work.

"What are you still doing here? Just leave me alone."

"Not until you tell me what he's up to."

She snorted. "How can one person be so dense? Why can't you take your nosy self away before you get hurt?"

"What do you mean about me getting hurt?"

"Seriously? How many warnings do you need?" She sat upright, her eyes filled with hate. "You are not wanted in this town. Go back to your big city and leave me alone."

"Did you have something to do with the boys tagging my house and the rock thrown through my dad's window?" I was getting a creepy-crawly feeling up my spine. I had envisioned the scenario as me rescuing the mayor from an unscrupulous detective. Not once did I really think this attractive woman who led our city could have been violent.

Beatriz stood and wobbled to the credenza at the far end of the room. She rummaged through her black leather satchel for a moment, then extracted a white envelope that looked similar to what she had given to the detective. She walked back and, towering over me, thrust the envelope into my face. When I didn't take it from her shaking hand, she dropped the envelope into my lap, tottered back to her spot on the couch, and collapsed. The bag clattered to the floor beside her bare feet.

"What's this?" I pointed to the envelope but didn't touch it.

"Consider it a gift." The mayor's head rested on the back of the cushion, her eyes closed.

Using the edge of my shirt to keep my fingerprints from the envelope, I opened the flap and saw a stack of green one-hundred-dollar bills. I didn't bother to count the money. She was trying to bribe me when her threats didn't work. "Why are you giving me this?"

"Let's just say there's more where that came from if you leave me alone and stop snooping."

"As long as Detective Miller keeps trying to pin Russ's death on me, I can't leave it alone." Someone needed to find justice for both the victims. While they might not have been nice people, I'd begun to think Russ had been a tortured soul. I hadn't known Grant long, but I supposed greed was his downfall.

Beatriz rolled her eyes. "What if I get Harvey to leave you alone and drop the case?"

"That won't work and you know it. There are too many people, including my father, who will demand the killer be caught and brought to justice."

"Cases are unsolved all the time and evidence can easily be lost or contaminated."

"Why would you want that to happen?" And more importantly, how could the mayor convince Detective Miller to drop the investigation? What did she know about him? I tossed the envelope onto the coffee table in front of me, then rubbed my hands over my face.

"You won't drop this, will you?" Her voice was resigned, almost melancholy.

"I can't. It's not the right thing to do." I stood. "I wish you would reconsider and help me find justice, no matter what went on between you and Grant. You know where to find me if you change your mind."

"Sit back down, Ms. Carmichael."

"Unless you have something useful to tell me, I don't need to waste any more of my time."

She bent over and rummaged in her satchel again. Instead of another white envelope filled with money, she withdrew a shiny black gun and pointed it at me. "I said, sit down."

My skin felt clammy, and I plopped back down on the couch.

"Give me your phone."

"I sent my dad those photos. He knows I'm here talking to you." Okay, that last bit was a lie. I hadn't thought to tell him I was visiting the mayor since I hadn't thought she was capable of violence. I shrank back from the hate-filled look she gave me. What would I do if he didn't get that text in time? I hadn't heard from him, but I reminded myself that wasn't unusual. Besides, he had told me he had to be in court today and would need to turn his phone off for a while. He would see it and come looking for the mayor.

She walked over to me and pointed the gun at my face. "I won't ask again. Give me your phone."

I complied and released my breath when she sat back down and placed the gun beside her. She turned my phone on and her laugh cut through me. "Really, Carissa? You need a better password than 1-2-3-4. Didn't your father teach you anything about security?"

I didn't answer. What was the point?

"Hmmm, this is unfortunate. Harvey will need to deal with the chief after we deal with you." She flashed the text with the photos toward me. "His death will be on your head, but since you'll already be long gone, I guess it won't matter much."

"Why? What do your dealings with Detective Miller have to do with killing the both of us?" *Where is my dad? Why hasn't he responded to my text?* "For all you know, my dad is on his way here. He knows I'm here."

"You need to tell better lies than that. I know for a fact he's sitting in a courtroom in Thousand Oaks right now and has been for most of the day. You certainly haven't spoken with him, nor has he likely seen these photos yet." Her laugh cut through me again. It was sharp and held an edge of anger. "That gives us plenty of time to take care of you, and Harvey can make a plan to deal with the chief. Maybe something like what happened to Grant. You know the county really should do something about that dangerous stretch of road. People are so careless these days. It doesn't take much for a tragic accident to happen."

CHAPTER FORTY-FIVE

Had she just admitted Detective Miller killed Grant? I needed to keep her talking while I figured out how to get away. Maybe the tequila would make her sleepy and I could sneak out of her house. "I heard Russ was blackmailing you, so I can see his death making sense, but why did Grant have to die?"

Beatriz reached over and poured another shot. She stared at it but didn't drink it. "You have nothing figured out. Just like the chief. Things going on under his nose and he doesn't have a clue."

"So, why don't you enlighten me?"

She glanced at her watch, picked up her phone, and made a call. "We have a situation here. You need to come to my house stat and help me get rid of the problem." Beatriz rolled her eyes. "No, I'm not going to take care of her all on my own. This is your fault, so you have to help me."

The detective's voice boomed over the airways as he yelled at the mayor about her ineptitude. I hoped he would abandon her since I thought I'd have more of a chance of escaping from tequila-shooting Beatriz. If he got involved, I was a goner for certain.

When the call ended, Beatriz tossed her phone onto the couch. "Your father will be leaving the courtroom in about an hour. Harvey's on his way since we have to get out of here before the chief sees your text."

"Leave? Where are we going?"

"We can't shoot you in my house. Too much forensic evidence." She poured the golden liquid back into the bottle and shook her head. "There's a lot of wilderness and so many wild animals up in the mountains to cover our tracks. It's a very convenient way to get rid of a body."

"If I'm going to die, why not tell me what this is all about?" I needed to stall our departure. I didn't stand a chance if I got into the car with this woman.

She pursed her lips, stood, and took my phone to the French doors that opened onto the courtyard.

I watched as she tossed my phone into the fountain. It splashed as it hit the water. I hoped insurance would cover a replacement if I lived through this ordeal.

"We can't have anyone tracking you through your phone." Beatriz locked the doors, then sat back down. "Once we take care of you, Harvey will take care of the chief."

I wanted to cower behind the couch. I wanted to cry. My father needed to be warned and, since I was the only one who knew what was planned, I had to find a way. It disappointed me that any effects of the tequila seemed to have vanished. The mayor appeared clearheaded and steady, which would make it harder for me to get away and save my dad.

Her phone chimed with a text. She looked at the screen and grinned. "Harvey will be here in twenty minutes. That busybody next door leaves for work in fifteen, and I can't afford for her to see us together."

Twenty minutes. Twenty minutes to find out why my life would end, unless I escaped. Twenty minutes to find a way to warn my dad. "While we're waiting, why don't you tell me what happened? I'm assuming you're the one who bashed Russ's head?"

"I suppose it doesn't hurt to tell you since we have time to kill." She laughed, although it sounded like a cackle. "An ironic choice of words, isn't it?"

I waited, letting silence fill the air.

Her gaze flitted to the tequila bottle, then she sighed and put the aqua-tinted cashmere throw, which had been draped across the arm of the couch, over the bottle. "Nope. I can't claim responsibility for that, although I lured him to your shop so Harvey could do the deed." She rubbed her eyes with the backs of her hands. Mascara and eyeliner smears appeared on her cheeks. "He'd been blackmailing me and probably half the town. But it wasn't over an affair. Grant, Harvey, and I are, or I should say were, in business together. I let Grant know who was having financial trouble with their orchards, and he swooped in and got the land for next to nothing. Harvey provided some of the financing and all the brawn if the owners didn't see things our way. After we pressured Victoria to sell her parcel of land to us, Russ found out about our partnership and wanted a piece of the pie."

"Even if you got your hands on cheap land, there's no way development would ever be granted. The City Council would never allow the permits to pass."

Beatriz cracked her knuckles and rolled her shoulders. "You're wrong about that. I have enough dirt on the council members and I've found blackmail is a wonderful tool.

You'd be surprised how no one lives a squeaky-clean life anymore. I knew I'd be able to get them to pass development and zoning laws with a little pressure. So far, we have a resort and an outlet mall planned."

"Why kill him in my shop? I haven't done anything to you to deserve being set up for his death."

"You were convenient. Russ was going on and on about wanting me to stop you from opening your shop, and then Grant overheard your altercation with him. Russ was conceited enough to allow me to lure him into your shop by promising a tryst after we'd trashed your merchandise. Harvey followed us in and bashed the fool's head." The mayor cackled. "Men can be so gullible if a pretty face shows them some attention. But you have to admit, the timing was perfect, from our point of view. With you as a suspect, your father would be kept as far away from the investigation as possible, so Harvey could spin the evidence in any direction we wanted."

"You're the one who demanded Detective Miller be assigned to the case."

"Of course." She shrugged. "Harvey had some evidence over a little indiscretion his boss was involved in, in case he wanted to assign someone else. We didn't need to use it until your attorney started throwing a fit and demanding Harvey be removed from the case."

It still wasn't making a lot of sense to me. I wasn't seeing the whole picture yet, and my mind struggled to fit the pieces together. "Why did he want my dad's job? He tried to push him out when San Francisco blew up in my face."

"If Chief Carmichael was out of the picture and Harvey was the chief of police, he'd have more leeway to pressure property owners to sell us the land we want. And I certainly didn't want anyone to interfere with my involvement in getting the council to approve our plans."

"So why would he kill Grant if you were all partners?"

"Harvey is Grant's nephew. With Grant out of the picture, Harvey now has full control of the development company. Grant never wore a seat belt, so the odds were in our favor that a bad accident would kill him. We didn't expect anyone would associate it with Russ's death. Why couldn't you have stopped snooping when you were warned?"

"So it was you or Detective Miller who tagged my place and threw the rock into my dad's house?"

"Harvey's hoodlums did it." She grinned and wiggled her eyebrows. "It's amazing what kids will do these days in order to keep out of prison and earn a little cash in the process."

"And the creepy text?"

"I planned it and Harvey sent it with a burner phone he confiscated." Her eyes turned bright. "See, I know what it's like, as a woman, to think someone's stalking you. Since you wouldn't stop, I thought we could frighten you off."

The crimes kept pointing back to greed. Could that be why the pair got rid of Grant? "Surely, if the plans are approved, there'd be enough for you to split the profits three ways?"

"True, except the company isn't making any money and, in fact, it's in financial trouble. Grant had a sizable life insurance policy that benefited the company. It'll come in quite handy once the check is issued." She looked like the cat that swallowed the canary. "Plus, Harvey and I have more than a working relationship. It was love at first sight when we met at a fundraiser a couple of years ago and it didn't take long to find out we're both willing to take a few shortcuts to get what we want. With just the two of us running the entire show together, we'll have more money than we'll know what to do with for the rest of our lives. We'll be together forever."

The exchange I saw between the mayor and Detective Miller didn't look like an amiable relationship, much less a romantic one. There had been a coldness on the detective's face, not one of endearment. And she had been so angry she'd pushed him. Why was she giving him cash? It looked like a bribe or a blackmail payoff to me.

I had no idea how the two would last in business together, much less a romantic partnership. This was something I would not share with the mayor. She was volatile enough without me pointing out the fallacies of her plans. I pressed my lips together while I looked around the room for something I could use to attack her with. There wasn't anything but soft throw pillows.

Her phone chimed with another incoming text.

I watched in horror as she read her message.

She pointed the gun and motioned for me to stand.

I swallowed hard; my mouth went completely dry. My heart banged in my chest like it wanted to escape all on its own. I stood and looked around the room again. There wasn't a vase or a statue or even a lamp I could throw at her.

"Harvey's almost here. Walk slowly toward the kitchen and keep your hands where I can see them." She waved her gun at me as she stood. "We'll go through the kitchen doorway and into the garage, then I want you to get in the driver's seat of my car. Once you're there, keep your hands on the steering wheel where I can see them. Do exactly as I tell you—or else."

CHAPTER FORTY-SIX

Beatriz waited until I was just past her before she took a step to follow. Her foot must have caught in the cashmere throw she'd tossed over the tequila bottle because she tripped and started to fall. The throw slid to the floor, and the bottle fell over, banging the top of the coffee table.

The second I saw her off balance, I spun around and kicked her knee.

The gun flew from her hand, and she tried to slow her fall with both arms.

I pushed her flat onto the floor and scooped up the gun. While I hadn't practiced shooting a gun for a long time, I had enough experience to be comfortable holding it. I wasn't a law enforcement officer's daughter for nothing. Growing up, my dad trained me in self-defense and handling a variety of weapons. That training rushed back to me.

She tried to lift herself up from the floor, but I pushed her right back down with my foot.

"Stay there and don't move. You ought to know I can fire a gun if I need to."

She moaned. "You don't have to do this. We'll make you rich if you let me go."

I rummaged through her satchel for her cell phone. I was sure my phone was completely fried. I found it and encouraged her to give me her password. She didn't use 1-2-3-4 like I did.

"I don't have to give you anything." Her voice snarled at me like a caged tiger.

My hands shook as I inspected her cell phone while I tried to figure out how to gain access before Detective Miller showed up. I finally realized I only needed to hold her face up to the phone and it would unlock. *Gotta love technology.* I straddled her back and struggled to lift her head from the carpet. Since I hadn't seen a landline in the house and I'd heard her nosy neighbor drive away, her cell phone was my only choice. My life and my dad's life depended on me. I had to find a way to warn him, so I wasn't very gentle and pulled her hair much harder than needed. In the end, I was rewarded with an unlocked screen.

I called 9-1-1. The second the call connected, I started talking. "Peg, this is Carissa. Send all police units to the mayor's house immediately. I'll explain once they're on their way."

I hoped I had conveyed the sense of urgency without sounding hysterical. It only took a moment for Peg to assure me several black-and-whites were on the way.

"You need to warn them that Detective Miller killed Russ and Grant."

A car door slammed in the driveway.

"I think he's in front of the mayor's house and he's armed."

"Oh good lord, Carissa. Hold on and I'll tell them."

I saw Beatriz move as she tried to crawl toward the door. She must've heard Detective Miller arrive as well. I pushed her back flat to the ground and tapped the gun on her shoulder to remind her I was watching—and lethal. Well, that was an exaggeration, but she didn't need to know that. She had locked the front door, but I worried he might have a key. If he did, what would I do?

Peg came back on the line. "They will proceed with caution. Where are you and the mayor?"

Sirens approached, but they still sounded too far away. "The mayor is Detective Miller's accomplice. She held me at gunpoint, but I have control of it now and the mayor is subdued."

The front door handle rattled and someone banged on the heavy door. "Beatriz, let me in."

Afraid the mayor would warn Detective Miller, I dropped the phone and quickly slapped the palm of my hand across her lips and held it tightly in place. I hoped she wouldn't bite, and I hoped she couldn't feel the tremble in my hand.

"Are you still there?" Peg's voice was a bit higher than normal. "ETA is less than a minute."

I left the phone on the couch where I had dropped it and kept my hand over the mayor's mouth. I wasn't about to give her a chance to warn her accomplice. I lowered my voice to a whisper. "I'm here. Detective Miller is trying to get in, but I don't think he has a key."

The sirens got louder and Detective Miller must've heard them, too. He stopped banging on the door. I caught glimpses of him as he ran past windows. When he reached the backyard, he tried opening the French doors, but they were locked too. Detective Miller saw me standing over the mayor with the gun in my hand. His eyes became huge saucers and his shoulders fell. By the time the sirens were in front of the mayor's house, he had tucked his gun back into the holster and headed toward the tall wooden fence that separated the yard from the neighbors.

I relayed the information to Peg, who informed the responding officers.

Boots pounded on the concrete sidewalk and a flash of uniforms went by.

Detective Miller had made it to the top of the fence, but before he could drop to the other side, loud barks and snarls split the air. It made him hesitate just long enough to give the officers a chance to reach him.

A large black snout snapped at Detective Miller's hands as he grasped the top of the wooden fence. More snarls and barks kept him from disappearing into the neighbor's yard. Five officers, guns drawn, charged the detective. He fell from the fence and held his hands in the air.

Once he was handcuffed, I scurried to the French doors and threw them wide open, sliding the gun onto the back patio. I placed my hands above my head and called for them to come arrest Mayor Torres.

After the pair were led away in handcuffs, Bryon let me call my dad on his cell before I went to the station to give a statement. It sounded like he was in a crowded room. There was loud chatter and a few laughs in the background, along with the tinkle of ice in glasses.

"What's up, Bryon?"

"Dad, it's me."

"Why are you calling me on Bryon's phone? Is everything okay? Are you safe?"

"I'm fine, but I'm guessing you didn't get my text?"

"Hold on a sec. Let me get to a quieter spot."

I waited a couple of minutes and wondered where he

was. Still at the courthouse? Or had he stopped for something to eat on the way home?

"Carissa, stay away from the mayor and Harvey. You shouldn't have followed them on the trail. I'll have Bryon bring them both in for questioning." Dad apparently had opened my text with the photos attached while he found a quieter spot to talk to me.

"It's okay, Dad. They've already been arrested." All I heard was complete silence for a moment. "Are you still there?"

"Yeah, I'm here. I thought I heard you say they've been arrested."

"That's right."

"Please tell me you didn't put yourself in danger by getting involved."

"I'm fine. Really." At least I'd kept the shivering out of my voice. Barely. The realization of having a gun pulled on me and certain death in the Topatopa Mountains was beginning to sink in. My limbs quivered so hard I almost couldn't keep the phone to my ear.

Bryon gently pried his phone from my grasp and took over talking to my dad. He gave his chief a brief overview and, even from where I sat, I could hear my dad's siren come to life as he peeled out of the parking lot, on his way to be with me.

CHAPTER FORTY-SEVEN

I spent most of the night giving my statement to a new detective from Los Angeles—over and over and over. Despite not getting home until the wee hours of the morning, I felt remarkably awake. I unlocked my shop as the sun peeked over the tips of the mountains. It was a few hours before our soft opening. I had worried this day would never come, especially after the near tragedy of the day before.

Just before I walked through the doorway, a for sale sign on Mystic Valley Candles' door caught my eye. I pitied Victoria and hoped she found peace wherever she moved to. I also hoped my new neighbor would be companionable.

I entered my shop with an armload of carryalls stuffed full of chilled lemonade bottles, then locked the door behind me and switched on the lights. The glass apothecary jars gleamed in the light, and Ashley's artful arrangement of merchandise drew my attention. After making a pot of the Celebration Tea Blend, I refilled a few reed diffusers with Celebration Blend essential oils and set them around the room. I arranged a self-serve drink dispenser on a table close to the popcorn machine.

A knock sounded on the glass door, and I nearly spilled the cup of tea I'd been holding. The sound of a key being inserted into the lock reached my ears, and I willed my heart to stop pounding. How long would it take before I stopped being startled?

"The gang's all here." My dad poked his head into the room and opened his arms for a hug. "Happy opening day, sweetheart."

I rushed to hug him and saw my friends entering the shop behind him. Ashley led the way, followed by Mari and Misty, each carrying a bouquet of flowers. And right on their heels was Jasper, carrying a platter of cookies. When he saw me looking at him, he shrugged and gave me a lopsided smile that made his dimples deepen. All of a sudden, I wasn't quite so upset at him.

Mari and Misty fussed with the arrangements, moving them from spot to spot until they both agreed where the bright blooms looked best. Ashley and my dad worked together to hang the photo booth backdrop, which left me standing alone with Jasper.

"Congrats on your opening." He handed me the platter piled high with an assortment of buttery cookies. "My gift to you. I know you're doing the popcorn machine now, so I'll cancel your order and refund your deposit."

"Are you sure?" I placed the cookies on the counter. "I would have reinstated the order, but you weren't available, and well..."

"Yeah. I heard Lacie gave you a hard time." He ran his fingers through his hair.

It was hard for me to not stare at his sculpted bicep that stretched his T-shirt as he moved his arm.

"I'm sorry about that. And I'm sorry about flying off the handle like I did."

"You were under a lot of stress. I understand." I really didn't, but what could I say? The guy brought me cookies and was trying to apologize. "Is business picking back up now that the patisserie has reopened?"

He flinched. "It's hit or miss. I don't know what happened."

"Really? No one's told you?"

"No. What happened?" He looked around the shop like he wished he was anywhere but here, standing in front of me.

"Lacie happened."

"What are you talking about? She was a lifesaver and stepped in when I needed the help." He finally looked at me with his bright green eyes, but his brows dipped together as if he saw something disagreeable. "I've hired her to work full-time. It'll give me the chance to take some time off during the week instead of living in the bakery practically every waking minute."

I gulped. He didn't need to suspect I was jealous, but someone needed to tell him. "Maybe you should keep a close watch on her, especially when you're not in the shop. She, ah, doesn't have the best people skills, and it's been observed she might scare some of your potential customers away."

He puffed air through pursed lips. "That's ridiculous. She's one of the friendliest women I've met."

I'll bet. I'd seen the way Lacie gobbled the baker up with her eyes. But I didn't say that. I wanted to keep my relationship with Jasper civil. "All I'm saying is you might want to consider putting in a security camera and observing what's going on when you're away from the shop. It might bring back some of your customers if you can identify what the problem is."

"I'll think about it." He gestured around the shop. "It looks great. Good luck with everything. Maybe once you get settled, we can try that dinner again."

"I'd like that." I smoothed my hair down and wondered if I should pin him down on a specific day and time.

But before I could figure out what to say, he walked out of the shop, back to the patisserie, and back to Lacie. I couldn't and wouldn't worry about it, except that I'd have to figure out her schedule, so I'd know when it would be safe to sneak in and get my Triple Chocolate Roll. I didn't want to admit to myself I'd enjoyed the time I'd spent with Jasper and had looked forward to getting to know him better. Maybe it would happen, but, with Lacie in the picture, I didn't have high hopes.

Ashley called me over to the photo booth wall and we all took turns taking pictures individually and in groups. It took mere minutes for her to post all the photos on social media sites. The comments started pouring in with congratulatory remarks.

Bryon dropped in to check on his popcorn machine. He helped Ashley fill it with the pre-popped popcorn, and it didn't take long for them to start an animated conversation about popcorn and their favorite black-and-white movie classics. I observed the pair and thought I saw some sparks between the two.

Just before I unlocked the front door and removed the closed sign, Mari squeezed my shoulder. "I'm so proud of you, Carissa. You will be fine."

My arms wrapped around the tiny woman. "I can't ever thank you enough. This wouldn't have been possible without you."

"My heart is full, knowing my work will carry on without me."

"Don't say that! You've got a lot of years left ahead of you." I looked at her nut-brown face. "Promise me you won't leave for good."

Mari held my face between her hands. "No one can make that kind of promise, but I'll be here as long as I'm able." She reached over and twisted the knob to unlock the door. "I'll be back this weekend to provide some complimentary reflexology mini-sessions. You've got help in the shop, so it's time you started providing treatments again." She opened the door, and then darted down the sidewalk. I watched until she disappeared around the corner and worried about what she'd left unsaid.

As customers, mostly friends, entered the shop, I shook off my worries and welcomed them all to Aromatherapy Apothecary. Chatter filled the air, along with laughs as people hammed it up for photos and munched on the popcorn and cookies.

We stayed busy throughout the day, and I was grateful when Dillon arrived at two. A tour bus of senior ladies had just pulled up in front of the shop and twenty or so women streamed through. Dillon was a natural charmer, and the ladies flocked to him. I was impressed that he had studied, without my prompting, the basic oils and what they were beneficial for. By the time I turned the closed sign and locked the door at five, I was dead on my feet. Ashley and Dillon both looked fresh and ready for more. They had hit it off, and I was more than relieved.

I had just plopped onto a chair when there was a knock at the door. Dillon peeked through the window, then rushed to unlock the door. "Hey, it's your dad and my mom."

With an inward groan, I smoothed down my hair and stood. I wanted a hot bath and a warm, snuggly bed. I didn't want an awkward meeting with the first woman my dad had deemed important enough to introduce me to since my mom died.

"We come bearing celebratory champagne for us and sparkling apple cider for the minor." My dad thumped Dillon on his back. "Mari and her friend, Ira, will be here in a few minutes."

"Thanks, Dad. Are plastic cups okay? I didn't think of stocking champagne flutes."

"No worries. We thought of that, too." He pointed to the woman behind him. "Let me introduce you to Sandy Andrews. Sandy, this is my daughter, Carissa."

Dillon bounded over, flung his arm across her shoulders, and kissed the top of the auburn-haired woman he towered over. "This is my mom. She's the best."

I held my hand out to shake hers, but she reached and pulled me into a hug. "It's wonderful to finally meet you, Carissa. I've heard so much about you from Rob and, of course, Dillon can't say enough nice things about you."

Momentarily stunned at being hugged by a stranger, I froze. But then her pure orange and jasmine blossom fragrance loosened something in my brain and I relaxed. A calmness and a rightness washed over me, and as she murmured her appreciation for all I'd done for her son and my dad, I knew I'd gladly welcome her into my family.

Dillon beamed at me as he stood behind his mom and gave me two thumbs up.

I smiled and gave him a wink right back.

When Sandy stepped away from me, her hazel eyes glittered. She turned and took the picnic basket my dad held. "Shall we get the celebration started?"

"Sounds good to me." Mari pushed through the front doorway. "Let me introduce you all to Ira Babcock."

The tall, thin man made Mari look almost doll-like. He waved a tanned, gnarled hand. "Thanks for including me."

I walked over and shook his hand. "I can't thank you enough for the still. Please let me know what I owe you."

He patted my arm after he'd extracted his hand from mine. "It was a dust collector, so I'm happy to see it being put to good use."

"It saved me. I was able to have the Celebration Blend ready for the opening." I swiped tendrils of hair from my heated cheeks. "The new still should arrive in a couple of weeks and, between the two, I'll be able to keep up on production. But if you ever want it back, please let me know."

"Nope. It's all yours." He put his arm around Mari's shoulders. "Besides, I've got to keep out of trouble and keep her happy."

Her grin told me there was more than friendship going on between the two. I hoped that meant she planned on staying in Oak Creek permanently.

We took turns introducing ourselves while Sandy and I set out the assortment of cheeses, cold cuts, and crackers. Ira Babcock reminded me of the former mayor's gatekeeper, Irene Babcock. I'd have to ask if he was related to her, but I'd leave that for another time. My dad deftly opened the champagne, without spilling a drop, then filled the crystal glasses Sandy had packed. Dillon helped himself to the sparkling apple cider.

Once we all held our filled glasses, I raised mine in a toast. "Thank you for making my dream come true. To family and friends, new and old, may you have love to share, health to spare, and friends that care. My life would be meaningless without you, so thank you for being a part of it."

AROMATHERAPY BASIC CARE GUIDE

Use the amounts of essential oils indicated for each condition, mixed as directed below with a carrier oil, such as sweet almond, coconut, grapeseed, macadamia, safflower, sunflower, olive, or avocado. Be sure to use organic, non-GMO, non-processed oils.

Before using a new essential oil, rub a drop of the blend on a small patch of skin. Wait an hour to make sure no allergic reaction occurs before continuing with treatment.

Abrasions

Mix 5 drops of lavender oil in a small bowl of warm water. Gently clean the abrasion with the mixture and pat dry. Apply 1 drop of lavender oil on the skin surrounding the abrasion, but do not apply directly on the wound.

Chapped Skin

Mix the following essential oils together: 2 drops geranium, 2 drops chamomile, 1 drop lemon, and 1 drop lavender. Blend in 2 teaspoons (10ml) carrier oil. Massage a small amount of the blend into the chapped area as needed. Ideal for the face.

Dry Cough

Mix together 3 drops eucalyptus and 2 drops thyme essential oils. Add in 1 teaspoon (5ml) carrier oil. Massage a small amount over the chest and back two to three times daily.

Earache (non-infection)

Mix together 1 drop lavender and 1 drop chamomile essential oils, then add 1 teaspoon warmed (not hot) olive oil to the mixture. Soak a piece of cotton wool in oil and wring out. Place gently in the ear.

Massage the following blend around the ear area, up the neck, and across the cheekbone: 2 drops chamomile, 1 drop lavender, 1 drop tea tree, and 1 drop geranium mixed with 1 teaspoon (5ml) carrier oil. After massaging oil into skin, apply a warm compress to cheek and ear area.

Headache (general tension)

Mix together 3 drops lavender and 1 drop peppermint oils with 4 drops carrier oil. Massage blend around the temples and base of the skull, along the hairline.

Heartburn

Mix together 3 drops cardamom and 2 drops peppermint oils with 1 teaspoon (5ml) carrier oil. Rub a small amount of the mixture over the upper abdomen.

Hiccups

Place 1 drop chamomile oil in a brown paper (NOT plastic) bag. Hold the bag over the nose and mouth and breathe in deeply and slowly through the nose.

Insect Bites

If there is a stinger in the skin, remove it. Apply undiluted lavender oil to the bite.

Sinus Issues

Mix together 5 drops rosemary, 5 drops geranium, 2 drops eucalyptus, and 1 drop peppermint oils with 2-1/2 teaspoons (12.5ml) carrier oil. Massage a small amount around the neck and in front of and behind the ears. Using 1 drop of the blend, massage over the cheekbone, the nose, and the forehead, avoiding the eye area. Blot oil with a clean tissue, then use the tissue to inhale as needed. You may add an additional drop of the mixture in the clean tissue to inhale.

Sore Throat

Mix together 5 drops chamomile, 1 drop thyme, 2 drops lemon oils with 2 teaspoons (10ml) carrier oil. Massage a small amount over the throat and behind the ears.

These products and information are not intended to diagnose, treat, cure or prevent any disease. Anyone suffering from disease or injury should consult with a physician. If you are currently on medication, please DO NOT STOP taking your medication as prescribed by your physician. Please consult a health care practitioner before making any changes to your medical routine.

Do not attempt to ingest essential oils. They are for topical use only.

LAVENDER

Lavender is one of the most popular essential oils. Research shows lavender has been historically used for over 2,500 years, starting with the ancient Greeks, Persians, and Romans.

Gentle on the skin, lavender essential oils can be used at full strength for a variety of symptoms, such as skin infections, cuts, rashes, itching, sunburn, headaches, acne, and insect bites.

When diffused, lavender is also beneficial for relieving stress and boosting your mood. It can help promote relaxation and improve sleep.

RECIPE:

Jasper's Triple Chocolate Rolls

These sinfully decadent chocolate rolls are Carissa's favorite treat at Jean-Luc Patisserie and the proprietor, Jasper, makes sure he always has some on hand to tempt her to visit. While these may be labor intensive, Carissa would agree they are worth the effort to make if she couldn't buy them from Jasper.

<u>Ingredients</u>

Flour Paste:

2/3 cup milk (2% or whole)

1/4 cup (35 grams) all-purpose flour

Dough:

2/3 cup milk (2% or whole)

1 large egg plus 1 large egg yolk

3-1/2 cups (478 grams) all-purpose flour

1 package (2-1/4 teaspoons) yeast (rapid-rise or instant)

1/4 cup (53 grams) granulated sugar

1-1/2 teaspoon salt

6 tablespoons (77 grams) unsalted butter, cut into chunks, room temperature

Topping:

3/4 cup (154 grams) brown sugar, packed

6 tablespoons (77 grams) unsalted butter, melted

1/4 cup dark corn syrup

2 tablespoons water

1 tablespoon unsweetened cocoa powder

1/4 teaspoon salt

Filling:

4 ounces (112 grams) bittersweet chocolate, chopped fine

4 tablespoons unsalted butter

1/2 cup (112 grams) semi-sweet chocolate chips

1/2 cup (112 grams) semi-sweet mini chocolate chips

Instructions

Flour Paste:

Whisk the milk and flour together in a medium bowl until smooth. Microwave on high power for 30 seconds. Remove bowl and whisk vigorously. Return to the microwave and heat for another 30 seconds. It should thicken to a stiff paste. Whisk until smooth. If the mixture isn't thick, heat in 15 second increments, whisking after each cycle, until thick paste forms.

Dough:

Whisk 2/3 cup milk into the thick flour paste until smooth. Pour into the bowl of a stand mixer.

Using a dough hook, add the egg and egg yolk, then slowly add the yeast and flour. Mix until flour is incorporated, and the mixture turns into a mass of dough.

Stop the mixer and allow the dough to rest for 15 minutes.

With the mixer speed on medium and, using the dough hook, add sugar and salt to the dough. Knead for 5 minutes. Add butter and continue to knead an additional 5 minutes, scraping down the bowl as necessary. (Dough will be sticky.)

Cover the dough with plastic wrap. Allow to rise at room temperature until doubled in size, about 1 hour.

Topping:
While the dough rises, whisk all the ingredients together until combined. Pour into the bottom of a greased 13 x 9-inch or you can use a 12-inch round metal baking pan. Spread the topping to the edges and set aside.

Filling:
About 30 minutes before dough is done rising, melt the bittersweet chocolate and butter. You can use a double-boiler or microwave at 50 percent power in 30 second increments, stirring after each until melted. Refrigerate 30 minutes until firm.

Putting it together:
Place the dough on a lightly floured surface and sprinkle top of dough with a light dusting of flour. Roll dough to form an 18 x 15-inch rectangle. The long side should be parallel to the edge of the counter.

Stir the bittersweet chocolate mixture until it resembles frosting. Spread over the surface of the dough rectangle, leaving a 1-inch border at the top edge. Sprinkle chocolate filling with chocolate chips.

Starting with the long end nearest the counter's edge, loosely roll the dough into a log, toward the unfrosted edge. Use your hands to push in the ends to create an even thickness as necessary.

Place the log seam side down and slice into 12 rolls. Place, cut side down, into the coated pan. Cover with plastic wrap and allow to rise until rolls are puffy, about 1 hour. The rolls should be touching after rising.

Heat oven to 375 degrees (F).

Remove plastic wrap and bake rolls on the middle rack for about 20 minutes. You may want to place a baking sheet on the lowest rack of the oven to catch any drips from the chocolate rolls as they bake.

Once the rolls are golden brown, cover loosely with foil and bake an additional 10–15 minutes longer, until rolls reach at least 200 degrees at the center of the bread.

Remove baking dish from oven, discarding foil. Run a knife along the edges of the pan. Place a large serving platter over the baking pan and carefully invert the pan and platter. Remove pan and allow rolls to cool 15 minutes before serving.

Notes:

While these rolls take about 4 hours to make, a lot of the time is hands off, waiting for the rolls to rise.

Be sure to use a metal baking pan, not glass or ceramic.

When rolling the dough out into a rectangle, use a light hand with flour. The dough should remain a bit sticky.

ACKNOWLEDGMENTS

It's true, it takes a village to bring a book to life! I'd like to start out by thanking Harbor Lane Books for taking a chance on me and bringing my story to life. Many thanks for working to make my manuscript the best it could be.

I never would have conceived of the Aromatherapy Apothecary series without the inspiration from my bonus daughter, Briana, who introduced me to the many benefits of aromatherapy. Thank you for sharing!

My gratitude to Maggie Stauble for linking me to a variety of aromatherapy Facebook groups and especially for connecting me to A.C. Stauble, Clinical Herbalist and The Traveling Herb Farmer. I am deeply indebted to A.C. for sharing her extensive expertise with me and answering my countless questions. https://www.travelingherbfarmer.com/

A chance conference breakfast encounter with Jane Lassell Hoff, Forensic Anthropologist, provided me with in-depth knowledge about our sense of smell and how remarkable it is. It helped me understand the correlation on how aromatherapy works with our brains. Thank you for taking an interest in my project and taking the time to share your expertise with me.

To my beta readers, Dan (I never knew how handy it would be to marry an engineer who has both a logical mind and the patience to find the plot holes!), Kathy Keith, and Janet Clause, I appreciate your time and willingness to read my unpolished manuscripts.

And most of all, thank you to family, friends, and readers who give me the inspiration to face a blank page and start writing.

Kim Davis writes the Aromatherapy Apothecary cozy mystery series, the award-winning Cupcake Catering cozy mystery series, and the middle grade fantasy adventure The Board Game Chronicles series. She has also written several children's nature articles published in a variety of magazines.

Kim Davis is a member of Sisters in Crime, Mystery Writers of America, and Society of Children's Book Writers and Illustrators.

She lives in Southern California with her husband and rambunctious mini Goldendoodle, Missy, who has become an inspiration for several plotlines. When she's not spending time with her granddaughters or chasing Missy around, she can be found either writing on her next book, working on her blog, Cinnamon, Sugar, and a Little Bit of Murder, or in the kitchen baking up yummy treats to share. To learn more, please visit http://kimdavisauthor.com/

ABOUT THE PUBLISHER

Harbor Lane Books, LLC is a US-based independent digital publisher of commercial fiction, non-fiction, and poetry.

Connect with Harbor Lane Books on their website www.harborlanebooks.com and on social media @harbor-lanebooks.

facebook.com/harborlanebooks

x.com/harborlanebooks

instagram.com/harborlanebooks

threads.net/harborlanebooks

pinterest.com/harborlanebooks